Summer of the Eagles

Jackie Clay

Jackie Clay Atkinson 2022

~ ~ ~

Mason Marshall Press
Medford. Massachusetts

This book is a work of fiction. Names, characters, places, and incidents are entirely the product of the author's imagination or are used fictitiously and are not to be construed as real. Any resemblance to actual events, locales, organizations, persons, or anything else is entirely coincidental

Published by Mason Marshall Press.

Cover painting by Jackie Clay.
Cover scan by Image-Tec, Methuen, Massachusetts.

For information, please contact:
Mason Marshall Press
P.O. Box 324
Medford, MA 02155

ISBN-10: 1-63247-009-8
ISBN-13: 978-1-63247-009-6

PUBLISHED IN THE UNITED STATES OF AMERICA

Coming June, 2015: *Autumn of the Loons*

After a lifetime of pain and struggle, Jess Hazzard finally hung up his gun, buried his demons, and found happiness in the mountains of west Wyoming with his dear wife, Julie, their daughter, and her young son from a previous marriage.

Life was good until the day he returned home to find the love of his life brutally beaten and raped, and their son, Keith, kidnapped.

Now Jess must master his rage and strap on the Frontier Colt he long prayed he would never again have to wear, to pursue a ruthless madman and his vicious gunmen, save their son, and avenge Julie's violation.

To receive email notification about Jackie's books, including when *Autumn of the Loons* and other titles in the series become available, please email your request to jackieclaybooks@masonmarshall.com or follow us on Twitter. @masonmarshallpb. or on Facebook (Jess Hazzard Series at www.facebook.com/JessHazzardSeries) or (Mason Marshall Press at http://on.fb.me/1IB5JzP)

Your email address will be kept strictly confidential.

To Bob Fuller and my husband, Will,
both of whom kept my dream alive.
Thank you.

Chapter 1

An eagle screamed as it circled high, a speck in the hazy blue above the Wyoming Territorial Prison in Laramie. Below, the gates swung open just enough to allow a lone man riding a sorrel to pass through. Thin the horse was, but proud, lifting his feet lightly, arching his neck so his chin nearly touched his chest. His golden tail swished at the tenacious flies clinging to the newly seared prison brand on his left hip. Then he broke into a smooth jog. It was early that summer morning, but already dust rose in little puffs, marking the trail, as the rider made his way to the top of the nearest ridge.

There, he reined the sorrel to a stop, watching the eagle float gently upward, taking advantage of the air currents, drifting, soaring, almost joyfully. The sun played on the man's thin, hard face as the eagle's shadow passed. The dark brows that rose where they met gave a perpetual watchful, cautious look, but deeply shadowed blue eyes conflicted with this impression. They could be as cold and hard as steel or laugh with boyish mischief even when his lips did not. And during the five years he spent in a grim hellhole they called a cell, no one ever saw even the merest hint of a smile.

Those endless years changed him. Broken or bitter were the alternatives, but Jess Hazzard's spirit was incapable of being broken by those he hated. He was a wild, free thing they caged and abused, but never broke.

A trim man, with a rider's lean hips and wiry build, he sat watching the eagle for long minutes before his eyes drifted instinctively to his back trail, narrowing ever so slightly as they caught the prison in the distance. Quickly turning his gaze from the buildings, as if somehow the mere sight could draw him back, he looked out over the hills of dry grass and sage toward the vacant, hazy horizon to the west.

An overpowering feeling shot through him. He wanted – he needed – to be as far away as possible from this place and from people. He longed to spur the sorrel into a run, but he knew the old horse had to be spared such foolishness if he would make it down the long, difficult trail ahead of them.

The gelding under him shook his head and pawed the ground impatiently, wanting to move on. With a tremble inside, Hazzard raised the reins, letting the horse break into a gentle lope.

Freedom.

Four hours later, he had lost the feeling of near panic; that somehow they would run him down and drag him back to the prison. The muffled, rhythmic beat of the sorrel's hooves as he moved along had a soothing effect.

Stopping to rest the horse by a small, rocky stream, Hazzard began to take inventory of his situation. He had a horse that could not take much hard work or rough traveling. *Horse!* He thought bitterly of the powerful, fast moving bay they took from him when he was jailed, and the two hundred dollars he had in his wallet. In exchange, when he was released, they gave him this tired, old horse and an empty wallet. They left him a saddle bum.

He had no food, coffee, or salt. He owned one shirt, worn and threadbare, a pair of pants in not much better shape, and stained and worn dark shotgun chaps. His hand fell to rest on his old Frontier Colt. Absently, he slipped it out fluidly and spun the cylinder. Only five cartridges. And his Model '73 Winchester was empty. He had his belt knife but no axe. A saddle blanket but no bedroll. A good rope, saddle, bridle and hackamore, a canteen, a pair of spurs, and a worn, black, alkali- and sweat-stained hat. He dug into the mildewed, jumbled bundle in his warbag. Mice had nested in one corner, eaten all but a small crescent of soap, and urinated on and rusted his razor. There was a small tin with fishing line, matches, and a few hooks. He tossed the bundle down in disgust. Five years was a long time.

He was in no shape to travel far, even living off the land, but there was no choice.

His eyes lifted to the northwest, thinking of the miles he wanted to put behind him. Maybe Idaho or Canada? But before he went far he needed to pick up a few dollars and get better outfitted. The very thought galled him. He had absolutely no wish to mix with people right then, not for any reason. He needed solitude to heal the wound in his soul, but he had to find some sort of temporary work before he moved on much further. He did not need much, only to replace the basic gear he lacked. Maybe he could stand a few weeks' work somewhere. Maybe.

As he followed a well-traveled wagon road west, he could not know that ahead of him by two days, a traveling drummer, who had the Devil's own gift of gossip, spread far and wide the news of his release.

By mid-day, Hazzard began passing smaller ranches. One after another, he passed, hesitating, then riding on until the sight of a small bunch of mustangs milling around in a corral, freshly branded and snorty, made him turn through a ranch gate. They were fresh-caught and still had knotted manes and rolling eyes. His gaze lingered on the animals. Maybe he wouldn't have to mix with folks much if he could land a job working those broncs. Hazzard never was a sociable man, even at his best, but just then, riding up to that house was the hardest thing he ever did.

A big red hound came bawling out from under the porch, announcing his arrival. Soon after, an old man, face seamed, wrinkled, and weather-beaten brown, walked out of the dark interior of the house, shading his eyes and squinting against the harsh glare of the noonday sun.

"Can I help you, Mister?"

"I was just wonderin' if you might be needing any help...maybe with that bunch?" He nodded toward the horses in the corral, now stopped, as one, alertly facing them.

"Well now, ain't that fine! Just yesterday, I was tellin' Annie I had to git into town an' round me up a bronc stomper. Pete up and quit on me two days ago." The old man was studying the sorrel as most ranch men are prone to do. When his eyes sharpened, Hazzard knew he saw the prison brand. "I'm sorry Mister, I don't need no help now. You see..." he stammered, edging warily toward the door.

Something like a sigh went through Hazzard, an old feeling. "Yeah, I guess I do." He swung his horse around and again started west. He wondered at how gossip of his release traveled faster than he had, and how much farther from Laramie and the prison it had spread.

The road was rutted and dusty. After two more hours of travel, a fine powder had settled on Hazzard's clothes and face. There must be water somewhere close, but after riding through several arroyos and rock-strewn creek beds, all were dry. At best, he found a fat toad, resting in the sparse shade of a curled up piece of dried mud, in a hole where a spring had been. He had done without water before, but the old gelding was beginning to drag his feet from weariness and thirst.

When Hazzard finally saw a stagecoach stopped at a small relay station ahead, he was not only thinking about a job, but more urgently, water. The place was not much to look at. The paint peeled off years ago, leaving a dull gray of weathered wood. In places the corrals were tied together with rope and rawhide. But there was a pump and full watering trough.

A tall man with a heavy black beard carried water and feed to a tired team in a nearby corral. He glanced at Hazzard.

"Mind if I water my horse?" Hazzard asked, stepping down.

"Naw. Help yourself," he muttered, continuing on with his chores.

Closer, another man, red-faced and bald, was puffing from exertion as he hurriedly threw harness on a fresh team. Leaving the sorrel tied and drinking from the trough, Hazzard walked up to the red-faced hostler.

"Can I give you a hand?"

"Shore 'nough. God, it's hot!" He shrugged toward the last set of harness on the rail. "If you want, you kin throw that on that bugger of a bay over there. Watch 'im, though. He's ornery as they come!"

Watching the hostler nervously flit here and there, poking the horses with hames and slapping harness on them, Hazzard could see where any horse could get "ornery" in a hurry.

Five minutes later, with the fresh team hitched, the stagecoach rocked out of the yard in a roll of dust, scattering multicolored chickens in its wake.

"Well, that does her 'till tomorrow mornin'. Come on up to the house. The wimmin oughta have some grub left fer us. You look like you could use a meal an'a cupa coffee," the bald hostler wiped the sweat off his red face with a much-used bandana.

Hazzard nodded his thanks, walking back to the sorrel. He loosened the cinch and patted the old horse. Then, leaving him to nibble on sun-bleached hay in the manger, he quickly rinsed the road dust from his face and hands, wondering if others could smell the prison stench on him like he could. Cupping his hands under the trickle from the pump, he drank gratefully the first fresh, cold water in many years. Quickly rinsing out his canteen, he also filled that. You never knew when you might desperately need water, or when you may need to leave a place fast.

Walking toward the house, he ran his fingers through his thick black hair, pushing it into some semblance of order. He somewhat self-consciously entered the kitchen. This would be the first time in five years he sat at a table to eat, and the first time in five years he saw a woman.

The meal was nothing fancy, just some warmed up fried potatoes, cold ham, and thick slices of bread with plenty of fresh butter and jam. But right then, it tasted better than the expensive meal he once ate in a fancy Denver hotel with elegant marble on the front.

A matronly woman in a clean apron, evidently the wife of the red faced hostler, kept slipping the platters to Hazzard, even when he politely refused. Their daughter, a pretty, blushing blond girl about eighteen, kept his coffee cup full.

"Are you sure you can't eat another piece of pie?" she asked for the third time.

"No ma'am. There's just no more room."

"Alright. Ned, Della and I are going out to the garden. We've got to get water to that corn or it'll be dried out by evening. I'll leave the coffee pot here for you men."

"Della, tell Art to come on in for something to eat. I'll be out there as soon as I go check the chickens. I surely do wish Art would come when I call him!" She took off her apron and went out the door.

"Art's my brother," the hostler said. "He stops here once in a while, but he's sure no help. Never can tell when he'll up and leave on us."

"You wouldn't be needin' a little extra help around the place, would you?" Hazzard asked cautiously.

"Well...yes an' no," he began with hesitation. "Yeah, I could use the help, but I jest can't have a 'breed on the place...'specially no ex-con. Manager's real fussy about things like that, an' he'd have my hide. Me, I don't care. Could sure use you." There was no viciousness in his voice, but the words still cut.

"I better be riding on, then." Hazzard pushed back the chair and stood. "Thank your wife for the meal."

Hazzard tightened the old sorrel's cinch and swung wearily into the saddle. *Damn! Why does it always have to be so hard?*

For the remainder of the day, he kept the sorrel to a slow but steady jog westward, unconsciously trying to leave those who knew of him far behind, and perhaps running from himself.

The elevation grew higher and trees began to dot the hills. Even the air seemed cooler as the sun began setting. Finally, bone weary, he dismounted in some tall cottonwoods next to a small spring-fed waterhole. The sorrel trembled and stood somewhat spraddle-legged.

"What's the matter fella? Legs a little sore, eh?" Hazzard felt down the tendons in his front legs, feeling some heat in them. "Sorry boy. I guess neither one of us has been on the trail lately."

He unsaddled the old horse and walked him down to the water's edge. After leading him in, he gently rubbed the soreness from them until nearly dusk. It was mindless work, but it allowed Hazzard time to begin absorbing the small things around him, things that seemed insignificant enough, things he missed all those years in that dark cell, like the smell of horse sweat, the far-away song of a coyote, moonlight on the water, and the whisper of a slight breeze in the trees overhead.

He sighed and straightened up, taking time to rinse the saddle marks from the sorrel's back. Then he led him through the trees, picketing him to graze in the lush grass. Listening to the gelding hungrily eating the grass, he lay down at the base of a big cottonwood. Looking up into infinity, the stars were so much brighter and bigger than he remembered. And there were so many of them! Today was the first time in five years he saw a tree, and somehow, the impact of this grandfather cottonwood was strong as he felt its rough bark against his cheek.

Never again will they lock me up! A bitter swell of anger surged through him as he rose to his feet and stalked off toward the water, unable to rid himself of the hatred. He could still smell the stench of the prison about him, clinging, vile, and haunting. His right hand instinctively dropped to the worn, sweat-stained walnut butt of his .44. He drew it with blinding speed. *I will never go back! Never!* Jamming it into the holster, he forcibly turned from his thoughts, and reached for the last bit of soap in his warbag.

At the icy water's edge, he stripped off his clothes and waded in, carrying his clothes with him. He scrubbed his hair, face, and body, then his clothes until the soap was gone and his body shook uncontrollably from the cold. It felt good to be clean, really clean again.

He lit a small, smokeless fire, hung his clothes close, and sat naked before it, enjoying the comforting, familiar warmth.

Then he thought back to his small cell, and those rats. Day or night, they scurried back and forth along the stone walls. If he didn't leave some bit of meager food out for them, he might wake up with one or two of them chewing on his foot, instead. Those damned rats, squeaking, as they fought in their holes, punctuated by the coughs of other prisoners off in the dark.

Tonight, his "pets" were far away, thank God, and the air was clear and sweet, not putrefied by the smell of twenty men crowded into one small, filthy cell block, meant to house ten. Hazzard was glad he was in solitary most of the time. He preferred his own company. But he heard the fights erupt nearby because one man would persistently urinate in the corner, making the stale air even more rank and unbearable.

The foul, rotten stink of that prison seemed as if it would never leave him, even as he sat naked before his fire, absorbing the fragrance of the sage tips he placed on the coals, trying to purify his soul from the smell and abuse which seemed engraved upon him forever.

Again his thoughts drifted back, unbidden. If a man did anything to annoy his guards, and sometimes it was damned little, perhaps they wouldn't haul away the slop bucket for a week. Or maybe they'd "forget" his ration of water in the sweltering heat of summer.

Then there was Blueson, the night guard. He was built like a bull, and, like a bull, could suddenly turn insanely vicious on a prisoner with his fists and lead-tipped quirt. Hazzard heard men talking in the exercise yard outside his window. Two men were killed in a week by beatings Blueson gave them. One was a simple-minded farm boy who Hazzard befriended. Twice Hazzard felt the sting of his lashes. Only twice. He had no scars on his body from that whip. But he carried them, nevertheless, in his heart. These things he would never forget, nor would they leave him in peace, even this night.

Unconsciously, he drew the sage smoke to his body, deeply inhaling its fragrance. He was hungry, but by the time he set a rabbit snare and caught one – he sure couldn't waste a bullet – it didn't seem worth the trouble. He had a very good meal that day, and it would last him for a while. Why he even had pie! A cup of coffee would taste good, but he didn't have any. The gauntness about him told of the years of poor, scant meals, but the taste of freedom was worth more than just food.

As his clothes were still damp, he sighed, banked the small fire, and lay back against the base of the cottonwood. The grass was soft and the night warm. Realizing how tired he was, he stretched and yawned, finally feeling a kind of contentment. He fell asleep listening to the night birds cry as they winged their way after insects. It began as a peaceful rest, but a haunting ghost invaded his dreams – hate. Ever since he could remember, he was distrusted, feared, and hated, one growing from the other. It all came back in a flood as he fell into a deep sleep. Sweat beaded on his taut face. Suddenly, there was a snap in the brush and Hazzard bolted upright. Instinctively, his hand found his .44. Even in his half-sleep, it was out and cocked, every nerve alert and waiting.

The sorrel snorted gently from his grazing near the willows and looked a question at Hazzard. He'd only stepped on a small branch while grazing.

Easing the hammer back on his Colt, Hazzard sighed, holstered it, and looking back up at the bright stars, sighed. If only he could know the simple peace the old horse enjoyed as he grazed in the velvet night!

When he awoke, the sky showed gray streaks of dawn over the rolling sage hills to the west. Maybe things would be better today. Maybe he would be far enough away from Laramie and the prison.

Morning dawned clear, dry, and bright, telling of the heat soon to follow as the sun slid higher into the cloudless sky. Stiffly, Hazzard stretched and rose, out of habit checking his horse as he shook out his now-dry clothes and dressed.

He rode on for the better part of the day, moving slowly to spare his horse, always headed northwest, across the dry, rolling sage hills. He saw a few cattle, scattered here and there, a large herd of mule deer and three pronghorns, but no small game. Maybe, if nothing else showed up, he could snag a couple of trout out of the North Platte, still many miles away.

The trail he followed was a heavily rutted stage road, leading through the parched grass past widely scattered ranches and a few cow camps. Nothing very promising.

An hour before sundown, a neat, well-built ranch, nestled in a narrow grassy valley, sheltered by high ridges, made him draw rein and study it. There was stock in the corrals and the hills were dotted with fat white faced cattle, grazing peacefully. The house, built of lumber, was painted white and sat on a small hill. It had curtains hung neatly in the windows and a low picket fence around a flower bed. *Maybe...*

He touched the sorrel's sides with his spurs and rode toward the house. Two girls, in their early teens, wearing plain gingham dresses and bare feet were walking toward the house. One carried a basket of eggs and the other a pail of frothy fresh milk.

Hazzard stopped in the yard to wait for them, tipping the brim of his worn hat with his fingertips as they neared.

"Girls. Is your father here?"

"You damn bet I am! And if you want to stay in one piece, turn around with your right hand in the clear!" A cold, harsh voice growled from the porch of the house behind him. "Linda, Nancy, get in the house. Now!"

As the girls hurried to obey, Hazzard carefully reined the sorrel around to face their father, his hands held lightly on the reins. He faced a tough-looking man of sixty, with a steel-gray mustache and eyes to match. In his hands, he cradled a twelve-gauge shotgun, with both hammers fully cocked.

"Easy, Mister. I'm just lookin' for work," Hazzard said quietly.

"You keep your ass in that saddle and your right hand high when you ride out. Do you think I'd let a half-breed ex-con with your rep work here when I have a wife and three girls? Now git!"

Chapter 2

Two weeks' riding brought Hazzard northwest, past the huge gray belly of Independence Rock on the Sweetwater, and across the barren dry hills just south of Lander. He traveled more than two hundred miles on four trout and a piece of back strap he stole from a grizzly guarding a freshly killed mule deer. The old sorrel hadn't liked that one bit, but Hazzard hadn't eaten for two days, and was nearly desperate for a good meal – desperate enough to bluff off a thousand pound bear that was in a killing mood.

Hazzard paused at the top of a long hill to let the sorrel blow, glancing up to the noonday sun. A good rain would sure lay down the trail dust, but there was no sign of a rain cloud, or any cloud, for that matter. The trail forked here, going southwest toward South Pass and northwest toward Fort Washakie. His mind and memories traveled both trails. South was Idaho, Utah, and California, maybe. North, through the Togwotee Pass, Colter's Hell – Yellowstone, they called it now – and Jackson's Hole, where more than once he camped with the outlaws and rustlers who used the out-of-the-way area.

While he rested the sorrel, he quietly slipped his Colt out of its holster, turning it in his hand. His speed with the worn Frontier earned him enough respect to go there and not be bothered, but even the idle thought sickened him. He felt like a wounded old bear, just wanting to go somewhere and be alone until something within him mended.

Almost angrily, he settled the .44 back into the holster and again looked in both directions, as if looking for some sign. He guessed it really didn't matter anyway and let the horse have his head. Without hesitation, the sorrel jogged forward to the fork, then swung northwest. The choice was made.

Four days later, deep into the afternoon, Hazzard rode into the Tripp Ranch yard. This was a big spread, with four barns, a ten acre tight network of corrals and pens, a big, sprawling house with a porch all across the front and a bunkhouse near the biggest barn. Perhaps big enough that one trail-worn, half-starved man could get lost in long enough to earn a trail stake. Maybe his luck finally changed. He was far from Laramie now.

Hazzard was directed to the owner, Matt Tripp, near a pen where several hands were treating a bawling cow with screw worm. Over the lowing of cattle and shouting of men, they shook hands, and Hazzard was hired.

Behind them, three ranch hands stood watching. "Jeesus Kerist!" exclaimed the oldest in the trio, "That's Jess Hazzard the Boss just hired! I seen him meet Ed Nevvins in Bozeman a few years back. Nevvins was hell on wheels with a gun, but Hazzard cut him down just like that!"

"I thought they had him locked up," the other older man mused thoughtfully. "Something about a woman."

"Don't know, but that's him, alright. No mistakin' him. A little older and thinner, but the eyes...them cold icy eyes...yeh, it's Jess Hazzard, all right!"

In awe the youngest, a boy of nineteen peered through an unkempt shock of brown hair. "Jess Hazzard! Here? You sure? He looks like a trail bum to me."

"Don't even think about it, Jerry," the old hand said sharply. "That 'breed has the quickest gun I've ever seen...and I seen 'em all in my time. Don't mess with him, kid. Them others you took was nothin', d'you hear. Nothin' compared to him!"

"Aw, hell," replied the boy with sarcasm. "He's a old man. Must be forty or more. He sure ain't much."

"Jerry!" called Mr. Tripp from beside Hazzard, "Come here, son, and show our new hand the bunkhouse and where to stable his horse."

Hazzard glanced to the boy across the yard from him. He would have been a handsome boy but for his eyes. There was something hard about them that did not fit the youthfulness of his face. And there was a smirky quality about his mouth that boded trouble. The boy worried Hazzard. Not many men wore a gun belt, holster hung low, tied down, much the same way his own Colt was carried. The boy obviously considered himself a gunslinger. The only difference was the newness of the gun and holster the boy wore, compared to the worn smoothness of his. A bad sign.

He led the sorrel, walking next to the boy. Hazzard didn't miss the looks of the other hands behind them, still watching. The boy was close-mouthed and tight as he walked, but when he finally spoke, the pieces fit, with the blood-chilling finality of the click of a hammered-back gun.

"Jess Hazzard, eh? I heard stories about you an' I expected more. They said you were fast...chain lightening." The boy spoke in a taunting voice, the echo of the ghosts Hazzard had heard so many times before.

"That was a long time ago," Hazzard replied quietly. He continued walking toward the barn, but he knew what was coming and suddenly wished he was still on that long, dusty trail, alone.

"Well, I'll tell you what I think," Jerry continued, savagely eager. "I think that reputation of yours came from a lot of saloons and drunk cowhands!"

Hazzard stopped and turned to the boy with no anger in his eyes. "Back off boy," he said quietly, suddenly weary. This happened so many times before.

"Old man, I don't back off from any man! What's the matter? Prison take the starch outa your backbone?" The boy stepped away meaningfully, his hand above his holster. "Tell you what, I'm gonna count to five and draw. An' unless you ain't got the guts for it, you'd better take hold of that gun. Not many men around here would put up with a 'breed that rapes a woman like you did in Cheyenne! ONE!"

"Let it go boy, it's not worth it." Hazzard's gravelly voice was just above a whisper.

"TWO!"

The men from the bunkhouse, barn and corrals stepped out to see what was happening, milling about uneasily.

"Jerry! Let him alone! He's gonna kill you! Matt! For God's sake, go get his pa!"

There was the sound of running feet and muttering from the gathered hands.

"Stay outa this Clint" the boy exclaimed angrily. "I can handle this myself! THREE"

"Are you sure you're ready to die?" Hazzard asked quietly. "Just let it go."

"FOUR!" Tension mounted in the boy's voice that you could cut with a knife.

Hazzard dropped the reins of the sorrel and stepped away from him. In a heartbeat, Hazzard wasn't just another trail bum, a worn old man, but straightened to face him with the deadly calm of a rattler before he strikes. Calm and sure. Sweat suddenly beaded on Jerry's forehead and lip. He could feel it trickle down his back, under his shirt as his count faltered.

"FIVE!"

As the boy's clutching hand touched his gun butt, Hazzard's .44 blurred and was leveled at his chest, hammer back. His eyes were cold as ice and the boy paled as he stared death in the face. His hand fell limp and the barnyard was silent, waiting.

"The next time you try something like that, you might not be so lucky," Hazzard said bitterly, swinging back up onto the sorrel. "You grow up before you strap that gun back on, boy."

He slipped his pistol back into the holster and spun the horse around, touching his spurs to its sides. He left the deadly pale boy bent over and retching, his body shaking uncontrollably. A roar of laughter burst out in the yard as the boy's father and the old hand gathered next to Jerry.

Jerry looked up at the rider, fading into the distance, and his eyes hardened as he wiped a hand over his mouth. "I'll kill that bastard. I'll kill him! No matter what it takes!"

"You didn't do so good today, Jerry," the old hand gently reminded him.

Jerry's voice rose from a whisper to a shriek, "I'LL KILL HIM!"

Hazzard rode until the land turned to red rock and barren hills, and the moon rose after dark, as if to ease the hurt. He drifted aimlessly northward, listening to the night sounds close around him. With the instincts of a wild animal, he often checked his back trail, expecting pursuit, but none came. Finally, some sense of soothing came into his still-tense body and his mind ceased racing.

To his left, in the dark, he knew rose the east slopes of the mighty Wind River Mountains, rugged, steep and wild. Out there and somewhere close by were hundreds of square miles of rough, empty country, broken by rivers, canyons and rushing streams.

When he awoke the next morning, he heard the brawling rocky little stream beside him, tumbling on toward the Wind River. The sky showed the pink glow of dawn, but was clouding over. Maybe it would rain later.

Saddling the sorrel, he glanced about, knowing he wouldn't stop again soon at a ranch or town. Somehow he would get by with what he had. Further up in the mountains, fish and game were plentiful, as were edible wild plants. Maybe he could fix up a camp and just stay put for a while. Living off the land was a part of him and much better than dealing with people. Hazzard mounted stiffly and turned his shirt collar up against a wind that blew an icy fog before it.

He rode on for half the day, through miles of twisting trail and towering rock cliffs and spires, making wide detours around the small town of Lawson and Fort Washakie. He also rode past any signs of habitation. There would be no more looking for work, no more hate and rejection. He had enough.

The old gelding was tired and the going was slow, but Hazzard was going nowhere, so it really didn't matter. The gray clouds above grew denser, angrier, as they slowly climbed in elevation, but still didn't rain. The air was calm and even the magpies and jays ceased their fussing. The only sounds were the muffled beat of the sorrel's dragging feet and the occasional ring of Hazzard's spurs.

Then, shattering the silence behind him and to the east, came the crack of a rifle, followed by the sharp, echoing report of a pistol. Again the rifle barked and all was silent.

With his heart pounding in his chest, Hazzard reined in the sorrel and listened. *It sounds like someone rode into trouble. Maybe it's a hunter. But the pistol shot? No, something's wrong.* He hesitated, then spun the horse around in the trail and touched his spurs to the sorrel's sides.

He rode fast, but with extreme caution, for there was no telling what he was riding into. As he rounded a pile of boulders, he spotted the prone form of a man, sprawled, face down in the dirt ahead. He yanked the sorrel to a stop as he slid his empty Winchester from the scabbard out of habit, and searched the hills around. To the south was a rider up on the ridge. The big black he rode reared high, fighting a heavy hand on the reins. The rider pulled up a rifle and snapped off a shot at Hazzard, then yanked the black around to plunge out of sight in a mad run. He was too far to make out features and too fast to get off a shot. There was only the sound of fading hoof beats, joined by other horses in the distance.

Hazzard paused, holding the excited sorrel to a standstill and sliding the Winchester into the scabbard as he listened to the now faraway hoof beats. Something fierce within tore at him. *You've been in enough trouble in this life. Get the hell out of here, before you get into something else!* He glanced down to the man in front of the sorrel's feet. He lay very still, a pool of blood welling into the sand beneath his head. *Maybe he's still alive. Maybe he needs help to stay that way. No*, his heart screamed, desperate to avoid more grief.

He reined the horse away savagely, his jaw working convulsively with the struggle within him. The sorrel took but a few steps when Hazzard stopped him, swiftly stepping out of the saddle, again scanning the rocks and sage, listening hard for any sound. Then he dropped the reins and knelt beside the unconscious man.

He was big, clearing six feet three, having the arms and build of a blacksmith. His tawny hair and common plaid shirt reminded Hazzard of the Swede lumberjacks and tie hacks back east.

His breathing was steady and strong. Ripping off a piece of the man's shirt tail, Hazzard daubed the blood away from the wound. It was a deep slash, running about four inches along his head, just beneath the hairline. Once the bleeding stopped, there should be no great damage.

Hazzard ripped lengths of bandage from the man's undershirt, rolled one into a thick pad, then fastened it over the wound with the other. He watched for a few minutes to see that the blood did not soak through the bandage. Then, after leading the sorrel close, he bent to lift the limp, unconscious man, who outweighed him by a hundred pounds. It took three tries but, summoning all his strength, he finally shoved him across the saddle.

Slowly, carefully, he led the horse back up the draw a little ways, taking time to brush out his tracks and sift sand over them. With the wind that was blowing, in a few minutes there would be no sign of his passing to all but the experienced tracker.

At a brush-choked spring, nestled in a group of large boulders, well hidden from any rider, he made camp. He was not sure who he was helping. The man had no wallet, no papers. Was he an outlaw? A marshal? Or just a cowhand who had been robbed? Hazzard had no idea. But no one deserved to lie bleeding to death or to die from shock.

It was getting dark and because they were now at a higher elevation, the damp, foggy wind began cutting like a knife. Soon it would rain. Hazzard was glad, because he knew it would further conceal their camp, but he also knew he and the man would suffer from the cold. After unsaddling the tired sorrel, he staked him nearby to graze, knowing he would give warning of any approaching riders, no matter how stealthy their approach.

A cold mist began to drift in, closing the valley with a bone-chilling swirl of fog. After covering the injured man with his saddle blanket, Hazzard sat down in the sparse shelter of a boulder to wait for the night to pass. It would be unsafe to build even a small fire. Not only could someone searching for them possibly see the blaze, but the smell of smoke carries far in moist, clean air.

The wet night became colder, and Hazzard tried to huddle closer to himself, wishing for a dry bed and a cup of boiling coffee. *Coffee would sure taste good now, as would a nice thick venison steak! Maybe I can get somewhere soon, where I can put up a good camp, make a bow and arrows, and at least get a deer. Then I'll have fresh meat and be able to smoke some jerky too.* His mouth watered uncontrollably. Seldom in his whole life had he been this hungry. He really had to stop doing this to himself, he thought ruefully.

He got up, tucked the blanket closer around the injured man, and again sat down to wait for morning. As miserable as he was, he felt like he would never sleep, but finally exhaustion overcame him and when next he opened his eyes, it was to the sun filtering through the misty morning haze.

A heavy dew dripped off the rocks and brush, giving the sound of rain, but there had been none and the day offered warmth. Hazzard still shivered uncontrollably. He stood, studying the hills around him, searching, listening, and watching his horse. Nothing was out of place. He built a small, sheltered fire with wood he gathered last night and shoved under a rock ledge to keep dry. The warmth from the fire, reflected off the rock wall, quickly warmed the little camp.

Pulling off his wet shirt, Hazzard propped it close to the fire with some small sage branches and held his hands out to the fire's warmth. Immersed in weary thought, he watched the steam begin to rise from the shirt. He got up and turned his back to the fire, vaguely wondering what the day would bring. Glancing toward the injured man, he saw the blankets rise and fall normally, and was glad. Again, he turned toward the fire's warmth and dozed.

The snap of a dry branch brought Hazzard awake and instantly alert. But everything was as it should be. The old sorrel had only stepped on a clump of dead sage. Hazzard glanced watchfully around the hills. He knew he was in no shape for a gun battle, with only five shells in his .44 and an empty Winchester.

After slipping on his warm, dry shirt, now fragrant with sage smoke, Hazzard again looked down on the injured man who seemed to be resting comfortably, then went to the sorrel. He pulled the picket rope loose and vaulted on the horse's wet back, guiding him with the rope halter.

It was a hard climb to the top of the rock-strewn ridge above them where the rider on the black had briefly appeared yesterday. Slipping off the sorrel, Hazzard quickly read the story of the man on the black horse. Two men, both mounted, had ridden to the ridge from the southwest. One dismounted and smoked two cigarettes, waiting, while the other rider held both horses. The smoker was not a big man. His boots were about the size of Hazzard's, but much less worn. Here, near the big rock, he knelt down and fired two shots with a rifle, a .44-40. The other man shot once with a .45 pistol. The brass glittered in the dew. The smoker reloaded, as did the other man. Then both men rode down the slope, toward the injured man.

The rest of the story, Hazzard had pieced together last night. The smoker briefly knelt by the injured man and then took his horse. The other man led the smoker's horse up the slope and the smoker, probably hearing Hazzard's approach, charged up the slope after him on the stolen black.

Hazzard remounted and turned to the brink of the ridge. From here, he could see at one sweeping glance a view empty of riders for miles. He could see the closeness of the mountain slopes, green with pines and fir, and remembered the country just west, through Union Pass. It was good country, quiet country. What wouldn't he give to be enough at peace with himself to stay somewhere, to ride around a piece of land and call it his own.

Then he scoffed at himself. *Me? A homesteader? A rancher? Some things are just not meant to be.* He touched his heels to the sorrel and started carefully down the rocky slope toward the camp. He jogged the sorrel back slowly, but after climbing the slope, the old horse snorted and pulled at the halter rope, wanting to go. He was glad to see the horse was rested and fresh.

As Hazzard tied the sorrel back on his picket, he saw the wounded man stir slightly, disturbing the blanket. The morning was still damp and cool, so he straightened it and threw a few pieces of wood on the small fire. The flames licked hungrily at the pitchy branches, sending warmth through the small camp but making little smoke.

Maybe this man was on the wrong side of the law, but whoever shot him, left him to die in the trail, and stole his horse wasn't much of a man.

Absently, he slipped his .44 from his holster. His eyes were shadowed soberly as he fingered the trigger and felt the smoothness of the walnut grips in his hand. How much he would give to never use it against another man. Being a gunman was a hell of a lonely way to live, and die.

He holstered the Frontier and reached over to check the bandage covering the man's wound. At that movement, the man's eyes flickered and opened. A look of confusion and pain crossed his face as he struggled to sit up.

"You'd better not try that for awhile yet. You lost a lot of blood back there." Hazzard laid a restraining hand on his shoulder.

The injured man groaned slightly and pressed a hand to his head, feeling the bandage. "Yeah, I see what you mean. How bad is it?"

"You'll live. Could have been a lot worse."

"I was ridin' home from Lawson." He reached into his hip pocket. "Empty! Kind of figured that. I had $500 from a bunch of horses I sold at the fort. I rode into that draw and somebody started shooting." He paused, remembering. "My horse! A big black gelding?"

"They got him, too. I saw someone ridin' a black up on the ridge when I came up. He took a shot at me, then was gone." Hazzard could see the stolen horse bothered the man much more than losing the money. "Good horse?"

"Yeah. If I ever find out who got him..." He winced as he sat up.

"I guess you're lucky he wasn't a better shot," Hazzard said quietly.

"You're right. I owe you a lot of thanks," he said, feeling the dried blood on his hair and shirt. "Looks like I'd have bled to death if you hadn't ridden up." He offered his hand, big and powerful. There was a smile in his green eyes. "Name's 'Seen' Thursten." He caught the questioning look in Hazzard's expression and grinned. "Yeah, I know. It's spelled S-E-A-N, but Ma got the name from a book she liked and didn't know it was Shawn, so for years they called me 'Seen' so the name stuck." He chuckled a bit. "I have a ranch west of here, over on the Upper Green, about twenty-some miles."

Hazzard returned the grip, feeling a sort-of connection. Maybe it was only the open honesty in the handshake, or Sean's easy ways. "Hazzard. Jess Hazzard."

If Sean recognized the name, he gave no indication. He unsteadily got to his feet, swaying dizzily. With a hand, Hazzard reached to balance him. "Easy."

"I think I'll feel better if I walk around a little. Where was that bastard shooting from?"

"Up there, on the ridge, in those rocks," Hazzard gestured.

"Show me the spot?"

"You feel like goin' up? It's a rough climb, and that's quite a gouge in your head."

"Not really...but he meant to kill me. I want to see his tracks."

Hazzard led the way back up the draw to the spot he found Sean, marked grimly by a rust-colored blood stain and tracks. Sean glanced at the spot, then up to the top of the ridge.

"He was up there, with another man, along those rocks by the dead pine."

"Show me."

Hazzard led the way through the rocks and brush to a point halfway up the slope, where he stopped and waited for Sean to catch up. He was pale and out of breath but game and determined. He nodded and Hazzard continued the climb, trying to pick the easiest route to the top.

He showed Sean where the riders came up and the one dismounted. In the dirt were two distinct boot prints where the smoker waited. Sean knelt on one knee to study them. They were made by a man quite a bit lighter and with a smaller foot than himself. A man about Hazzard's size.

It seemed as though Hazzard could read his thoughts, for he carefully stepped down next to the clearest track. Then he withdrew his foot and looked at Sean. Sean did not need to look down to know there was a difference in the tracks and regretted letting doubt enter his mind. He caught the flash of anger in Hazzard's eyes as it was replaced by bitterness, or was it sadness? It was like he was expecting to be doubted.

"I better go saddle the horse," Hazzard said quietly and turned back down the slope. "Stay here and I'll bring him up."

There was little to breaking camp, just putting out the fire and saddling up the sorrel. Hazzard returned on the horse and dismounted beside Sean to let the horse catch his wind. He wished the horse did not carry the prison brand, so big and plain. As the sorrel turned, it was in painfully plain sight.

Hazzard saw Sean's eyes rest briefly on the brand, as men do in the west, but there was no change in his expression. No suspicion, fear or loathing. And he wondered at this man he helped.

"You feel up to ridin'?" Hazzard asked.

"Yeah, I guess so. But that horse won't be able to stand us riding double for the ride across the mountains, to home. It's a hard climb all the way up. We can cut maybe eight miles off, by taking the old elk trail instead of the pass, but it's still too much for him, double."

"I know. We'll try somethin' different."

Sean watched with curiosity as Hazzard reached into his saddlebag and pulled out a leather bundle. Sitting on a boulder, he pulled off his boots and, in their place, slipped on a pair of calf-high Apache moccasins. Hazzard was thankful the mice shredded his spare clothes but left the moccasins untouched.

"Now we'll see how soft I got," he said, placing his boots carefully in the open saddlebag and buckling it closed. Then he stripped to the waist, rolled his shirt up, and shoved it into the top of his warbag.

"You lead the way. They're your mountains. Mount up," he said, tightening the cinch. "We'll try a jog once we hit the trail, till the climb gets bad."

Sean heard of the Indians doing this – one on a horse, the other alongside, on foot, keeping pace – and he never really believed it could be done for any distance. But watching Hazzard's fluid pace and even breathing, he wondered if he had been wrong.

At first Sean's head throbbed unmercifully with the jolt of each hoof beat, but as he rode, it slackened some and he began to watch Hazzard with much interest. He was always right alongside, only occasionally grabbing the stirrup when the going got rough or the trail too steep, never seeming out of breath. Sweat glistened on his bare back and shoulders. But he ran on, seemingly tireless.

It was past noon when they paused to rest at a small, clear stream. They were in the pines now, and the fresh air had a woodsy smell to it. They were far above the sage and red rock.

"How's the head doing?" Hazzard asked, as he unsaddled the sorrel to rest him.

"Kinda feels like I have two heads, but it's a hell of a lot better than being dead!" He grinned. "I get the feeling you've done this before. We came a lot of miles, mostly up."

Hazzard was kneeling at the edge of the stream, splashing the icy water over his head and sweaty shoulders.

"Was a time I could go fifty miles across the desert without stopping. I guess I got rusty, though." There was no brag in his voice. It was more like he was ashamed to have run only fifteen miles. For a moment, with his wet, black hair and the dusky color of his sweaty shoulders, he looked like an Indian, wild and free.

He drew a deep breath and sighed, grateful for the rest. Looking down their back trail, he saw, for the first time, how steep their ascent had been. The foothills spread out far below them, lost in the blue haze of the distance. Only rock, mountain tops and eagles were above them. The trail they followed was narrow, curving, and faint, but it was a good trail, packed well by years of deer and elk winding their way through the mountains. Pretty country, and quiet.

He glanced back to the old sorrel, who was starting to wander off the trail, following the lush grass on the bank of the rocky stream.

"Whoa, Sorrel!" he called to the horse, who stopped stock-still in his tracks, ears swiveling. Turning to Sean, Hazzard explained, "He might not be the best horse now, but someone, somewhere, spent a lot of time training him. He sure knows what *whoa* means!"

Hazzard rinsed out his mouth with the icy water, but drank only a few sips. Drinking too much cold water after a long run would cause painful cramps. He stood and caught up the sorrel, running his hand lightly down the gelding's neck.

"He's cooled down, if you're up to travelin'," he said, swinging the saddle blanket and saddle onto the horse's back. Hazzard felt sharp, gnawing hunger pangs. *A cup of coffee would be good right now, too!*

As he jogged along next to the sorrel, he felt strange, but could not figure out why. Maybe it was because he was light-headed from lack of food. Or maybe it was the thin air. He felt like the barrier he built around himself was crumbling. The wall between him and any other person, his shell of self-preservation, was slipping away. *Why? How? This man's a total stranger.*

He suddenly realized he felt younger, cleaner, as if he was starting a new life.

It was almost dark when they came to a hill overlooking a broad valley. Directly below them, in a small grove of tall pines, was a log cabin and outbuildings. There were two corrals behind the barn with several horses grazing lazily in the dusky light. Far out in the valley, a herd of elk mingled with a small herd of red cattle.

"Well, this is home," Sean said, with a touch of pride in his voice.

"You've got a place here some men'd give their souls for," Hazzard replied, barely audible. He watched the elk raise their heads and trot off the meadow into the trees at the sight of them.

"It's been a lot of work, and I never run out of things that need doing. But it's good country. Kind of remote, but good country. Let's go on down and get something to eat. I'm starved."

Hazzard felt his stomach tighten with hunger pains. *You have no idea. No idea.*

Later that evening, after they finished a hefty dinner, complete with steak, potatoes, and homemade bread, a cold wind began to gust down out of the mountains. Sean lit a small fire in the stone fireplace that dominated the far wall of the cabin. There was a clap of thunder, echoing in the valley and shaking the very ground. The two men sat down in front of the fire, soaking up its warmth as they enjoyed a second cup of coffee.

"How that bushwhacker knew I had anything worth taking, or even that I would be going back that way, is beyond me," Sean said. "But not only did I lose my best horse and saddle, and my best rifle, but now I have to catch and break another bunch of horses to make up for the money I lost. That money was supposed to buy supplies and feed. Without it, I'll have a real tight winter." Sean shook his head at the prospect. Then he looked up at Hazzard with an idea in his eyes. "Say, you wouldn't be interested in a few months' work, would you? Don't know how I can get all the work done alone that needs done now."

"I'll help you all I can. Shouldn't be too much of a job to run in a small bunch and get 'em broke. But I don't know how long I can stay. Somebody'll find out an' there'll be trouble. There always is." Hazzard looked down into his coffee, hoping Sean wouldn't ask why. A confusing swirl of emotions roared through him. Here he was, in almost desperate need of work, offered a job working horses in a country he liked, by a man he could almost trust, yet he was deeply uncertain about staying.

"Jess, tell me one thing. Are you on the run?" Sean asked simply.

"No. Not the way you mean it, anyway," Hazzard answered quietly. "Trouble just follows me, like a hound from Hell."

Sean rose, satisfied, throwing his grounds into the fire. "I can't pay much, and I'll probably work us both to death," he warned lightly, wondering if this dark, quiet man ever smiled.

"I'm not worried about the pay. Like as not, I won't be stayin' long, anyway."

"You might be surprised. These mountains have their own sort of magic. They put a spell on a man, if he lets them." Sean banked the fire for the night. "I still remember the first time I came up to this valley with my wife."

"Wife?" Hazzard was taken by surprise. There was no woman's touch evident in the cabin.

"She was killed over three years back. A raid by a bunch of renegade Blackfeet." A touch of pain reflected in his face at the memory. "We were just finishing the cabin."

"I'm sorry." Hazzard watched the big man stare into the fire. His sorrow was genuine, for he knew all too well the hurt that could come from something seemingly long past. "Sean, you've got to know. My father was a Chiricahua Apache. I was raised Apache. So if you'd rather I left, especially with your wife an' all, I'd understand." Even as he spoke, Hazzard cursed himself. *Why? Why do I always push everyone away some way or another? Here's a man I could like, who could be a friend, and I'm twisting a knife in him.* He knew it but could not stop. *Better he finds out now than later, when it will be harder for both of us.*

"Jess," Sean answered quietly. "You're not one of those Blackfeet. Around here, a man's judged by what he is, not by gossip and bloodlines. I've seen enough to say you're welcome to stay here as long as you want."

The rain fell peacefully on the roof. As a drop found its way down the chimney and landed with a hiss, Sean stood. "Well, let's turn in. If this rain quits, we'll take a look around for a bunch of horses tomorrow and let you get the lay of the land. My son's with a neighbor. You can use his room. We kinda have been using the other room for harness repairs and junk. Looks like a rat's nest in there right now. We'll have to clean it out. If you get cold, there's an extra blanket on the chair at the foot of the bed."

Later, Hazzard stretched out on the bed, savoring the luxury of the evening. *A full meal, and a good one at that, eaten in peace. Coffee, a roof over my head in the rain, and a real bed with a patchwork quilt and even a pillow! A man could get spoiled.* It was a long way from last night, when he huddled, shivering, with an empty belly and no prospects of a life.

He looked around, seeing shiny stones, special bird feathers, a crudely built little boat, and all the things a small boy picks up and treasures. Somehow it all brought a peace to him, as if there was something in the world besides hatred and killing.

Morning came quickly and Hazzard was up with the first streaks of dawn, feeling a strange excitement. The rain stopped sometime during the night, leaving the grass wet as a mist of fog drifted through the clearing and wandered up into the pines.

The horses all nickered from their stalls as he turned the latch on the barn door. Limping slightly with the stiffness of over-stretched leg muscles from his long run the day before, he watered the old sorrel. He watched the clear water in the trough ripple slightly beneath the gelding's velvet lips. It was these little things he missed most in prison, the things that made life worth living, especially when a man had nothing.

"Well fella," Hazzard said, stroking the gelding's smooth neck, "maybe one of these days you can retire and loaf around in knee deep pasture." There was a gentle wistfulness in Hazzard's voice. "Like that, eh?"

He heard steps approaching, and the latch opened on the barn door. Sean walked in, his hair wet and freshly combed away from the dark, ugly scab on his head. Today he wore no bandage and the wound looked nasty but healing.

"Morning. Looks like I overslept a bit," Sean said with a guilty smile.

"Mornin'. You needed it. Most men'd be laid up a couple weeks with that." Hazzard nodded at the wound.

"I'd better ride over and get Scotty this morning. I leave him over to Old Ernie's place when I have to be away. If you want, you can ride up the valley and look things over a little. There's a lake several miles up the trail and an abandoned homestead. Only the barn left, but you can't miss it. We'll meet you up there. Then, maybe we can look around for horses."

An hour later, they were mounting their horses. For a time, they rode together, eastward, with Sean doing most of the talking. Then, at a fork in the trail, he turned north and Hazzard, south, up the valley toward the mountains.

Beneath him, the old sorrel jogged contentedly, not even spooking at the sight of a cow moose and her long-legged calf crashing off into the willows at a small creek. There was abundant game sign. Fresh tracks of moose, elk, and deer showed this would always be a good hunting area. At the river, the water was muddy with the tracks of a small herd of mustangs crossing a shallow ford.

Hazzard studied the tracks for a few minutes while the sorrel drank his fill. Then he looked about him. The grass here was good and there was water enough to take care of a lot of stock, even in a dry year. It was warming up well, as the sun rose higher in the sky, lending a steamy atmosphere to the trail. The rain from last night's storm had almost soaked in, but in spots, puddles still lay on the trail. It would be a pleasant day.

In an hour, he came to a rise, heavily timbered with pine and fir. As he rode over the ridge, he was surprised by a large, emerald-clear lake before him. Straight across, a huge, square topped mountain peak jutted upward, seemingly rising from the depths of the lake. It was guarded on both sides by many miles of the mighty Wind River

Mountains' vast wilderness.

He rode on down to the clearing at the lakeshore, seeing a large log barn, grown to grass and weeds, a sad evidence of a life that had once been. Only a few burnt logs remained of what had been a small cabin.

He rode past the barn to the edge of the rocky shore, where the crystal clear water washed the smooth stones. He saw many fish in the lake, including large trout cruising the depths. It was paradise for someone who loved trout as much as he did! The wind shook the pines high above, sending fat drops of rainwater down on them. The sorrel shook his head to rid himself of the irritation. Then he suddenly pricked his ears, staring to the west.

Instinctively, Hazzard slipped the thong from his .44, loosening it in the holster. He looked where the horse's ears pointed, every nerve taut. It could be a wild bunch, but they would surely catch his scent in that direction. Sean and his boy? Too soon. A bear?

At first he couldn't hear or see anything but the whispering pines, but he knew there was a horse out there and close. Too close. Then he heard the faint sound of many shod horses and the creak of wet saddle leather.

He realized he was in the open, reined the sorrel toward the other side of the river, and put his spurs to his sides. Usually when that many men rode together, that far from anywhere, it meant trouble, and he had already had his fill.

Hazzard crossed the river at a run and was almost to the draw on the other side when he saw them. He counted about twelve men in slickers, riding into the clearing. A chill swept over him as he turned the sorrel, stopping to face them across the river. Three hundred yards separated them. Damn! Only five shells!

The old horse sensed the tension, snorted and half-reared, trying to turn and run. But Hazzard held him in firmly. *Maybe...maybe, they aren't...*

"There he is! Get him!" a voice shouted. The call was repeated and they came thundering after him, as a pack of hounds bays a wolf. A shot cracked through the still air. And another.

"There's who?" Hazzard muttered, unbelieving, as he jerked the old horse into the brush choked draw. *Why the hell are they after me?* He spurred the horse into a desperate run. *Maybe if I can reach the pines.*

The brush was thick. Branches whipped his face and ripped at his shirt. Closing behind him, he heard the riders crashing as they hit the brush. The sorrel stumbled and went to his knees in the tangled branches. But he managed to stagger to his feet, throwing himself onward, giving all his old heart had to give. Another shot burned past Hazzard's head. *Too close!* He pulled his .44 from his holster and turned and quickly fired two shots at the nearest riders. His horse was running too hard in the brush for accurate shooting, but he was gratified to see the riders pull back a little. He holstered his gun and leaned forward against the horse's neck, knowing the old horse could never hope to outdistance those behind him. Turning to fight would be suicide, with only three shells left in his Colt. *Maybe I can reach the rocks ahead.*

Something like a giant fist smashed into his back, driving the breath from him. Then he heard the sharp report of a rifle. He tried to urge the horse faster, but couldn't bear the pain. It was all he could do to cling to the plunging horse. Swaying low, weakening by the second, the laboring horse gave a burst of speed, sensing his rider's need. Hazzard did not have the strength to urge him on. His right hand fell from the saddle, his fingertips reaching for his Colt. But he was unable to feel it.

"He's done!" voices cried excitedly.

Suddenly, a low branch caught Hazzard in the head and everything exploded black as he fell from the plunging horse, face down and bleeding in the mud.

As Sean rode into Ernie's yard, he gave a shrill whistle. He looked around the still yard, and then saw a blond little boy with mischief in his blue eyes peep out from the open door of the barn loft.

"Pa! How come you're back already? What happened to your head? Where's Satan?"

"Ran into a little trouble, Son. Somebody took a couple of pot shots at me. They got Satan and the money from the horses."

"They stole Satan?" the boy asked, unbelieving.

"Afraid so. What are you doin' up there?" Sean rode closer.

"Watchin'," the boy answered mysteriously.

"Watching what, Scotty?"

"They might come back."

"Who?" Sean threw a leg over the saddle horn with a smile. This might take some time.

"Them men that had that 'damn breed' caught."

"Scotty," Sean scolded. "You stop talking like that."

"Well, that's what they said! That damn half-breed," the boy protested. "He was all bloody, an' tied up, an' looked dead. But a posse don't hang a dead guy, do they? Boy he had a skinny ol' horse!"

"You makin' all this up? You know what I told you about tellin' stories, Scotty."

"This is really, honest! Honest, Pa!"

"Then you tell me more. Who were the men?"

"Men from town. A posse. They said he robbed an' killed people."

"When were they through here?"

"Just now! Uncle Ernie told me to clean the harness while he caught a hurt cow, an' they rode right through the yard." The boy paused for a breath. "They caught him up by the lake. An' they sure sounded mad!"

A shadow of chilling uneasiness touched Sean. Could it be Jess Hazzard?

"What did the man they had look like," Sean asked.

"I dunno. He was so muddy it was hard to see. I didn't want to look. There was lots of blood, Pa!" Fear showed in his eyes as he tried to remember more. "He was ridin' a skinny old sorrel horse."

They must have Hazzard! But he said he wasn't on the run and he believed him.

"Scotty, I'm going to find out more about this. I think there's been some kind of mistake. You stay right where you are and you tell Ernie. Understand?"

"All right, Pa."

Sean wheeled his horse around and picked up the trail. It wasn't hard to find with more than a dozen shod horses traveling east in the mud.

When the dull blackness began to fade, Hazzard opened his eyes and tried to straighten up in the saddle. A silent gasp of agony came as a stabbing pain ran through his back and chest, taking his breath, making his fingers tighten on the sorrel's mane.

Through his blurred vision, he could see the rumps of horses ahead and the backs of riders. Leaning heavily on the sorrel's neck, he saw his hands were tied to the saddle. As he looked down, he noticed a sticky mat of clotted blood on the horse's shoulder and the saddle. He could hear blood trickling from his chest steadily, splashing down onto the horse. His head spun and he felt like he would be sick. *So damn weak. They shot me and it's bad, seeing how much blood I'm losing.* He forced his hands back to the holster at his hip, just reaching it. His hands trembled with the effort. At least he would not die alone. But the Colt was gone, the holster terribly naked and empty.

Then a Voice spoke loudly behind him, bringing him back from near-unconsciousness.

"I say we should string up the dirty bastard right here and now! Take him on into town an' some lawyer might get him off with a few years, like before. Let's see him pay. Now!"

Several others took up the cry and before long, the fever was hot, and the roar of voices, loud.

Hazzard became aware the sorrel was standing still and he struggled to focus his blurred vision. Ahead, one man was throwing his rope over a branch of a big cottonwood.

So this is how it ends. A vaguely-familiar voice was saying something behind him. None too gently, they tossed a loop over his head and jerked it tight, tying it off to the tree's trunk. Drawn upright by the rope, Hazzard almost passed out from agony.

The Voice was urging, behind him. Hazzard caught some of the words – bank and Thursten. But he could not make any sense out of what was being said. He knew it would be soon. Part of him begged for death's softness and the end to his torture. But a small part of his soul stubbornly demanded that he fight as long as he was able, any way he could, to cling to life. Damn the Voice! Who here hated him this much?

"Whoa fella," Hazzard whispered to the sorrel, his words gravelly with pain.

The Voice yelled and the sorrel half-reared in confusion, nearly throwing Hazzard.

"I'll move that damn horse!" shouted the Voice. "Give me that quirt, Tad!"

There was some talk behind and Hazzard waited for the jerk of death. The old horse couldn't stand much longer for him.

Nothing happened.

Another voice was speaking and Hazzard struggled to hear.

"You heard me! The first man that so much as breathes is going to die. Tad! Hold that sorrel! What the hell is this all about?" the new voice demanded harshly.

Where did I hear that voice before? Hazzard fought for breath against the rope's strangling grip.

"Yesterday, he robbed the bank in town and killed two men an' we thought he'd killed you. Jerry, here saw you down on the trail, thought you were dead. Came to get help!"

"Not good enough. Yesterday, he chased off the bushwhacker who shot me and stole my horse and my money, and spent the night nursing me so I didn't bleed to death. I saw the tracks and it wasn't him. And he sure didn't have time to ride to town and rob the bank!" He motioned with his rifle. "Now loosen that rope. Right now!" There was an icy chill in Sean's voice that Hazzard had not heard before.

The mob's fever cooled abruptly, leaving the Voice alone, still clamoring for a hanging.

"Now we're sorry, Sean, but how's we to know? Just figured it was the 'breed anyway. Jerry said he saw him ride around town like he was plannin' something. An' everyone here knows his reputation."

Hazzard felt the rope go slack and felt himself slipping from the saddle. Numbly, he fought to stay on the horse, but his strength had poured out with his blood. He was unconscious before he reached the ground.

Chapter 3

Hazzard tried to move but he couldn't seem to even turn his head. Just keeping his eyes open was difficult. He tried to make sense of his surroundings, but the room swayed around him in a fog. *I'm on my back...in a bed?*

He looked at the room, the log walls, a window above the bed, the deer antlers on the wall, and was sure he'd never been there before. *Where am I?*

He heard faint steps approaching the door across from him. Slowly, the door creaked open a crack, and a little tow-headed boy peered in at him. Their eyes met. The boy look startled, jumped back, and ran off. In a few minutes a heavier step approached, and Sean Thursten walked in.

"Well, I see you're with us again." Sean smiled as he came over to stand by the side of the bed.

"I...remember...them tryin' to hang me." Hazzard's voice was rough from days of pain. "That was you that stopped 'em?"

"Yeah. That was a week ago. You almost didn't make it. I had 'em send Doc Stone up here. He rode all night to get here, and he never rides. Don't remember ever seeing him on a horse. But he says if you keep quiet for a few weeks, you'll mend good as new."

Something akin to panic gripped Hazzard. "I can't just lay here!" He struggled to sit up but fell heavily back with a grimace of pain.

"Now don't try that again," Sean said sternly. "Sure, you'll be okay. But you've got a hell of a hole clear through you and it's not pretty where it came through in front. Doc says if you start bleeding again, you could die. So lay quiet, will you? I don't want to be burying you." A smile formed behind Sean's sternness.

"Not much choice, is there?" Hazzard asked, his face grim.

"Listen Jess, all you have to do for a couple of weeks is take it easy and put a little meat on. I ain't really a bad cook at all. I even bake bread! You rest."

"I can't expect you to mother me while I just lay here," Hazzard said with helpless frustration.

"No more than I could have expected you to stop and help me in Red Canyon. I would have bled to death and you know it." He touched the healing wound across his head gingerly. "Right now you'd better rest. I've got some soup on. It'll give you strength if you can eat some."

Hazzard looked at Sean and their eyes met. "I can't figure you out, but thanks."

Sean smiled at the confusion on his face, then walked to the kitchen where the smell of beef and vegetables hung heavily in the air.

Scotty was sitting on a chair, dangling his legs back and forth, watching the steam rise from the pot. "When's he goin' Pa?" he asked.

"I don't know. Not for quite a while yet. He was really hurt bad. Why?"

"I don't like havin' him here! He's a Indian, like the ones that killed Ma! I can't sleep at night with him in there."

Sean looked at his son for a long minute, absorbing his words and what lay behind them. Had the blind hatred he felt after the death of his wife shown so, that even a three year old boy saw it? Maybe if he had met Jess Hazzard under different circumstances, and knowing him to be part Indian, the anger he knew might have come between them. But he didn't want to think he would be like the men in the posse. As it was, he could not help but like the man.

Sean sat down across the table from the boy. "Scotty, do you remember that wolf cub we raised?"

"Sure, Drifter."

"Well, you know how everybody said wolves were born mean and that he'd turn on us one day?"

"Uh huh, but Drifter wasn't like that. He was just like a big ole dog! He even slept on my bed!"

"But people said he was an outlaw. That he was bad, remember?"

"Yeah. But we knew better, huh?"

"Well, in a way, Jess Hazzard's that way. Just because some folks with Indian blood are bad, I guess people don't give the rest a chance to be anything else. I wouldn't call those men who shot Jess exactly good, would you?" The boy shook his head. "From what I've seen, Scotty, he wants the same things any man does, but he's just not had a chance to have them. Can you understand?"

Scotty frowned for a second. "But doesn't he have a ranch or kids, and stuff?"

"No, I don't think he's been that lucky." Sean mussed Scotty's hair affectionately. "You know what? Maybe if you'd forget about him being part Indian and give him a chance, I'll bet he'll be a good friend."

"Okay, Pa." The boy did not sound totally convinced. "I'll try."

As the days passed, Hazzard found his strength slowly returning. At first, he had all he could do to raise his head enough to eat. He even found it difficult to read for any length of time. But in two weeks' time, he could sit on the edge of the bed, unaided. And in three weeks, he walked across the room to the window. Three long weeks gave him a lot of time to think, and to mend more than his wounded body.

He stood, leaning on the window sill for several long minutes gazing at the trees, pasture, and outbuildings. It was so good to see the trees and sky again! Perhaps he lingered a little too long, for he began to feel shaky and light headed. Behind him the door opened.

"Pa had to go work on some fence. I brought you some breakfast he fixed." Scotty stood across the room with a plate and cup of coffee.

"Thanks." The boy watched soberly as Hazzard painfully made his way back to the edge of the bed where he sat down gingerly.

For the first time, Scotty remained in the room alone while Hazzard ate. It did not go unnoticed. The boy had only remained with him if his father was in the room or, at best, quietly watching him from the doorway. He could understand. It was nothing new in his life. But it bothered him that the son of a man like Sean Thursten would be leery of him.

"Your horse is getting fat, Mr. Hazzard," Scotty said shyly.

"You must be takin' real good care of him, then," Hazzard replied, not wanting to spook the boy into leaving.

"I do! I brush him every day and lead him to all the good grass."

"Thanks. He's a good horse. He saved my life. I'll bet you could handle him just fine. You ride yet?"

"Just a little. Mostly with Pa. Pa's always worryin' about me. He says that one of these times, he'll find me my own horse. One that'll be safe. Most of our horses are for men to ride. I sure wish we had just one kid horse!"

Hazzard knew just how the boy felt and smiled at his impatience. Then, without thinking, he began to talk.

"I wanted a horse of my own when I was about your age, too. Trouble was that no one worried about me gettin' hurt. The day I decided I could ride by myself, I jumped onto my father's war pony from a rock. I wasn't used to spirited horses and that pony wasn't used to boys sneakin' up on him. He spooked and dumped me off right in a big patch of prickly pear. They had to dig a couple hundred spines out from my leg. See?"

Hazzard slid his pant leg up, revealing a patch of small white scar. Then he stopped, suddenly feeling that he shouldn't be talking about "Indian" things to the boy.

"Gee, I bet that hurt!" Scotty exclaimed, impressed.

Hazzard shrugged with relief and said with a wry smile, "Not as much as my pride did when I found out that night the whole camp knew about it."

"What's that brand on your horse? Looks kinda funny," Scotty asked innocently.

"Well, it's a brand that the prison uses on their stock. I had to spend five years in prison, and when I got there they took my horse. Big bay gelding with lots of sand." Hazzard's eyes clouded with the memory. "When I got out, they gave me the old sorrel."

"But what happened to your other horse?" Scotty asked, puzzled.

"I don't know. I guess some guard took him. I never saw him after that first day. But it's a good thing, maybe, because Cody would never have stood like the old sorrel did, and I'd have been hung, for sure."

"Why'd you have to be in there?" Scotty asked shyly.

"A man who was my partner lied an' said I took his money...hurt a woman. Folks believed him, not me."

"But that isn't fair!" Scotty protested.

"Maybe not, but I wasn't in a position to argue much. It was lucky the woman got a conscience maybe and ran off before the trial or I'd still be there...or worse." Hazzard smiled ruefully.

"Scotty!" Sean called from outside. "You can run the cow down the lane now. I've got the fence fixed."

"Okay Pa," Scotty shouted. "I gotta go now. See you later, Mr. Hazzard."

"Jess," Hazzard corrected. "I don't feel too comfortable when anyone calls me 'Mister'. Last one to do that was a judge."

The boy tried the name. "Okay, Jess." Then he smiled. "See ya!"

Again, Jess slowly made his way to the window and watched as Scotty swung open the heavy plank gate by the barn and drove the little blue roan milk cow out to pasture, her bell clanking cheerily.

Scotty looked back at the house and waved at Jess. He smiled and raised his hand in return. Maybe it wasn't such a bad thing that he had been forced to stay.

He was barely back on the bed when Scotty came running in, scarcely pausing to open the door. "Jess! Jess! The cow's chokin'. Her collar's twisted on a stub. She's down an' I can't get her collar off an' I can't find Pa!" Tears were streaming down his face. "She's gonna die!"

"Take it easy, Scotty," Hazzard said, getting up. "Let's see if we can do something to help her. Hand me my knife."

"Pa says you're not supposed to get up."

"Where is she?" Jess asked, walking out ahead of the boy.

"Over there!" He pointed to a place in the trees where the little blue cow thrashed convulsively.

Jess thought to the time he easily ran fifty miles across the Arizona desert. And how hard it had been today for him to cross the ten feet to the window. Shaking his head, he started for the cow.

One step at a time...just one more step...and another. For the boy. Sweat beaded on his forehead as he covered a hundred feet without pause.

He was near enough to see the cow's bulging eyes and blue tongue. The collar was twisted so tightly on the pine stub that it was sunk deep into her neck. Then he was beside her, kneeling – or was it falling – next to her, leaning on her, grateful for the support of her body. He pushed the sharp knife down on the collar, and with the last of his strength, he slashed through the leather. It parted with a loud crack and the cow fell away from him, twitching and gasping. Great whistles came from her throat as she sucked in sweet air.

Jess set the knife down, afraid he might fall on it. He could not raise himself from his knees nor shake the black haze before his eyes. He was trembling from weakness and could not seem to catch his breath. He gradually became aware of Sean rushing up, clearly concerned. "Scotty told me about the cow. Are you all right?" he asked.

Jess accepted Sean's hand and, with great effort, got to his feet. "Guess I overdid it a little. I'll be okay. Just a little shaky. "

Sean's reprimand was gentle. "You know that cow wasn't worth you coming out here and risking opening that wound."

"Yeah," Jess said quietly, looking at Scotty with a smile in his eyes. "I know."

Jess continued to grow stronger every day, until only an occasional twinge reminded him of the new scars he carried. Once again, the old sorrel wore a saddle. The rest and good care did the horse a world of good. His coat gleamed and he gained two hundred pounds, taking the rough look away from him and seeming to take away many years from his age. He looked like a different horse entirely. Even the prison brand was healed and haired over so it didn't scream to be seen.

The two men jogged their horses through the sage flats, up the hills and into the edge of the trees.

"We've got two bunches of horses to run together, then we have to drive them all down this way to the catch pen I built," Sean said, leaning forward in the saddle, pointing toward a shadowed clearing. "There! You can see it now."

Jess could just make out a few dark posts and rails among the trees.

"Trouble is, I've used it twice and the horses are getting wise. I almost lost them when I ran in the last bunch, and that was only three months ago."

"They'll be cagey, alright." Jess studied the area. "How about adding wings up there where all the dead brush is..." He motioned with his hand, "...and bringing them down to the pens. That way they won't suspect anything until they're in too far to do anything about it."

Sean nodded. "Might just work. What do you say we start first thing in the morning?"

"Shouldn't take long with both of us workin'. Maybe a week."

"You sure you feel up to starting that much hard work? Maybe we better wait a few days longer." Sean watched Jess flex his shoulder, working the stiffness out.

"I need to get to work, Sean," Jess said quietly, but firmly.

"I know. It's just that I never saw a man shot up so badly, like you were." Sean was clearly troubled.

"You haven't been out here long, have you?" Jess asked with a wry smile.

"No, I guess not. We came west from Minnesota six years ago. Not much gunplay back there."

"A little quieter there," Jess agreed. "I brought a bunch of horses in to Duluth from the Dakotas several years back. Might have stayed if there was any mountains." He smiled. "I was born in them and I guess they're in my blood."

"I was raised about fifty miles south of Duluth, just off the Military Road to Minneapolis. My father came over from Sweden, married my mother in New York, then headed west to log. I grew up with an ax and crosscut. Never got used to carrying a gun, even when I came here."

"It's just as good you didn't," Jess said. "Once you put it on, you can never take it off." He pressed his spurs against the sorrel's sides and started down the trail toward the catch pen.

Sean watched him go, knowing the bitterness in Jess's voice was not meant for him. Such turmoil in a man's eyes! It was as if he was waging some kind of terrible war within himself, always on guard, scarcely even at peace except, maybe, when he was with Scotty. Perhaps his small son was not such a threat to him. He grinned. Jess Hazzard might not be aware of the power of a child's trust. Sean's grin widened as he rode after him.

All week long, lodge pole posts and rails were cut, brought in along the trail to the catch pen and carefully set. Wherever possible, existing trees were used to keep the area as natural as possible. Dirt piles were carefully removed where posts were tamped in and bright, raw cuts on the rail were darkened by rubbing in handfuls of dirt. Not even a small accumulation of sawdust or wood chips was left on the ground, and when they were finished, neither rider nor horse could see the wings from the trail, even when looking carefully for the fence.

"You see, Scotty," Jess explained at the cabin, over a cup of coffee, "those horses are wild as deer and probably smarter. If we drove them down, somethin' as small as a fresh stump could spook them and your pa and me could never force 'em back."

Jess dumped the grounds in his coffee cup into the fire and rinsed it out. Then he dipped out a basin of water to wash off the day's sweat and dirt. "Ain't it about your bedtime, boy?" he asked, unbuttoning his shirt.

"Aw darn. Just a few more minutes?" Scotty pleaded.

"Your pa's gonna be back in a couple minutes and you're supposed to be sleepin' now. If you ain't in bed..."

"Aw, alright," he mumbled, heading for his bedroom.

Jess was just toweling off when he heard the bedroom door open. There stood a guilty-looking Scotty, reaching for a dipper of water. "I'm thirsty," he mumbled.

Jess smiled to himself, drying off his wet hair. Then he became aware Scotty was staring intently.

"Does it hurt?" the boy asked, his eyes wide.

"What?" Jess's brows knit with a puzzled look.

"That." Scotty pointed to the gnarled knot of white on Jess's chest.

"No. Not anymore." He smiled at the boy's frown

"But it sure used to. A lot. Didn't it?"

"Yeah. I guess it did."

"I'm real sorry those men hurted you like that," the boy blurted as he turned and ran back to bed. "G'night."

Jess looked at the door of Scotty's room and felt something drift through his insides, a warm glow that hadn't been there for a long, long time.

Chapter 4

The mustangs, wary of the noise and activity in the valley, stayed in the high country for nearly two weeks. But at the end of that time, Jess found some fresh horse sign at the far end of the valley, near the vacant old homestead, nearly to the lake. Cautiously, he trailed the signs until he could make out specks grazing unconcerned in the distance.

Concealed in thick brush, he sat on the old sorrel watching the horses grazing quietly and drifting slowly west, toward their trap. *The horses can be driven soon.* He felt a smile go through him. *It will be good to be working with horses again.* Something in him yearned for the physical strain, the concentration, the exhilaration of feeling the surge of a leaping, fighting bronc under him. It was the only time he felt free, the only time thoughts of his past were buried. Gone. No longer was he a half-breed gunman, drifting in search of something which eluded him. He was nerve, muscle, and sinew, fighting with everything in him to stay aboard a horse that threw more than nine hundred pounds into every explosive leap. Still smiling, he quietly turned back toward the ranch.

As Jess jogged into the yard on the sorrel, he saw Sean in the barn aisle, saddling his bay. "Any luck today?" he asked hopefully.

"Yeah. They're back. Must have been twenty head with a roan stud."

"Good. The other bunch should be back, too. Let's round up Scotty and go over to Ernie's and let him know. He said he'd cook and tend camp for us. To tell the truth, I think he's lonely over there by himself. Tough old batch. He'd never admit it, though. He's kind of stuck on Scotty. Has been for years. Spoils him rotten! He said he didn't want Scotty left alone while we were off running horses."

Sean's face clouded. "Seems like ever since.... Even when he was little, I'd have to leave him alone, once in a while. Maybe for just a few minutes. And I'd worry every minute I was gone. God, it was terrible! You don't know the things that can go through your mind...what could be happening."

"I know. But pretty soon, he'll be ridin' along with you."

"Yeah. I suppose so. He's growing up fast. Being a father's harder than I thought it would be... 'specially with him having no ma."

Jess lowered his eyes, seeming to study the stitching on his saddle horn for a minute. "Sometimes I wonder what it's like... havin' kids...a family." His voice was strangely soft. "But it's somethin' I don't let myself think about much. Not many decent women'd have much to do with a 'breed, let alone marry one." Jess felt the old hurt well up and shook it off.

Sean smiled. "I don't know. You might just find one with more sense than most."

Jess sighed and stepped down from the sorrel. "It's hard bein' part Indian in a white man's world...or even in an Indian's. You saw it in that posse. The viciousness and hate. I used to handle it with this." Jess's hand dropped to touch the dark, smoothly worn butt of his .44. He raised his eyes to Sean and smiled almost shyly. "It didn't work. Things just got worse. The only thing worse than a 'breed is a 'breed with a fast gun hand." He turned and started away, uncomfortably, as if he had revealed too much. "You want me to go find Scotty?"

An hour later they entered Ernie's yard, Sean with Scotty riding behind him on the broad back of the bay and Jess alongside on the sorrel. Jess felt himself hanging back, feeling a certain tenseness inside. Surely, Ernie knew about him. Was the peace of the last few weeks going to be shattered? Maybe it was the peace he felt for the short time he was at Thursten's. It would make facing another hate-filled man, especially a friend of Sean's, even harder. Then the uneasiness was replaced by awe.

Jess expected Ernie's place to be like that of most of the old bachelors he ran across in the west – slightly rundown, sometimes bordering on shambles, with broken glass plugged with burlap sacks in windows, a porch, slightly caved in, and piles of trash in the yard.

Nothing could be further from what he saw. Ernie had a small, neat cabin with a well-made barn and a variety of whitewashed outbuildings, each with an orderly set of stout pens. There were bright curtains at the windows and even flowers growing here and there in flowerbeds, gay splashes of color against the huge spruces of the windbreak.

And signs! There were signs, all neatly painted, hanging everywhere: "Don't spit on my roses!" "Keep your damned horse out of my bird feeder!" "Danger, goose crossing!" and more.

Jess was still reading the signs with amusement, when he heard footsteps inside the cabin. The door opened and the old man stepped out onto the porch, shading his eyes to look up at them. Ernie reminded him of a typical prospector or camp cook. He was short, spry, bewhiskered with stubby silvery white whiskers that grew from everywhere on his face and ears. His sharp, lively gray eyes swept across Jess, then flew to Sean and Scotty.

"Well, hi there, Sean. I suppose you finally got a bunch of horses ready to run, eh?" He carefully scrutinized Jess with his head tilted like a banty rooster. "You must be Jess Hazzard, eh? Heard 'bout you. Light down."

Jess stepped off the sorrel and started to offer his hand. But he was dismissed by the old man. "I don't shake hands with a man until I know him well enough to know if I want to or not. Ain't much one for po-liteness. Foolish idea, anyway. I just got a little dinner ready. You boys put up the horses. Mind you, watch for the baby ducks by the water trough! Come on Scotty, I got something special to show you."

Sean and Jess led their horses toward the barn and the whitewashed pole corral next to it.

"So that's Ernie," Jess smiled, feeling a dizzying spin of relief. "Don't think I ever met anyone quite like him!"

"And you never will! He's an odd duck, but a good friend. He used to be a prospector up in Montana, but decided to settle down here. He gave his half ownership in his last mine to a friend in Utah and moved here. It was an abandoned old ranch and nothing much to look at. But for four years, he cleaned, built, fixed, and bustled around like a mother hen.

"He has a couple hogs, chickens, some Scotch shorthorn cattle, geese, ducks, a team of oxen, a burro, and a tame skunk!"

"Skunk?" Jess asked, looking around.

Sean laughed. "Yeah. Homer lives in a hole under the south wall of the barn. He usually only comes out at night. Ernie keeps him to catch mice. He does as good a job as a cat and doesn't kill the birds around the cabin, either. Ernie's made pets of them. They'll eat right out of his hand."

"Sean! Jess!" Ernie's voice boomed over the quiet yard. "Come on an' eat. My good bread's gettin' cold!"

In the morning, with the mist still rising from the river, Sean, Scotty, and Jess arrived at the catch pen with the wagon. Behind, were tied Sean's big bay and a powerful, liver-chestnut gelding. At first, Ernie was nowhere to be seen, but on closer inspection, Jess could make him out in the shadows, sitting on a moss covered log. He caught the slight flick of a black tail among the trees further away.

"Now Scotty," Sean said seriously, "I want you to stay right here on the wagon while we try to run this bunch in. Don't get down until I come after you or Ernie says it's okay. You can help Ernie unload the wagon, but be quiet and mind him. Understand? Our winter supplies depend on us bringing in these horses."

The boy nodded solemnly.

"He'll do fine," Ernie snorted. "You two git an' bring in a good big bunch!" He dismissed them with an impatient gesture.

They rode without speaking, in a wide sweep, to come up behind the biggest bunch, two miles from the pens, hoping to drive the larger bunch into the closer, smaller one, to mix the horses and bring in the entire herd. If something went wrong, the horses would be nearly impossible to trap, and fall was roaring down on them like a freight train.

One old mare lifted her head, giving a loud, whistling snort as she caught sight of them. Suddenly, as one, the herd broke, flowing down the valley, toward the waiting pens.

The band ran easily and well, with Jess and Sean flanking them enough to keep them running straight but not pushing them hard enough to panic and scatter the horses.

Suddenly, a small, dark, powerfully-built stallion burst into sight from the brush with a small bunch of mares. The most striking thing about him was the length of his silver-streaked black mane and tail. They flowed and cracked about him as he ran, making the stallion look as if he were flying just above the ground.

Sean groaned. "That's the Hawk! He's too wise to traps! We're going to lose them. We have to stop him!"

Jess, only lengths behind the thundering stallion, lashed the chestnut with his reins, angling closer. He knew Sean was right; they could not hold the herd if this horse was smart about traps. He would turn the herd away from the wings in time to escape.

Jess loosened his rope and spurred his horse closer, until flying clumps of dirt began to hit his chest from the stallions pounding hooves. Together, they flew into the wings of the trap, a blur beside Jess. The herd was following them into the trap when suddenly, the stallion spotted the wings. His ears pointed toward the poles and his nostrils flared red.

Jess shook out his loop and reined the bay closer to the stallion's hind quarters. Only seconds! Already, some of the herd was hesitating, as if they knew something wasn't right.

With a wild spin, the black stallion turned to the nearest rails, ears pinned back in determination and hatred. He was either going to jump the fence or crash into it! Jess swung his rope twice overhead and prayed it would fall true.

The sweat-darkened stallion reared as the loop tightened on his neck, his forefeet pawing the air in front of him. An instant later, instead of fighting the rope, the furious horse turned on Jess's mount and Jess found himself in the middle of a cyclone! The chestnut reared against the vicious attack of the smaller horse, desperately trying to escape.

The stallion was fast and savage as he attacked, biting with strong, vicious teeth, pounding with his hooves. The chestnut was teetering on his hind legs and the stallion drove him still higher. Jess swung the rope hard against the stallion's wicked face, his teeth bared and breath panting, only inches from his own, but the horse never gave an inch of ground.

Feeling the chestnut going over backwards, Jess jerked the rope loose from the saddle and jumped free. There was a loud crash as the chestnut hit the ground. The stallion did not let up his attack on the downed gelding until he saw Jess on his feet, snubbing the rope to a fence post only yards away.

With what could only be described as a roar, the stallion snaked toward Jess with pounding forefeet and bared teeth. There was no time to get through the fence. Jess was pinned against the poles. He managed to tie off the rope before the horse hit him.

The stallion slammed into him with his shoulder, crashing him against the pole fence, spinning him heavily to the ground. When Jess looked up, there were two hooves, coming down fast, only inches from his face!

Rolling fast, Jess was relieved to hear a loud crack as the stallion's feet hit the lower rails of the fence. The rails gave Jess just enough protection that he was able to get past the rope's length before the enraged horse splintered the rails in his rampage, scattering them as so much kindling.

Breath coming in ragged gasps, Jess got to his feet, brushing the dust from his clothes, relieved and amazed to find that he was still in one piece.

"Jess! Are you alright?" Sean asked urgently, stepping off his puffing bay.

"Sure. Did they all go in? Did we get the horses?"

"Yeah. Was close enough, though. Do you always take chances like that?"

"You said 'stop him' so I stopped him." Jess smiled, catching his breath. "You're the boss. Now what are you going to do with him?" Jess looked from Sean to the storming stallion that was tearing out mouthfuls of splinters from the post he was tied to.

"Hell, I don't know. The ranchers from here to Lawson have a $50 reward for getting him off the range. You've sure earned that!" Sean looked again to the stallion, who suddenly stopped, nostrils flared red, head up, staring at them with his little ears intently pricked forward. "I hate to shoot him. I don't much like killing a horse and he's a purebred Morgan from back east.

"Two years ago, they roped him and took him to the Lazy 70, west of here. Some of the best riders hereabouts tried him. They say he's really savage. The last rider to try him got pitched off into a corral gate. The stud hit it so hard the hinges snapped. He drove Wes right through the gate, scattering saddle in all directions. Then he took off and has run wild since. Now he's an outlaw through and through. And Wes is still crippled."

Looking at the raging stallion, Jess could easily believe that. But there was something he admired in the Morgan. Maybe it was his eyes. Behind the hate that blazed in them so fiercely, he saw, not a killer, but the eyes of a good, honest horse that was pure grit, that had absolutely no quit in him at all. He worked with hundreds of horses, and felt strongly the little stallion could be more than an outlaw that terrorized ranches scattered over fifty miles.

Sean was reaching for his rifle when Jess stopped him with a hand on his arm. "Let me try him, first," Jess said softly.

"Huh?"

"I need a good horse. Old Sorrel can't stand hard riding anymore. Not the kind I'm liable to need from him. I need a horse with sand...one that's willing to give more than's reasonable to ask of him.

Let me try him."

"Jess, he's a killer. Plain and simple."

"They say that's what I am, too."

"You're welcome to your pick of any horse in the herd. There's some good horses there. Take one of them."

"There's something about him, Sean." There was a stubbornness in his quiet voice. "I won't try him 'till the others are broke, just in case something happens."

Sean's eyes were troubled. "It's not that. If you want him, he's yours. You may be pretty well healed up from that gunshot wound, but he's going to be the most horse you'll ever sit...or try to."

"Yeah. I know. Maybe that's why I want him."

"Pa!" Scotty shouted, running up, "Is that the Hawk Jess roped?"

Sean nodded, holding the boy back so he didn't get close to the stallion.

"Is that what he's called?" Jess asked, his eyes on his new horse.

"Yeah. He's a Morgan from Vermont, grandson to Black Hawk, himself. Cost the rancher who brought him out here seven years ago, as a two year old, over $1,000! But I think he mostly got that name because he can fly away from anyone trying to catch him, like a hawk."

Chapter 5

It was almost dusk, two days later, when Jess and Sean rode out of the corral on tired horses. After a long day of riding wild mustangs, they were exhausted. The dust raised by the churning, bucking horses made the darkening clearing look like fog settled early.

Not wanting to miss a thing, Scotty sat the whole time, spellbound, on a log near the corral. The riding fever in the boy was hot as he ran to his father.

"Can I ride with you, Pa?" he pleaded.

"Sure." Sean smiled and leaned down. "Come on up." He reached down for the boy's hand and pulled him up until he could put his foot on top of Sean's toe. Boosting the boy up behind him, he clucked the horse to move.

The ride to camp was all too short for Scotty. "Can I ride him by myself?"

"I'm sorry, Scotty," Sean explained, "both Red and Tom, here, are just too much horse for you. I'm afraid you'd get in trouble."

The boy didn't say anything, but his head hung as he slid down to the ground and walked toward camp, his boots scuffing the dusty ground in dejection.

"I guess he's about ready to have a horse of his own, but there isn't a gentle enough horse on the place I could trust him on," Sean explained to Jess as he stiffly dismounted and loosened his cinch.

Jess was watching the boy thoughtfully. It was hard to see such a little boy so sad.

The next morning, Ernie stirred up the fire and headed into the woods to gather firewood. Passing the picket line, his head jerked up. There was an extra horse tied at the far end! Jess Hazzard's old sorrel. "Hummmp," the old man muttered in false gruffness. "That damned fool. Hazzard must have rode half the night to go back to Thursten's and get that horse!" But his gruffness melted, for he well knew why the horse was there. He, too, saw the sad little boy without a single horse to ride here at horse camp. "The damned fool," he repeated, blowing his nose loudly, as he turned to see if anyone was nearby to see him.

The clear stillness of the morning air was broken again by dust and bawling horses. One after another, the mustangs were roped, tied, and saddled. They chose twelve horses to break, making six apiece to work with daily. Jess grew to admire Sean's natural skill with a rope. Likewise, after only a few horses, Sean knew that if anyone would ever stand a chance of riding the Hawk, it would be Jess.

Sean liked the way Jess handled a horse. He rode a bronc without spurs or quirt, and stayed quietly with the horse until it lost its terror and responded to the pull of the hackamore, slowing to a trot. There was no "showing the horse who was boss," beating, or other violence. Those horses soon came to trust a rider.

Jess worked each horse for fifteen minutes after it stopped bucking and calmed down. Then he would dismount and mount several times. The horse was still spooky, but quickly responded to the gentle handling.

Finally, all twelve horses had been worked for a second time. After the last was unsaddled, Sean and Jess walked stiffly to camp for a well-earned cup of coffee and rest.

The smell of bacon and beans wafted through camp. And bread? They knew Ernie had been busy. Down in the clearing, Scotty happily rode the old sorrel, managing quite well by himself, overseen by the watchful eye of Old Ernie. Jess smiled and dusted off his chaps with his hat.

"You boys get at 'em all this mornin'?" Ernie asked, poking into his bean pot.

"Yeah. Every last one of them," Sean answered. "Can't say as I'm sorry. I never was cut out to be a bronc wrestler. But it's a way to buy winter supplies until we get our cow herd built up more."

"There's one more, Sean." Jess gestured toward the corral with his coffee cup. "There's the Hawk. I'm going to try him later on."

That afternoon, Jess picked up his saddle, blanket, and hackamore. He didn't say anything, but everyone knew this was the time and followed him down to the corral. Sean slipped the rifle out of his scabbard, just in case, before settling next to a corral post to watch.

It took nearly half an hour of intense struggle before the roped stallion was inside the corral, but foot by foot and inch by inch, he was worked, fighting, through the gate. With a second rope, Jess forefooted him and threw him to the ground. With a fluid motion, he had the stallion tied down securely, but even down and blindfolded, the Morgan thrashed about, trying to crush, bite, and kill his captor. Despite the thrashing, Jess managed to get his saddle on and the cinch drawn tight.

With one practiced move, Jess quickly slipped the bosal over the stallion's muzzle, past that wicked mouth. With the hackamore on, Jess was ready. There was no use for soothing words or soft strokes with this horse. He wasn't so much afraid as he was full of hate. After years of running wild, his first contacts with man had brought him fear, but he soon learned how weak a man really was. One swift kick and a skull would crack. One strike from a lightning-quick forefoot and one less human would torment him and threaten his freedom. A strong shoulder against their puny fences and he was free again. This time would be no different.

"Scotty," Sean cautioned as he caught his breath. "You can watch, but stay away from that fence. He might go right through it. No tellin' what'll happen now."

Jess stood back as the stallion leapt to its feet with a shudder. The Hawk was still handicapped by the blindfold and a Scotch hobble, which held one hind leg off the ground. Tension built in the corral as Jess drew the cinch tighter. *Soon... Soon...*

For a few moments, the stallion was still, but quivering with an ear cocked toward Jess, trying to sense the presence of the man near him. It was then Jess swung on, quickly found his stirrups, and in one fluid motion, set the horse free.

The stallion shook his head like a snake, realized he was free, and exploded! His head went down between his forelegs and he leaped into the air with a loud bellow of rage. His ears were pinned back and nostrils flared red. When he hit the ground, it shook. Again he leaped in the air. And again. His bucking was vicious and full of savage tricks. He spun, seemingly two ways at once, then burst into the air again. There was no rhythm to ride to, only explosions. Never before had Jess ridden a horse so fierce. He could hardly see, and heard only the grunting and squealing, the pounding, thundering hooves, the creak of saddle leather, and his own rough breathing.

Five minutes later, Jess's nose began to bleed, but he was still there, trying to find rhythm and balance in that savage bucking.

Nearly ten minutes passed and those who watched stood in awe, pressing against the fence, as though willing the stallion to stop, to give in. Something had to happen soon! A horse just couldn't keep bucking like that! And a man couldn't continue riding like that! A man couldn't take that much punishment.

The Hawk grew desperate, throwing himself against the corral fence, hoping to catch Jess's leg between himself and the logs. Sean drew a sharp breath and started for the fence. But Jess was a quarter of a second ahead of the Morgan. And the leg was not where it would be smashed. The stallion took the full force of the blow on his ribcage, grunting mightily.

Puffing hard now, the Hawk had foam and sweat running down his sides and legs. He was beginning to feel real fear. He had never been beaten before. His wicked cunning was lost and he bucked now out of terror. He must throw this man! For a few minutes longer, he struggled, his bucking losing its sharpness. Then he stood still with his head hung low between his quivering legs as sweat splattered from his body onto the dry ground of the corral.

Jess urged him to a walk, and for five minutes more, he slowly circled the hesitant, beaten stallion around the corral, their heaving breath blending together in the stillness. The horse was not the only one who was done in by the awful battle. Jess's hands shook on the reins and he felt like he was floating out of his body.

He managed to tie the stallion securely and began to walk from the corral. *Maybe if I just sit in the shade for awhile.* He took just one step before his legs buckled, and he fell against the corral, clinging to the logs. A moment later, he ducked between the rails and staggered toward the camp.

Sean ran up, taking Jess's arm. "Are you okay?"

"Sure." Jess stopped at the creek, squatted down, and splashed the icy water over his face and shoulders. The cold shocked him back to life.

"I told Pa you could ride anything," Scotty said.

Jess grinned sheepishly, like a boy. It was the first time they had seen him smile.

"Scotty, go get Jess a cup of coffee. It'll help clear his head," Sean said. "That was some ride!"

"You're damned right it was!" Ernie exclaimed enthusiastically. "I never saw a horse go so hard, for so long, an' I've seen a lot of broncs! Here, I'll help Scotty get that coffee for Jess."

Noticing a spot of blood on the front of Jess's sweat-drenched shirt, Sean frowned. "Open your shirt. Let's see if that wound opened up."

Jess protested, but opened his shirt front, revealing a little trickle of clotting blood from the white, fan-shaped knot on his chest.

"That isn't anything, Mother!" Jess laughed at Sean's concern. "Just a little split. See." He wiped the blood away with the back of his hand.

"Yeah. Guess you'll live, at that." Sean smiled, shaking his head as Jess stood and tucked his shirt into his Levis. Was this the quiet, somber man who came across the mountains with him, carrying little more than bitterness?

After a cup of coffee and an hour's rest, Jess went back to the corral and the stallion, still tied to a post. He approached the stallion boldly, but quietly. At the sight of his conqueror, the Morgan trembled and backed away until the rope was tight. The hate in the Hawk was gone, but in its place was a dreadful fear. Without a spur or quirt having touched him, he was bested, ridden to a standstill by this strange new enemy, and then quietly ridden until he panted no more.

Now the fear was almost more than he could bear. Not knowing why, he shook like a leaf as the man stepped steadily closer.

Jess was speaking to the horse constantly, but so softly only the horse could hear. Every muscle was corded and the veins stood out on the stallion's finely cut face as his flared nostrils breathed in the scent of this man. Steadily but slowly, Jess advanced, speaking now to the stallion in Apache, the tongue of his youth. There was no one else on earth, just then, only him and the horse. One quick movement, one slip or loud sound and the magic would be over. The horse would leap away, never to trust again.

Ever so gently, Jess blew into the stallion's fluttering nostrils, so close to those savage teeth. To those watching, it appeared Jess and the horse were talking to each other.

Slowly, Jess moved toward the stallion's shoulder, reached his hand up to touch, then stroke the glass-smooth, sweat soaked neck. Unhurried, he moved along his neck to the saddle, still speaking to the horse in Apache, as one would speak to another person.

He untied the cinch and slowly slid the saddle and blanket off, being careful not to let it bang the horse. The black stallion danced to the side as the weight of the saddle slid off his back, but did not fight.

Jess slipped the tie rope carefully over the stallion's tiny ears, then holding the reins of the hackamore, he turned and stepped toward the opposite side of the corral. The Hawk's first reaction was to fight the pull, but he quickly remembered his long battles with the ropes and stepped hesitantly after the man.

Together, they walked the length of the corral, then back to the center. Jess stopped him and slowly put his arm across the Hawk's damp back. At first the stallion wiggled his skin, trying to shake the strange touch off, but gradually got used to the feeling. Jess increased the pressure, both on the off side and across the stallion's round back. All the time, he talked to him, scratching his neck.

Then, he leaned his chest across the horse's back and swung on with a smooth, unhurried motion. At the new weight of Jess again on his back, he shied violently. Jess could feel the fight come into him and the muscles tense.

"Take it easy now. Just walk on out. You don't want to fight any more than I do."

He pressed his legs into the stallion's sides, urging him ahead. At first, the horse's movements were jerky and tense, but soon he moved with the flowing stride of a panther.

Jess lost track of time as he worked his new horse, getting the stallion used to him. He didn't work him hard, but just in big, looping circles at a walk and jog. Stop, start, walk, jog, slip off, rub the horse's sides and neck, back on, walk, jog, stop.

When Jess noticed the sun was sinking over the western peaks, he smiled, dismounted carefully, near the gate, and patted the horse's satin neck.

The Morgan no longer trembled. He was cooled down and relaxed. He still held a spot of caution and distrust, but even that was slowly fading. Way back in his memory, the Hawk remembered being brushed, eating grain from a box in a barn, nuzzling a quiet black man for attention. The picture was old and dim, but there again.

Jess tied the Hawk outside the corral, carried him a fresh pail of water, then walked back to pick up his saddle. After hanging the saddle and blanket on the corral to dry, he walked back toward camp, picking up firewood on the way.

Old Ernie waited in the shadows of the pines. "Been watchin' you," he began roughly. "You remember when you an' Sean rode to my place the first time?"

Nodding, Jess dumped the firewood next to the fire and brushed off his hands.

"I tol' you I never shook hands with a man 'lessn I knew him well enough to know if I wanted to. Any man that can be good to a little boy an' an outlaw horse is okay in my book." The old man offered his weathered, work-roughened hand. "You may be half-Indian, but you're all man."

Self-consciously, Jess reached to return the grip. "Thanks."

Sean called from the edge of camp, "Jess. Grab a cup of coffee and come see how Scotty's doing on your sorrel."

"Well, go on then," Ernie grumbled gruffly, clearing his throat, "Don't be standin' around here when there's fresh coffee. Git outa here an' let me get this bacon sliced for supper."

Jess smiled as he walked away. *I just passed some sort of milestone. Maybe there* could *be a place for me to settle down, make a life instead of just havin' a lifetime of painful wandering.*

He found Sean squatting on top of a hill that overlooked the clearing, below. Jess joined him, a cup of steaming coffee in hand. His eyes crinkled into a smile as he watched Scotty jogging Old Sorrel confidently in circles, "training" him, as Jess himself had done with the Hawk.

Sean gestured with his cup, chuckling. "Our new bronc stomper in training."

"We'll need him," Jess replied. "It'll take three or four horses tomorrow morning before I can loosen up enough to walk straight! How long you plannin' to work them before you sell?"

"About a week should do it. The army doesn't need lady-broke horses, just the rough off of them. Say! Don't forget the stockmen have a reward for the Hawk. I think they had in mind that someone shoot him. But all the poster said was 'removed from the range'. You sure did that, and $50 isn't bad."

"Makes me feel like a bounty hunter." Jess smiled. "But I've about worn out these clothes. More patchin' than clothes. And it won't be all that long before winter comes on."

His smile faded and his eyes became serious as he thought of putting together an outfit for the trail. For what? More fruitless, empty years of wandering?

Sean and Jess worked with the horses for seven days, until they showed no desire to buck and performed smoothly. All they needed now was some daily work for reinforcement.

"Well," Sean said as he stretched tired muscles, "I guess we got 'em this far. The only thing left to do is to ride to town and get in touch with Captain McMasters. He'll send a couple of men to pick them up. Last time, I hired John Miller and his oldest boy to help trail them in to the fort, but McMasters told me he'd be glad to send a crew up to bring in the next ones."

"When you plannin' on riding in?" Jess asked, refilling his coffee cup.

"Soon. You come too. A man needs to get away once in a while. And besides, you have fifty dollars waiting for you. You said, yourself, you need new clothes."

"But what about Scotty and the stock?"

"I have that all figured out. Besides, I might need a bodyguard after last time!" Sean chuckled.

Jess shook his head and quietly said, "If I go with you to town, there's liable to be trouble."

"Aw, come on. Why would anyone start anything? Especially after that fracas with the posse. They all went home feeling pretty sheepish."

"They don't need a reason. Guess it's part what I am, bein' fast with a gun. People just have to talk. And I've been here long enough for talk to have stirred up a lot of bad feelings. I don't think Jerry Tripp is ever going to let it lay." Jess followed a shrug with a resigned sigh. "If something does happen, try not to get mixed up in it. They can hate you as easily as they do me, just for havin' me here."

Chapter 6

Two days later, the three left the milk cow with Ernie and headed out. Ernie would haul hay over to the penned horses and take care of watering them until they returned. Scotty rode Old Sorrel through the morning sunlight, as happy as if he were riding a beautiful, spirited thoroughbred. They had no saddle to fit the boy, so Jess insisted they use his for Scotty. The boy's legs were much too short for the stirrups and the seat had to be made smaller by tying a rolled up blanket behind the fork, but it was much better than him riding the sorrel's backbone the twenty miles over to the Miller place where he would visit while the men rode in to town.

Jess rode the Hawk bareback, with only a blanket and hackamore. The black Morgan was still spooky, but was beginning to trust this man, something entirely new to him.

It was Scotty's first ride of any distance, and though a little boy can get awfully sore, he was game. He never complained, but later in the afternoon Sean noticed him squirming a little, as though trying to find a place on his bottom that was not sore.

"Do you want to stop for awhile?" his father asked.

"No sir! That Bobby Miller'd say I'm a sissy. Just because he's a year older'n me an' has his own horse'n stuff, he's always braggin' how far he rides. I'll show him!"

An hour later, they crossed the pass and arrived at a small ranch along a creek, nestled between two gently sloping sage hills. A wide assortment of chickens and loose pigs ran around the yard. Two good sized dogs ran to greet them, barking a welcome.

"That's Bobby, over there," Scotty told Jess.

A red-haired boy of seven or eight climbed down from the barn roof and clung to the fence rail with his bare toes.

"Ma! Ma! It's Scotty and Mr. Thursten. Hey Scotty!" he yelled, jumping down from the fence, running to meet them, "You got a horse!"

"Well...no." Scotty frowned a moment. "But I can ride him when I want."

"Aw well. I just got a new colt borned yesterday. You wanna see him?"

"Can I Pa?" Scotty asked.

"Sure. Here, let me take the sorrel."

The Hawk was suspicious of the sights in the barnyard. He danced nervously, neck arched and nostrils flared, trying to whirl and run every time a pig would start towards him.

"Sean Thursten!" A buxom woman of perhaps forty came out onto the cabin's porch. Her gingham apron had seen years of use but was patched neatly and clean.

"You've finally brought Scotty for a visit. How nice! How have you been?"

"Fine," Sean said, dismounting. "Jenny, this is Jess Hazzard. He's helping me get things in shape."

"Pleased to know you, Mr. Hazzard."

Jess tipped his hat. "Ma'am."

"Why isn't that the stallion that hurt Bob Crawford and Wes London?" Surprise showed in her voice as she carefully looked at the horse, her hands on her hips in concentration.

"That's him alright," Sean replied. "Jess roped him out of the wild bunch we ran in and broke him." Sean smiled at her astonishment.

"How in the world...? My goodness, he's a pretty one though!" Her hand flew to her mouth, her eyes twinkling. "Now here I am talking away. And after you rode this far, too! Come on in. I have a good supper on the stove."

"Sorry, Jenny, but we have a bunch of horses penned up and we'd better get on in to town. Could Scotty stay here while we're gone?"

"Why Sean, I'm insulted you even asked. Of course he can! The youngest kids love to have someone to play with. I wish John was here. I know he'd like to see you. But right now, he's out with the older boys, working on the irrigation ditch in the east pasture."

Jess slid off the Hawk, unsaddled the sorrel and carefully saddled the stallion.

"We'll stay awhile when we get back," Sean promised. "Is there anything you need from town?

"No, can't say as there is. We went in a month ago, so I'm pretty much set. Thanks though, Sean."

Chapter 7

It was the next evening when they finally reached Lawson. After getting a room at the one hotel in town, they rode on down the rutted street, toward Grey's Livery Barn, at the end of the main street. In front of the three saloons that made up much of the town, horses stood hipshot, patiently waiting. It was Friday night and the town appeared to be livening up. Loud voices and a heavy cloud of cigarette smoke escaped into the street. Jess rode easily, but his right hand was just a little closer to his holster and the thong was off the hammer of his .44.

A heavyset bald man stood in the doorway of the livery barn, leisurely smoking a cigar.

"Al, do you have room for two more in there?" Sean asked, stepping down from the saddle wearily.

"Sure I do, Sean. Been awhile since you been to town. Did they ever get the bastard that bushwhacked you?" Grey glanced at the Morgan. "Say, ain't that the Hawk?" His eyes widened in surprise. "Nah...couldn't be." But he cocked his head, studying the stallion closer. "Same size, same eyes, same build...and no brand."

"Sure is, Al," Sean replied. "Jess, here, roped him out of the wild bunch we ran in."

"You sure?" Grey slowly walked closer, examining the dark horse until, approaching too closely, the stallion flashed back his ears, striking at him with both front feet.

Grey leapt back as Jess yanked the Hawk back onto his haunches.

"Sorry," Jess said, stepping off the stallion. "You okay?"

Al dusted off his shirt front, laughing a deep, booming laugh. "Took off a couple 'a buttons, neat as can be! That's the Hawk, alright! Bring 'em on in. Have to charge you ten cents more for him though. Stud's like him's a lot of extra bother. And it looks like you're gonna have to take care of him yourself. Don't need to get me or my stable boy hurt by that killer."

Grey looked sideways, taking measure of the man, as Jess hung up his saddle after rubbing down the stallion and shutting him in a comfortably bedded box stall. "You really rope him?" he nodded toward the Morgan.

Jess nodded.

"Well, I don't know what you did to get 'im or tame him down like that, but I figure whatever it was, you sure earned that reward. Stop in my office, an' I'll give you the draft they left here...or I'll cash it, if you like, it bein' Friday night an' all."

"There ain't goin' to be someone wanting him...claiming him?" Jess asked, not wanting to lose the stallion who was working his way into his heart.

"Hell no! Not him! Who'd want a killer like him? Maybe you got him charmed. Wouldn't be nothin' but an outlaw for someone else. It's all he's been since the old mustang stud stole him with a bunch of mares from Old Man Kellerman's. Hell, even the Old Man said so. He even left the Hawk's papers with me, before he died, to go along with the stockmen's reward. Guess he kinda hoped someone would get the horse instead of shooting him. Come along. I'll get what's owed you."

Relief washed through him as Jess followed the huge mountain of a man. He already felt possessive about the little black horse, as though finally there was something that was his and his alone.

"Is Doc in town?" Sean asked as they walked into the office.

"Naw. Ham Martin's wife is down sick. Her an' the kids. Doc and Martha are out there for a few days, till they're better." Al Grey reached into his desk drawer and retrieved a bank draft and a piece of folded, yellowed paper. "Here's the Hawk's papers, all signed, and the bank draft. If you'll sign it, I've got that much cash."

He handed the draft to Jess, who quickly put his name to the paper.

Digging into his cash box, Grey counted out five ten dollar gold eagles. But Jess would only take three of them. "You see that Doc gets the rest," he said to Grey. "I still owe him."

Grey shrugged, poking the coins back into his cash box. "More'n Doc would have charged, but it's your money."

Satisfied, Jess slipped the heavy coins into his pocket and followed Sean out onto the street.

"Al's right," Sean said, as they walked down the dark street. "Doc wouldn't have taken that much."

"Let's just say it was worth it to me," Jess said with a wry smile. "Never know when I may need him again."

The Dead End was a small dining room with a much larger saloon attached. It stood in the center of town, between the livery stable and the hotel. As Sean and Jess walked toward it, relishing a late meal, they could both feel tension building. It was only a short four blocks to the restaurant, but several small groups of men, engaged in intense talk, grew silent as they neared. Then, as they passed, whispering grew. Jess's spurs rang softly in the stillness that felt unnatural on the busy street. All eyes followed them. Sean missed the cordial greetings usually exchanged on the street. He wondered angrily how word of their riding into town could have spread so quickly and why it was so different with Jess beside him.

They ate their generous meal in silence, each with their own thoughts. But the steaks were not improved by the bits of raw talk drifting to them from others in the room. It was not pleasant, being talked about. Generally, Sean enjoyed the din in the café. It added a sense of comfort to a meal in town, one he didn't have to cook for himself. But tonight it only made dinner miserable. Jess looked up at Sean once and shrugged. It was as he expected, as it always has been.

The sound of running boots on the boardwalk brought Jerry Trip's head up from the whiskey he was nursing at the bar of the Steer's Head, down the street. Tad Wilkerson burst through the swinging door, flushed with news.

"Jerry! Jess Hazzard's in town! I just saw him an' Thursten walk outa the Dead End."

The boy's eyes narrowed and his face took on a hardened, evil look, making him suddenly no longer a boy but a hate-hardened man. "You sure?"

"I'm sure. They passed me, as close as I am to you right now." Tad Wilkerson watched Jerry's face, then blurted out, "What're you gonna do?"

But even the false security of the whiskey he drank did not take away the knowledge in the pit of his stomach that even with his months of practicing with his Colt, he was not yet nearly a match for the lightening hand of Jess Hazzard. And the fear twisting his guts angered him beyond words.

"Jerry?" Tad waited, as a dog waits impatiently for his master.

"Leave me alone. Let me think!" He tossed down another glass of whiskey and pushed his way through the doors to the boardwalk outside.

Not fully understanding Trip's rage, Tad followed him to the darkened alley where he stood, intently watching when he spotted for himself Thurston and Hazzard walking toward them.

It was only a few minutes' walk to the hotel, along the oil lamp lit street, but the way led past the two other saloons in town, with men lounging outside of them. Sean could feel Jess growing whipcord tense as he walked beside him, but his friend continued walking in an even, measured stride, giving no outward sign he was troubled.

Then from the deep shadows near the Steer's Head, a somehow familiar, sarcastic voice cut the night. "They shouldn't let damn 'breed convicts walk the street with decent people." There was a silent whir of the cylinder of a revolver being slowly spun.

Jess continued walking, the slight flexing of his gun hand and the twitch of his jaw the only signs he heard the insult.

"Yeah," continued the voice, "you go right on. Only a man would get riled!"

Jess's jaw hardened as he recognized the voice. Jerry Tripp. But he continued walking to the hotel.

"You see what I mean," he said quietly to Sean as they opened the door of their hotel room.

"Yeah. Why is it Jerry Trip hates you so much? He's always been a mean, nasty kid, but he really hates you."

"It was back this spring. I stopped at their ranch, lookin' for work. The boy must fancy himself some kind of gun hand. He tried to prod me into a fight. Like tonight." Weary, Jess sighed. "He wasn't fast. Not even lukewarm. Maybe I should have killed him. But I'm just plain sick and tired of killin' and of men like him. I beat his hand before he got his gun started out an' left him standin' in the yard. The hands got a good laugh at that an' I guess it was harder for him to take than bein' killed." Restless, Jess paced to the window overlooking the town and dimly-it street.

"It'll only be worse tomorrow night. They know I'm here now. They'll all band together like street dogs, gettin' braver with talk an' drinkin'. Then one'll try provin' he's a real man. Maybe it'll be Jerry Trip. Maybe just some drunk cowhand. Suppose they do kill me? What in the hell do they think they're getting? Damnit, why won't they just leave me alone?" Jess asked vehemently, turning back from the window.

A slightly uncomfortable feeling overtook him, seeing the concern in Sean's eyes. *Did I say too much? Reveal too much of myself?* Jess sat down on the bed closest to the door and began pulling off his boots. He did not look up as a grim smile just curled the corners of his mouth. *It's always the bed closest to the door or a chair facing the door with my back to the wall in a restaurant.* He tossed the boots to the floor. *Hell, Jess Hazzard's not a man, but a damned way of life!*

They were both exhausted, not only from the long ride into town, but the strenuous weeks of the horse roundup and breaking. The beds felt good.

Jess looked around. The room was small and cheaply furnished, with one chair, two narrow beds, scarcely more than cots, and a plain wash stand. But it was better than sleeping on the trail. Or was it?

Sean found sleep immediately after pulling the blanket up around his shoulders but Jess lay awake, listening to the sounds of the night. In the distance, faint traces of off-key piano music tinkled from a saloon. Boot heels clomped down the boardwalk. Horses trotted off into the night, their hoof beats sounding hollow on the hard packed street. But night and the bed were soothing, and though sleep finally overtook Jess, it tormented him, as if an enemy. It was not the rest he needed. Instead, the Dream came back.

He had been free from it for months. Perhaps that was why it came to him so strongly, so clearly. The faces of all the men he fought, and killed. He heard their voices, the taunts, could see the fear and hatred in their eyes. He saw their hands move toward their guns, as if in some sort of horrible slow motion. And he saw them die, blood blossoming on their shirts, flopping and twitching in death in the street, blood pooling beneath them in the dust.

Sweat drenched his blanket as he tossed and turned, as if trying to escape the clutches of the Dream. The Mad Dream.

Sean awoke as Jess threw back the blanket and sat up, forcibly ridding himself of the torture. In the faint moonlight, Sean watched as Jess quietly stepped to the window, looking into the night. He was still standing there in the morning. The sweat had dried from his bare shoulders but he looked tired and somehow older.

Breakfast was eaten in peace. It was early and the only other people in the restaurant were the local merchants. The rowdies were still nursing hangovers from last night.

"I'm going to ride out to the fort and see what kind of deal I can make with Captain McMasters," Sean said, finishing his second cup of coffee. "You want to ride with me or stay in town?"

"I think I'll go over to the store first, before it gets busy. Pick up a few things. Maybe after that, I'll ride on out there to meet you. Never did like Bluecoats." Jess grinned.

Sean nodded, chuckling. "I have to get a few supplies, too, but I think I'll wait to see how I come out with McMasters first."

Just after eight o'clock, Jess walked into the merchandise-crowded aisles of the Lawson Mercantile. He was flooded by smells of leather, spices, tobacco, and oil. Because it was so early in the day, Mr. Sexton, the owner, was sweeping the floors, alone in the store. The big, heavily bearded bear of a man put down his broom.

"Can I help you?" There was only a mild curiosity in his voice.

"I need a few supplies," Jess said, his eyes drifting over the heavily-stocked shelves, suddenly aware that now he had enough money to put together a modest outfit to travel many miles. But he did not feel the need or desire to go.

Almost mechanically, he listed the things he needed most, watching Sexton writing on a small pad. "Three boxes of .44/40 cartridges, two sturdy work shirts, two pairs of Levis, socks, gloves, two wool blankets, a light tarpaulin, slicker, saddle axe, flint and steel, a small cooking pot, frying pan, and two bars of soap." As an afterthought, when he saw he still had enough of the thirty dollars, he picked out a used, but sturdy sheepskin-lined winter coat and half a pound of hard candy for Scotty.

As the pile in front of him grew, he felt uneasy, almost lonely at the thought of riding away from the place and people he almost felt he belonged with as part of a family and a small community. Deliberately, he did not buy food or coffee, as if that would commit him to the trail.

"You going to take that with you or do you want my boy to deliver it somewhere?" Sexton asked, studying Jess with sharp, dark eyes that lurked under heavy, bushy brows.

"Why don't you have him take it down to Grey's Livery. I'll pick it up there before I leave," Jess replied, turning to walk away. "Thanks."

"Thank you. It'll be there when you're ready for it."

Jess felt himself relax as he rode across the small river, marking the edge of town. The Hawk threw his head, splashing water with plunging forefeet, also glad to be on the move again. It was only two hour's ride to the fort and Jess was in no hurry, letting the Hawk choose the pace. Quickly settling into a mile-eating jog, the proud, dark stallion trotted southward on the main trail.

Perhaps an hour later, the Hawk snapped alert. Jess could see a rider coming toward him. Still half a mile away, Jess made out the long-legged way Sean sat on his bay.

"Our lucky day, Jess!" Sean called, riding closer. "They had a bout with sleeping sickness and lost a lot of horses. McMasters is sending men up to pick up our horses today. He was more than glad to pay fifty dollars a head, too!"

Jess felt Sean's contagious exuberance and smiled.

"You get your supplies?" Sean asked, reining in next to Jess.

"Waitin' for me, over at Grey's."

"Good. With this windfall, I can pick up a few supplies now and bring the wagon in before winter to stock up." Sean drew a deep breath. "I don't mind telling you I was plenty worried about how we would make it through the winter without them. I owe a lot to you. Without your help, I could never have gotten that second bunch in, let alone broke before McMasters found some other horses. I plan on giving you the sale price of two horses for wages."

"Whoa, Sean," Jess protested. "That's way too much."

Sean held up a hand. "No. Let me finish. We brought in two more horses than I expected, broke and sold them for a good price. When I get to the bank, the money for two horses is yours. I was feeling guilty that we might not get enough for the bunch, and here we are settin' pretty! No use in arguing. My mind's made up. You can use the cash and I'll feel better. After all, look how well we came out on that deal!"

Jess swallowed uncomfortably. *A hundred dollars in cash, decent gear, and a damned good horse. I feel rich, so why do I feel so uneasy when I think about leaving?*

The late morning sun beat down on them as they rode north through the sage-dotted red rock canyon. Far away, a magpie squawked in irritation and a raven took up the call.

"I couldn't talk you into staying on for the winter, could I?" Sean asked, remembering Jess now had his trail supplies. "I have a lot of hay to get up, firewood to cut, and I want to clear the ten acres below the hayfield. I could sure use the help if you don't mind that kind of work." He sounded weak, hesitant, knowing full well most cowboys hated any work that could not be done from the back of a horse.

Jess turned to him with an odd expression. "No, I don't mind that kind of work," he said quietly, fighting mixed feelings. To stay was death. It had always been so in the past. But the day was bright and he chose to ignore the whispers of dread from the darkness in favor of the new emotions flowing within him, sending him soaring until he felt as one with the eagles above.

"Some don't hanker to make hay and work with an axe," Sean was saying. "Say it's farmer's work." The big man looked at Jess with a slight curiosity in his eyes.

"I don't mind." Jess smiled. "I've cut my share of ties back in the Dakotas. And to my way of thinkin', there's more in a man building his ranch than building a railroad to cut the country apart."

"You'll stay, then?"

Jess nodded. "I'll stay."

Chapter 8

The two men talked as they rode the last miles back to Lawson. Their horses relaxed and jogged quietly, tails swishing pleasantly. Ahead, blue gray against the hazy sky, the jagged peaks of the mighty Wind River Mountains beckoned peacefully.

The town was busy. After leaving the horses at Grey's Livery, they walked down the boardwalk to the restaurant. The smell of fried food drifted out onto the street along with the pleasant hum of conversation. The café was crowded with noontime customers but they made their way through the crowd to the empty corner table. Jess settled into the chair in the corner, to face out into the room.

The hum in the restaurant stilled for a minute as eyes lifted to them. Then the conversation picked up again, but was more guarded and intense. And there were those who threw their money down on the table and left, in spite of half-finished plates before them.

Sean and Jess ordered and ate their meals. From Jess's relaxed attitude, Sean could not see any tension in him, but he knew it was there. Maybe it was the way his eyes seemed to soak up every movement, every noise in the room. He ate comfortably and his face was calm, but his eyes betrayed him, as if looking for that one man, that one gun.

Then anger flashed for a second into Jess's eyes as a small group of men began to gather near the door. Finishing their meals, Sean and Jess got up to head back downtown. Among those men, obviously looking for trouble, was Jerry Tripp.

Jess noticed how Tripp followed his every movement with hard eyes. And he knew.

Sean and Jess paused in the shadows of the livery barn door, watching the men, stopped now in front of the mercantile across from them. Waiting.

"Sean, it's happening already. Maybe it's that Tripp boy stirring them up." Jess sighed wearily. "They may call me yellow, but I'm leavin' now. I'll camp by that hot spring we passed an' wait for you there. If I stay in town, there'll be shootin'. They'll settle down if I go." Jess watched a knowing woman gather her small children in off the street. He felt the old pain shoot through him.

"Alright," Sean said, clearly troubled. "Maybe it's best. Jess...I'm sorry."

"It's okay. It's happened before. You couldn't have known." He turned to pack his supplies.

In minutes, he was gone, leaving Sean with only dust and an anger in his chest he could not explain. He stood, leaning on the corral fence behind the barn, watching the empty trail Jess had ridden only moments ago. Then he became aware of another man walking up behind him. Syl Davis, the stocky middle-aged sheriff with a drooping graying mustache and a trace of a belly over his gun belt, stopped next to him.

Hooking his thumbs in his belt, the sheriff looked uneasily about him. "Hello, Sean. How you doin'?"

"Okay," Sean replied, knowing full well the sheriff wasn't here merely to pass the time of day. "Just sold another bunch of horses. This time, I'll get home with the money!"

"Say, Sean, you know there's trouble brewin'. Talk of gunplay maybe. That Tripp kid's itchin' to run that Hazzard outa town...or maybe kill him. I want Hazzard outa my town. And I want him gone now!"

Sean resented the growl in his voice when he spoke Jess's name. "He already rode out. He wasn't running from that bunch of loafers. But he doesn't want any trouble. Sure seems like this town does, though." Sean's voice was unusually hard.

Sheriff Davis held his hands up in protest. "Whoa, Sean. It ain't anything like that."

"Well then, what the hell is it? First they shoot him down. Try to lynch him. Now they want to corner him into a fight he doesn't want. If he's the gunslick you all seem to think he is, he'd probably be out there in the street right now, facing one of them. Maybe you." Sean's blue eyes turned to ice. "He's worked hard for me. Been as good a hand as I could ask for. But one of these days I've got a feeling that someone's going to push him too far. Then all hell's going to bust loose."

"That 'breed's trouble, plain and simple. I just hope it don't come in my town." The sheriff turned and walked onto the street.

Sean stood by the corral until the blood stopped pounding in his temples and the anger lessened in his chest. No wonder Jess was so defensive, so bitter, when he first met him. To go through this, and worse, for years! How could a man help being worn raw?

He stalked past the livery barn, past the dissolving crowd, toward the door of the mercantile.

"Hey Sean, you're gettin' pretty low, havin' a 'breed workin' for you," yelled a jeering, half-drunk cowboy from the hitching rail of the saloon across the street.

Coarse laughter filled the street and Sean's face grew red with anger as he walked into the store.

The mercantile was dark, crowded with a new shipment of stock, not yet put away. Hardware, dry goods, and sacks of feed seemed all jumbled together, piled high in the narrow aisles. Sean was impatient, suddenly wanting to just get done buying and leave town behind him, but the clerk was busy waiting on a woman and there were two other women patiently waiting their turns. So Sean wandered through the shelves, looking at the widely diverse stock – pump leathers, nails, horse shoes, sewing notions, bolts of brightly colored fabric, clothes, tools, bits, harness.

Then in the small back corner that smelled strongly of mellow leather, which was used by the harness maker, Sean saw a new three-quarter rigged saddle. It was built just for a young boy. Horse sized, but small of seat and short stirrups. Sean cautiously turned over the price tag, fingering the carved design on the fender thoughtfully. Twelve dollars. He could remember paying twelve dollars for his working saddle, six years ago. Prices were sure climbing! But, he did get fifty dollars a head for the horses, and it'd sure make a nice Christmas present for Scotty.

Taking one last look at the saddle, he stepped to take his turn at the counter.

"Hello Sean," the thin clerk said, too politely, over his thick glasses. "Is there something I can do for you?"

"I want fifty pounds of flour, about ten pounds of sugar, ten pounds of coffee, two pounds of salt, a pound of baking powder, two sides of bacon, ten pounds of beans..." Sean thought about which supplies were dwindling and what he would need between now and the fall trip to town with the wagon.

"Will there be anything else?" the clerk finished writing, looking up.

"Wrap up about five pounds of salt pork and half a pound of licorice. And I'll take that kid's saddle, back there. But I'll pick up the saddle in a couple of months. I'll pay now."

The clerk looked down to his pad, as Sean finished his order and began to add the short column of figures.

Sean interrupted him. "Almost forgot. I need a couple of pounds of plug tobacco."

Sean paid without a word of explanation to the clerk's raised eyebrows, wishing Ed Sexton was clerking instead of Wilbur Henniger. Ed knew he always bought chewing tobacco for old Ernie.

"Do you want to take your supplies with you now or come back for them?"

"Can you have them hauled down to Grey's? I have to talk to Al about buying a pack mule."

"Sean Thursten!" A frail, elderly woman approached him, as he turned to leave. He almost ran into her. "You should be ashamed! Bringing up a youngster away from a church is bad enough, but with a heathen, a savage, living in the same house! Your poor wife, only dead three years, too!" The old woman gasped. "The Lord will surely bring down hell's fire on you. In sin the poor child's raised. Why the man's not even Christian!"

"Grandma, come away." A young girl tugged at the woman's dress sleeve, looking up to Sean with embarrassment.

"Oh Lord, forgive those who wander from Thee," she prayed, her watery eyes uplifted, as the girl led her away.

Sean turned and stomped out the back door. How the hell does she know he ain't a Christian? She's one to talk, after turning half the town against her son-in-law!

That night, in a hidden camp off the trail, Jess lit a small fire and began roasting the rabbit he shot earlier. Crickets chirruped loudly in the velvet stillness of the night and a wolf howled mournfully in the canyons far in the distance, echoing through the rim rock and red cliffs that surrounded the hot spring.

Deep in his soul, he knew it would happen. *It always had before and always will again. But damn! It still hurt. It about tore my guts out having people look at me that way, like I'm less than human.*

Jess ran his thumb lightly down the fine edge of his knife. He studied the small drop of blood welling up on his thumb. *One drop, full and red. Can theirs be more pure, less poisoned? Can they feel things I can't? Are they somehow more than I am?*

He closed his eyes and pictured Elijah, the old black man who found a fourteen year old boy, snake bitten and scared in the Georgia swamp, a thousand hard miles from home, a stranger in the white man's world. It was Elijah who tried to show him how to live in that confusing world.

He remembered what Elijah said. "Boy, when you kin look them right in the eye an' hold your head up, you're jest as good as them. When you hang your head, you quits bein' a man."

His thoughts drifted back to the soft, kind man who was a second father to him. He could see his gentle eyes, his weathered, wrinkled face and strong hands, and hear the violin music he played around a small campfire in the middle of the hidden island in the swamp. The memory tugged at Jess's heart. Elijah remained a man until the very end. Until the white slave hunters rode him down in the bayous of their hidden home.

Weary, Jess lowered his head into his hands, listening to the wind whisper of loneliness through the rock walls that sheltered his camp. Being alone in the wilderness could feel uplifting, cleansing. Being alone in a crowded town was hell.

Then his thoughts were interrupted as all at once, sounds ceased. The Hawk raised his head and stared into the blackness of the night, flaring his nostrils to catch a scent. His ears were pricked straight toward the trail. Even the wind paused and seemed to wait expectantly.

Jess stood up, tense, and listened as he slipped the thong off of his gun and moved silently away from the fire's light. There it was. The faint clop-clop of two horses walking along the road, turning off, coming closer. He crouched in the shadows, his hand on his gun, waiting.

Then there was a soft, familiar whistle. The one Sean used to call Scotty. Relief washed over him.

"Come on in Sean," he called, holstering his Colt. He squatted down by the fire and watched the fat from the rabbit slowly drip down into the coals with a loud hiss. Mindless fire-watching. He looked up to see Sean ride into the firelight leading a big, spotted mule wearing a pack saddle.

"Mind some company?" Sean asked, stepping down. "I have coffee."

Jess shook his head and accepted the bag of coffee. As Sean

unsaddled and picketed his horse, then unpacked the mule and picketed him as well, Jess carefully measured coffee into a pot of water.

They sat, hovering over the warmth of the fire, each with his own thoughts, waiting for the coffee to brew. The sharp wind blew, heralding the snows that would whiten the mountain peaks all too soon.

"It's starting," Jess began slowly, with difficulty. "Sooner than I figured. But it's starting and I'd best be movin' on before it gets worse. Tomorrow, I'll ride on north." The twitch in his jaw, the way he couldn't look at Sean, told more than words.

"You never hit me as the kind to run away from something," Sean said gently.

"Yeah. All my life, I've been in one scrape after another, an' met 'em head on. Maybe that's how it kept getting worse. Funny, though. I almost felt human lately." Jess released a weary sigh.

"I don't think anybody's fired up enough to come out to the ranch. It's mostly just talk. Whiskey talk."

"I know. This time. But one of these days someone will come. Maybe Jerry Tripp. Maybe someone else just lookin' for the name. You wouldn't want me to gun a man in front of Scotty, would you?"

Standing quickly and spinning in one liquid and lightning motion, he drew his gun and put five shots into the rabbit skin hanging in a tree, barely visible, ten yards away. There was a single, rolling roar, as one shot blended with the next. The skin twitched and leapt, as the bullets punched black holes into a spot, scarcely as large as a small child's fist.

Spent, Jess sat down and numbly reloaded the still-smoking revolver. "Sean, that could have been a man," he said, scarcely above a rough whisper. It was no brag, rather a somber confession of something terrible.

It was the first time Sean saw the power of that cold blue Colt, the blurring speed of Jess's hand. It chilled him to the bone. He never had any doubts Jess was good with a gun, but he was faster than he ever dreamed a man could be. Fast, calm, and terrifying. And it left a knot in the pit of his stomach, knowing Jess's words were truly spoken. In that brief instant, when Jess was drawing that revolver in a faintly seen blur, it seemed he ceased to be the man he knew and became the gunman, feared everywhere he rode.

"But how do I explain you just riding off? Tell me that." Sean looked directly at Jess. "Scotty would understand you fighting to protect yourself. It's not the same as gunning a man down, just to see him die. And what about you? You're not just some saddle bum, content to drift around all your life. You have to stick somewhere and make some sort of life for yourself. You know you want to...need to." Sean's voice was earnest, nearly desperate.

Jess was quiet for long minutes, weighing Sean's words, for he knew Sean was the only one who could see inside him, cut through the bitterness and pain.

Finally he sighed, giving up under Sean's direct, waiting gaze. "Alright, Sean. Maybe you're right. But whatever comes, it's my affair. I won't put you or Scotty in any danger. Whoever or whatever comes, stay out of it."

The quiet warning in his words reminded Sean of the buzz of a rattler. And it brought extra chill to the night wind.

Chapter 9

Late summer melted into autumn. Even a slight wind sent trembling golden aspen leaves falling with a quiet rustle, to carpet the ground underneath with yellow-gold coins. It had been a good time for Jess. Mowing and putting up the lush meadow hay near the river hardened his muscles, and the sweat he put into his work seemed to purify his body and cleanse his mind of the past.

On several rides to the wild lake above the Thursten ranch, Sean noted with some satisfaction that Jess was drawn to the abandoned homestead at the head of the lake. As they rested the horses, letting them graze the lush grass in the meadows near the old barn, Jess would drift to the hill overlooking the beautiful clear green lake and stand a long time, lost in thought, perhaps beginning to allow himself to dream.

Sean began to hear Jess speak of the homestead, from time to time. "Was me, I'd have put the cabin up here in the trees, so you could see the lake all year and watch the elk and moose come out by the river." Or, "A man could tap that spring on the hillside and bring water right down to the house and barn." They were small things, to be sure, but seeds, and they did not go unnoticed by Sean.

The boisterous pup Scotty smuggled home from the Millers' was quickly growing into his name, Bear, and while Sean and Scotty took the wagon, team, and pack mule into town for winter supplies, Jess stayed, content with the ranch and the mountains. The elk were beginning to bugle now, and he seemed to find time every day or two, to ride upriver to the old homestead in the early morning or late evening, just to hear the elk music echoing across the lake from the hills and mountains around it.

Only one thing troubled Jess now, a new and very different recurring dream. He dreamt not about shooting and death, but of a beautiful, dark haired young woman. And she was crying. He had no idea of who she was or why he would be having such a dream, but he, like his people, the Chiricahua, always set great store by dreams. Perhaps in time, its meaning would become clear to him. While he hated to feel the woman's sadness, the dream was not entirely unpleasant for him, as she would turn to him through a misty fog, as if asking for his help. Asking for him.

Two weeks after Sean and Scotty made their last, thankfully uneventful trip to Lawson, returning heavily burdened with feed, supplies and a few extravagances such as white sugar, as well as several wheels of cheese Old Ernie made, two smoked hams, two sides of bacon, seasoned pork sausage, and a bucket of lard from the Millers, Sean and Jess were once again busy with routine work.

They sawed wood from the ten acres Sean planned to clear, hauling some to the wood pile, where it was blocked and split for firewood and the best, sorted for building logs, fence posts, and rails. Work went quickly and easily, though it was well into November, when in a normal year the snow would be deep and the peaks heavily coated in a blanket of white lasting until spring. So far, there was only an inch of snow on the ground.

Jess was just backing the team up to hook onto a load of logs when he stopped, suddenly alert. "Sean, there's someone comin'."

"You sure? I don't hear anything."

"Yeah. Sounds like a single horse...trotting." His right hand brushed his coat back, clear of his revolver, and he slipped the thong free.

A cutter, pulled by a dark bay mare, came into view on the trail, just above them. On seeing Sean and Jess, the two heavily bundled people in it waved merrily.

"Hey!" Sean exclaimed, "It's Doc Stone and Martha! Tie the team and come on." The big man pounded the wood chips from his clothing and headed for the visitors.

Jess tied the team out of the wind, and followed Sean, relief flooding his being. Not trouble, this time, but, instead, he was about to meet the man who saved his life after he was gunshot by the posse.

They met the sleigh as it pulled up in the shelter of the barn. The horse was covered with a thin coat of snow, as were the bundled doctor and his wife. Shaking the snow from their hats and scarves, they pulled the robe from their laps. Doc Stone, a short but well-built man with graying hair and lively, good-natured gray eyes to match, stepped out of the cutter.

"Hello Sean!" The Doc patted the mare. "Do you have barn room for Ruby?"

"Sure. Plenty of room. Why don't you go on into the house with Martha? We'll put up your mare and rig."

Jess took off his gloves and helped Doc's attractive, silver haired wife from the cutter. She had smile-wrinkled, kindly eyes and pink cheeks from the cold wind.

She smiled at Jess pleasantly as she stepped down. "Oh! They didn't tell me you were such a gentleman. Thank you." Martha took his hand and gracefully stepped down.

Jess flushed. "You take them on in, Sean," he said, turning to unhook the horse. "I'll put her up. Won't take the both of us."

Sean needed no further urging and he escorted Doc and Martha through the yard to the cabin.

Jess rubbed the mare down and threw a light blanket over her to absorb the remaining dampness from her sweated coat. Then he bedded her well, brought her a pail of water, and threw down enough hay to keep her happy.

There was a great deal of bellowing and stamping from the Hawk's stall as he scented the strange mare.

Jess laughed. "You'll live without love, fella. Spring's a long ways off an' you don't have mares of your own yet!" He closed the barn door behind him and pulled the cutter out of the falling snow into the lean-to. Deciding they wouldn't be cutting much more wood that day, he walked back to the clearing and brought in the team, as well.

After caring for the team, he made his way back through the yard toward the cabin, stamped the snow off his feet and pants, then brushed off his coat as well as he could, and opened the door. Voices, engaged in warm, lively conversation, came from within. He felt the warmth from the fire and stepped into the room.

"Well!" said the Doc with a broad smile on his face, "I see another patient of mine made it! You certainly look a lot better than the last time I saw you! Put on a couple of pounds too. Good." The doctor reached out his hand to Jess.

"I hear I've got you to thank," Jess reached out and met Doc's strong grip.

"Think nothing of it," chuckled the Doc. "You're a walking advertisement for my proficiency! Pregnant women, gunshots, and rheumatism! Maybe I'll specialize!"

"Simon!" Martha scolded with a good-natured smile.

"What brings you folks out here, this time of the year?" Sean asked.

"A pregnant woman!" Doc laughed out loud, looking at his wife. "Jenny Miller's baby was born yesterday and she kind of wanted Martha with her. So I came along for the ride. Another great big, red-haired boy. And, as long as we were this close, we figured we would drop by."

"Glad you did," Sean replied. "Can you stay a few days, this trip?"

"We'd like to. But we're pushing our luck, having the pass open this long. Lucky it's been a dry year! We'd better leave in the morning. Don't want to gamble on this snow lasting too long or getting heavy."

Martha interrupted graciously, "But I've brought some things in the sleigh for a big Thanksgiving dinner tonight. Most of it is already cooked up."

"Is it Thanksgiving?" Sean blurted in surprise.

Martha and Doc both laughed. "You live too far out! Yes, it's Thanksgiving," Doc chuckled. "And you should smell that turkey! Twenty pounds and fully cooked, with stuffing, to boot! And I sat with him under me the whole way!"

"What can we do?" Sean asked enthusiastically.

"Well, I have the turkey, some rolls, bread, pies and some other things out in the sleigh," Martha smiled at Sean's bachelor-eager acceptance. "About all I'll need are potatoes, milk and butter."

"Oh boy!" exclaimed Scotty. "A real Thanksgiving dinner! Can I help?"

"Of course you can," Martha said kindly. "First you can get a good supply of stove wood for me, and a big dish of nice potatoes." She turned to Jess. "Mr. Hazzard."

"Just Jess, Ma'am."

She smiled. "Alright. Jess. Could I persuade you to go out again into the snow and get those boxes in the sleigh? There are three of them. I don't need to remind you to be careful of the pies and pickles in them."

"Sure, Ma'am. Anything else?"

"No. Thank you. Now let's see..." She turned away with the efficiency of a gentle drill sergeant.

By nightfall, everyone had that pleasant, over-stuffed feeling commonly associated with holiday dinners. Only Doc had ever tasted such food as they ate. Even the pup, Bear, had all he could do to thump his tail politely when someone walked by the spot where he lay.

Scotty helped Martha wash dishes and the men sat near the fireplace catching up on the past year's happenings, both in town and at the ranch.

Jess sighed comfortably. This sure was a change from the last year at this time when he had sat in his cold cell on the north side of the prison. The meal had been cold, soggy dumplings that may have had some turkey mixed with them. It was brought to the prison by the Laramie church women, doing their Christian duty of the year. He was suddenly very thankful the old sorrel chose the trail to the Wind Rivers.

A week later, winter hit the mountain valley full force. The snow quickly became deep and, at times, the wind, bitter cold, but in order to have the new pasture ready by spring, Sean and Jess worked nearly every day, cutting and hauling wood, making the clearing larger.

In spite of the cold, sweat flowed freely down Jess's face as they sawed on a big aspen. He glanced at Sean on the other end of the crosscut saw and grinned. Red faced and blowing, he worked with dogged determination.

The tree creaked, swaying slightly. Then, as they stepped back, slowly at first, then faster, it crashed to the snow-packed ground.

By now their work was automatic. They sawed the straightest pieces out of the aspen log and dragged it to the ever-growing pile by the fence. Jess then hitched the heavy team to the branches Sean lopped off and hauled them to one of the piles in the clearing to burn later on. Following that, they loaded lengths of the better tops onto the bobsled to pile and dry for firewood next year. They saved the straightest pieces of pine and fir logs for future building material and the smaller trees and tops were sorted for fence posts and rails.

That winter, they sweated, froze, cursed, and laughed at those logs. The harder nature made it, the harder Sean and Jess worked.

The teams struggled in the snow, then later in the mud. The horses strained against the logs they pulled through the deep snow. Often Sean and Jess limped back to the cabin. Trace chains snapped. So did their tempers. Reins were torn. And so were their hands. But always they were back the next day, ready to battle those trees.

Finally, there was only one pine left at the end of the day, in the middle of May. It still stood guard over the new clearing. They leaned wearily against it, wiping the sweat from their faces, the dirt from their hands. Spring was swelling about them, and they were finally nearly done. It was a small tree, almost insignificant, and both men felt a swell of victory. Soon this would be down, the clearing cleaned up, seeded, and would become a pasture until the stumps rotted away or were burned. Then it would be a good hayfield. In the high country, a rancher needed hay to winter his stock. As Sean's small cattle herd increased, so would his need for hay.

"Well, Sean, we got it licked," Jess sighed, pushing the hair out of his face, resetting his hat.

"Yeah. Sure was one hell of a job though! Let's go on down to the house and get a cup of coffee."

Jess nodded as he followed Sean. "Tomorrow, I'm gonna go out and see if I can't get us a deer. Sure hope there's more sign than there was last week. They should be all over the place by now, fast as the snow's been melting in the high country."

"You're not complaining about the salt pork again, are you?"

It was a standing joke between them. Every time Sean cooked salt pork and beans for more than two days in a row, Jess would quietly take down his rifle and bring home some fresh meat.

"Naw...not me," he grinned.

"Say Jess," Sean said, stopping in his tracks, "someone's coming. Looks like Sheriff Davis' gray."

Jess looked up quickly, a clammy feeling crawling up his back, a tight, painful feeling in his gut.

The sheriff's big, stout gray gelding jogged slowly down the hill and into the yard. The sheriff nodded to them, reining in.

"'Lo Sean...Hazzard."

"Syl."

"You look like you been doin' a little work."

The small talk screamed in Jess's brain. *What does he want?*

"Yeah. We've been clearing a new pasture north of the barn." Sean looked at him questioningly. "What brings you over the pass this early? Get that bushwhacker?" Sean asked hopefully.

"No. Not yet. You know old Walt Peterson?"

"Heard of him..."

"Well, last week he won a few dollars in a poker game. On his way home, he was murdered. Right in town." The sheriff looked at Jess. "Stabbed to death and robbed." The sheriff paused. "Three witnesses saw him." He gestured toward Jess with his rein hand, his right hand held close to his gun butt.

"What?" Jess snapped alert, eyes blazing in anger.

"There's three people say you murdered a harmless old man...for forty dollars."

"That's a damned lie! I ain't been any closer to town, than I am right now, since summer!"

The sheriff was glad Jess was unarmed, but even so, this was one job he'd gladly have passed off on somebody else. There was no mistaking the fire in Jess's eyes.

"Now I'm willin' to listen to reason. Where were you three days ago?"

Jess thought back confidently, then felt a sinking feeling grip his insides.

"Huntin'..."

"Anyone with you?"

"No."

"How long were gone?"

"Two days. There was no game out." Jess knew this was just long enough to slip the noose around his neck.

"It ain't the first trouble in town, either. There's been a lot of funny business around, since you showed up. Robberies, folks bein' shot. Now Peterson. Don't look so good." The sheriff shrugged his broad shoulders. "You'd better get your horse and come with me." He lay his hand on his gun, meaningfully.

Like a cornered cougar, Jess judged the distance between himself and the sheriff. In a whirl, his years in the territorial prison came back to him, and the vow he would never be behind bars again. If he moved fast enough, maybe he could get to the sheriff before he could shoot. He had a horse that could run, and even death was easier to face than a day in a cell.

But he glanced at Sean. And Sean looked him directly in the eyes and plainer than with words, pleaded with him to stop. It was the hardest thing he would ever ask of Jess.

The tenseness went out of Jess's corded muscles and he turned into the barn with helpless resignation. The sheriff rode to the door and watched him. Numbly, he pulled his saddle off the rack and walked towards the Hawk's stall. Then Sean was beside him. Jess looked up.

"Sean, I swear to God I never even rode near town." His voice rasped as he wondered if Sean doubted...

"What? Hell, I know that! But I thought you were going to get yourself killed out there!"

Jess shrugged in agreement. "I'd rather that sheriff shot me dead right there. They'll hang me for sure. And that trial, if there's even a trial, is gonna be hell."

"I know it'll be rough. But it'll be better if you just ride in with Syl. They can't have good witnesses. How could they see someone that wasn't there?"

Jess smiled ruefully. "You got a lot to learn, yet."

"Scotty and I'll start after you in the morning," Sean said, shaken. "We'll get us a good lawyer and start pounding the alleys to find out just what did happen. It's a small town and someone's bound to know. Just give us time."

"Okay." Jess's eyes lifted to the dark silhouette of the sheriff on his horse in the doorway.

Seeing them coming, Davis reached inside his coat for a pair of handcuffs. Something like a clawing panic hit Jess square in the chest. His eyes blazed a furious protest.

"I don't think you'll need them, Syl," Sean said quietly, again holding Jess back without a touch. "He's riding with you peaceable. He's done nothing for you to slap those on him."

The sheriff shrugged and slipped them back inside his coat, deciding to leave well enough alone. He could feel how dangerous Hazzard was, but even Jess Hazzard couldn't beat a bullet.

Jess turned to Sean. "Thanks, Sean," he sighed. "I'll see you." His eyes said more. Then he turned and swung effortlessly onto the Morgan.

Seconds later, Sean stood numbly alone in the yard. The birds were still singing, the new grass, still green, but a pall seemed to have settled over the world. It didn't seem real. He looked around, his mind not yet working. Where was Scotty? He'd have to get Ernie to come watch over things while they were gone. Was he wrong to have told Jess to go? He knew that only he had held Jess back from jumping the sheriff. Would he have made it to freedom? Suddenly, he felt the cold, heavy weight of responsibility.

A wave of sickness passed through him. Three witnesses were more than enough to hang a man. Especially when they were townspeople and Jess was a half-breed gunfighter they feared. Damn! He wiped the cold sweat from his face.

Sean went into the cabin and began packing his saddlebags, gathering bedrolls while he waited for Scotty. Was that Bear barking? Sean paused and listened. Yes, it was. Scotty must be coming. How could he possibly explain all this to him?

"Pa! Jess!" Scotty shouted excitedly. "Look what Bear caughted!"

Sean opened the door. Panting for breath, Scotty was running toward the cabin, his hands holding a big rabbit swinging limply by its hind feet. "Bear caughted it all by himself! I told him he could have some for supper." Scotty looked around, sensing something was wrong. "Where's Jess?"

Sean sighed. This was going to be hard. "Come in here and sit down."

Scotty looked puzzled but did as his father told him, while fighting a growing fear.

"The sheriff from town was here this morning. He said some people saw Jess kill and rob a man in town. So Jess had to go with him."

"He's a liar!" Scotty shouted. "Jess wouldn't do that! I know he wouldn't!" he exclaimed hotly, rising from his chair. "They're all liars!" His voice rose to nearly a scream.

"Easy Son," Sean put his hand gently on his son's shoulder. "I know that. But we'll have to go to court and tell a jury. We'll ride to town tomorrow and see what we can do to help."

"Those people from town don't like Jess! They're the same ones that shot him! They want him dead!" The boy's eyes were wide with fear.

"It'll be alright. Now go do your chores while I finish here, so we can tell Uncle Ernie what's happened." Sean put his arm around his son to comfort him. There was something wonderful in the boy's complete faith in Jess. A faith all heaven and earth could not shake.

Chapter 10

It was a long ride into town and it was made at a slower pace than Sean would have liked, but Scotty would not be left behind, and kept up well for a seven-year-old boy. Along the trail, Sean unconsciously glanced at the small, round prints of the Morgan, bringing a sickening reality to their ride.

Darkness was beginning to fall when they entered the outskirts of Lawson. Worn and stiff from the ride, Sean dismounted in front of the jail. "Stay here, Scotty. I'll only be a minute."

Sheriff Davis sat at his desk, reading some wanted posters. He looked up uncomfortably. "Sean." He nodded an abrupt greeting.

"Hello, Syl. Is it alright if I go back and see Jess for a minute?"

"He's not here, Sean."

Twenty miles down the trail, southeast of Lawson, a huge, gorilla of a man turned toward Jess, riding, hands bound, beside him. A marshal's badge was revealed on a stained and unkempt shirt front. His close-set black eyes sparkled like a snake's and his thin mouth broke into a cruel smile, revealing tobacco-stained teeth. One huge hand dropped to the heavy quirt that hung loosely by a thong on his saddle and his blunt, dirty fingers ran over the butt thoughtfully, almost lovingly.

"We'll camp here tonight," he said, snapping the quirt lightly across Jess's handcuffed hands for emphasis.

Jess felt a surge of anger at the uncalled for abuse, anger at being once again accused of something, though he was totally innocent, and anger at being turned over to this madman they called Marshal Blueson.

Jess remembered him well, all too well. He was a guard while Jess was in prison. "Mad Blueson" they called him there. Of course, no one dared call him that to his face for many times only a single word spoken at the wrong time, a hate-filled look, or even laughter would bring about a terrible beating and volley of oaths. Two men died under the rages of Blueson's insane ravings the last year Jess had been there. Until one of his spells struck, he could be almost normal. But once begun, he truly fit the name of "Mad" Blueson. How could he possibly be a marshal now?

Jess carefully lifted his leg over the saddle horn and slipped to the ground. He knew he must take great care not to stir Blueson's passion, for he was in no position to fight back, even to protect himself. At least the Hawk was still safe in town. He would have never stood for the mishandling Blueson would have given him. One of them would have been killed. Today he rode a placid livery horse that would put up no fight being unsaddled or tied by a madman.

"Over there," Blueson gestured with the quirt that was almost a living part of him. "Get down by that tree."

Silently, Jess walked to the small aspen and knelt down.

Blueson handcuffed Jess's hands behind him, to the slender tree, unsaddled and tied the horses, then returned to him.

"I knew I'd meet up with you again someday, Hazzard. I just knew it." His eyes peered into Jess's expressionless gaze, focused back toward the mountains and it irritated him. "Look at me, you bastard!" He flicked the tip of his quirt at Jess's cheek, leaving behind a slight trickle of blood.

In the way of his people, the Chiricahua, Jess neither flinched or changed his expression, though his heart swelled with bitter hatred.

"Must be the Injun. Or can't you feel nothin'?" He laughed coarsely then turned to make a camp before darkness fell.

Jess leaned wearily against the small tree. The handcuffs were too tight and they bit roughly into his wrists, cutting off the circulation, numbing his hands. For an hour he listened to a pair of coyotes yowl back and forth in the distance. But his thoughts drifted back to the ranch, his one island of peace and he clung to it almost desperately. He thought of Thanksgiving with Doc and his wife, of Christmas, when he and Scotty rode into the woods like a couple of boys, in search of a Christmas tree and throwing snow at each other. He remembered decorating the tree, Sean reading the boy the Christmas story from the Bible on Christmas eve, and the joy in Scotty's eyes when Jess made him a present of the old sorrel he loved. Peace on earth. It was like a pleasant dream. Now he awakened and was once more tossed into the seas of hell.

A prisoner of Blueson! It could get no worse. The huge man clung to the fire, mumbling to himself. He bent down to the coffee pot, burning his hand. He swore viciously, throwing the pot into the brush. When he looked up, the firelight caught his eyes with an uncanny glow.

"They let me go. After six years they fired me!" His voice echoed in anger. "Six years' work in that lousy hole an' what'd they do? Fire me! Just because some weakling scum couldn't take what they deserved. So a couple cons died. So what? There was too many of them anyway!"

Jess shifted his weight uneasily, trying to work some feeling back into his legs and hands. He could sense Blueson was quickly becoming dangerous, like a vicious dog. He lowered his eyes to avoid drawing his attention to him. He vainly hoped the madman would become so involved with his ranting that he would forget his prisoner just outside of the firelight.

"They laughed at me, so I just taught 'em to respect me. An' they fired me for it!" He slowly turned his head and his gaze riveted on Jess. "You all laughed at me behind my back, didn't you?" He rose silently to his feet. "Listen to me, damn you!" He slashed at Jess's face with his quirt, but Hazzard managed to duck so that his shoulder caught the blow.

"You son of a bitch! You never did learn any respect for a white man!" The quirt lashed out again, only this time, Blueson was closer. He did not miss. The tip sliced through the back of Jess's neck.

"You rotten bastard! You cons cost me my job! Damn you! Damn your rotten hide! Damn you!" His voice rose the roar of a charging bull.

Again and again the whip fell expertly on Hazzard's shoulders and back. He managed to keep his face protected, as he'd seen Blueson take the eyes out of a prisoner. But he knew he could not last for long under such an insane attack. The man's strength was incredible! Already, Jess could feel the strength draining from his body with the shock of each well-placed, cutting blow.

"I'll mark you so's you'll always respect me! You'll never forget how to treat a white man!" Blueson screamed.

Jess moved as close to the tree as he could, gaining as much room as he could. There was not much chance, but maybe. Blueson stepped toward him again and Hazzard kicked out with his boot at Blueson's broad forehead. The kick was well aimed, but the huge brute shook it off like an enraged bull. It took him by surprise, but only further enraged him. Like poking a stick at a buzzing rattler.

"Soooo You want to fight, eh? When I finish with you, you won't be so cocky!" he hissed viciously.

The whip fell with more force and became even more cutting, peeling off flesh and spraying blood in its wake. It sliced through Hazzard's shirt, through his skin. Muscles corded tight in Jess's arms as he strained against the handcuffs. They cut into his wrists as he prayed one might slip. They did not.

Slowly, he was beaten down by the rages of the madman. Finally he slumped and merciful unconsciousness ended his pain. He dropped to the grass which was wet by his own sweat and blood.

Not yet sated, Blueson lashed again and again at Hazzard's still body, until, finally growing tired, he kicked wickedly at Jess's head, turning away with a hysterical laugh when he felt the pleasure of his kick connecting with flesh.

Before dawn, Sean was on his way to Carter City. Following him by an hour or so, came Doc Stone, his wife and Scotty in their buggy. He could travel much faster alone. Excuses, Syl Davis had given him. But Sean knew the reason Jess had been moved to Carter City. The trial would be over a lot sooner. The judge was already there, Doc told him. There and waiting. Sean was terribly uneasy. Anger welled within him and he wished for Satan, remembering the powerful, untiring gaits of the stolen black gelding. He again urged the bay on south at a gallop.

Four hours later, Sean spotted the outmost buildings of Carter City. Not much of a town, he thought, riding past the tumble down, weather-beaten buildings that had once been a thriving mining town. Now it was just a tired hole.

There was the jail, in similar disrepair. Sean dismounted and quickly tied his sweating horse. He mounted the creaking steps to the marshal's office with one swift stride. On opening the door, Sean saw Blueson, filling the doorway into the cell block, as he leaned to put a rifle into its rack behind the desk.

"Yeah?" he snarled, "Whaddya want?"

"I'm Sean Thursten, from Lawson," Sean said, not liking what he saw of the marshal, "They tell me you brought Jess Hazzard here. Can I talk to him?"

"I dunno. What business do you have seein' him, anyway?"

"I'm a friend of his," Sean said, fighting down his dislike of the grossly-built man.

Blueson looked at him with cold eyes. "Didn't figure he had any friends. I'd haveta lock you in with him. I'm goin' fer breakfast..."

Sean could see the marshal did not want him to talk to Jess.

"That's okay. Lock me in with him."

"Yuh know, the bastard tried to escape last night on the trail." Blueson fumbled for his keys.

A sinking feeling again came into Sean's stomach. Something was very wrong here and getting worse.

"In here, Thursten." Blueson unlocked the door into the musty, dark cell.

Sean entered, hearing the raw clank as the marshal slammed the door and left. There was the smell of blood from the cell, sweet and sickening. "Jess?" Sean called in panic. Had the marshal shot Jess?

"Sean?" It was Jess's voice, quiet and questioning from the soft darkness of the windowless cell.

"Yeah, Jess. Are you okay?" Concern was strong in Sean's voice.

"Sure. Where's Scotty?" Jess hoped Sean would not see what he must look like. But he could not bear the boy to look upon him.

"He's coming. On the way with Doc and Martha." Sean's eyes were rapidly becoming adjusted to the dim light. And what he saw sickened him. Jess sat on a dirty bunk, leaning heavily on the stone wall for support, blood on the wall, on the bunk, his shirt in tatters, mingled with his flesh.

"God! What happened Jess?" Sean stepped closer.

"Nothin'..." He winced as he tried to straighten up, realizing he was slumped against the wall. Some of the thick scabs that had crusted on his back cracked and fresh blood trickled from them.

"Nothing my eye! Let's see." He drew a match from his pocket and lit it. Moving it from Jess's face to back, the big man was choked by gore rising in his throat. And he realized the blood smell was from his friend's body and face.

"Jesus Christ! Who did that? The marshal?" he demanded, straightening and starting for the cell door violently.

"Don't Sean!"

"I'll kill that bastard with my bare hands!"

Jess had never heard such anger in a man's voice.

"Sean! Sean. It'll heal." Jess reached up and grabbed his friend's arm. He could feel it trembling in rage. "It'll be alright. Don't cross him. I knew him back in prison. He was a guard. But he's crazy. Mad dog crazy. He's killed men for no reason with that quirt." It was hardly Jess's voice, as his speech was distorted by the swelling and bruises on his face.

"He had no right to do this!"

"He just went berserk. I was 'cuffed to a tree and couldn't keep away."

"The bastard!" Sean again turned quickly away.

"Sean! Give me your word you'll leave him alone. He'll kill you."

A wave of weakness hit Jess. He let go of Sean's arm, closing his eyes against the pain.

"Oh Jess. Is there anything I can do 'till Doc comes?" Sean asked in helpless frustration.

"Just stay outa Blueson's way. An' Sean? It'd be better if Scotty didn't see me like this." His hand made a weak gesture.

"Don't know if I can keep him away."

"There's things a kid doesn't need to know about. An' Blueson might hurt him."

"Yeah, I know. Try to rest and we'll be back."

"Thursten! You done yet?" Blueson's coarse voice rang down the hall.

"Yeah," Sean replied harshly, trying to keep the rage he felt under control. "Listen Jess. Hang in there awhile longer, till Doc comes. Maybe he can give you something."

Jess sighed heavily as Sean left. At least he spared his friend the worst of it.

An hour later, Blueson grudgingly allowed Doc and Sean into Jess's cell. Jess smelled a lamp being lit and heard Doc Stone rummaging through his bag.

"Why no human being in his right mind could have done that!" Doc exclaimed, taking a quick deep breath, seeing the extent of the savage beating. "He's the one who should be in here instead of Jess!"

Then his voice quieted, seeing Jess's pain. There was the sound of water being poured and something being mixed.

"Jess, take this. It will take away some of the pain."

Jess felt a cold cup and drank the contents quickly. Bitterness clawed his throat but the cool water felt good.

"Can you lie face down on the bunk, so I can do something for your back?" he asked kindly.

Jess felt for the edge of the bunk and lay down carefully, slowly. It was a long hour later when the long, swollen gashes were cleansed thoroughly of dirt, pieces of shirt, and caked blood. While Doc Stone worked, Jess lay, eyes closed, as if asleep. Only the sweat on his forehead, wetting his hair, and the white knuckles where his hands gripped the sides of the bunk showed what pain he knew. The laudanum did not help enough. Sean had to turn away to keep from vomiting.

"I can't sew them up. As dirty as they were and with all those bits of cloth imbedded, they would become badly infected," Doc said, gently smearing some warmed salve thickly on Jess's lacerated back. "There. You can sit up, if you'd like."

Jess let out a slow breath of air and shakily sat up, pushing the wet hair out of his face. He was trembling and felt dizzy. *Maybe it's the drug Doc gave me.*

"How do you feel?" Sean asked anxiously.

"I'm okay." Jess's voice was tired, strained.

"Do you want me to give you a rest?" Doc asked kindly. "Or shall I finish now?"

He was gently touching the welts and looking over the angry cuts and bruises on Jess's face and neck.

"Might as well get it over with," Jess answered, drawing a breath.

"This won't be nearly as bad. Some shallow cuts, bruises. Hmmmm" Doc studied the ugly bruise just above Jess's right temple. "What happened there?" lightly touched it.

Jess shook his head. "I don't remember. I don't think he got my head before I passed out."

Doc Stone shook his head is dismay and began examining him closer. "Sean would you go get me some more warm water?" He rummaged through his bag, thinking.

Jess felt it in his gut. *He knows. He knows.*

Sean's footsteps faded down the hall.

"I take it Sean doesn't know?" Doc asked gently as he continued his examination.

"No. I'm worried about him as it is. I don't want him flyin' off the handle and gettin' into it with Blueson. You can see what he's like."

"He'd want to know, Jess. Can you see anything at all? Light? Here, I'll hold up a match."

Hopefully, Jess listened for the match to be struck. He smelled the sharp, acrid sulphur fumes and strained to see even the suggestion of a light. Some sign he was not really blind. But there was nothing.

Only velvet blackness and despair.

"Nothing?" Doc asked softly, already knowing the answer.

"No." Again, for a moment, Jess felt the strangling panic he felt when he regained consciousness in the cell, to total blindness. Then, whether it was the drug that Doc gave him or just pure exhaustion, he felt tired and weak and wanted to be left alone.

Sensing his feelings, Doc gently laid and encouraging hand on his shoulder. "It may not be permanent, Jess. I've seen something like this last for only a few hours or days. Others...months. We'll know more in a week or so when the swelling goes down."

"Might not matter then. The trial's in three days." Jess's voice caught as weariness overcame him.

"What?" Doc demanded.

Jess nodded slightly. "Guess they want to get it over in a hurry."

"You just rest and concentrate on mending. Sean and I will make sure you get some justice! A good lawyer is first on the list. We'll get started, right now and we won't quit until this is righted!" Doc's voice dropped. "Sean's coming now."

Jess listened to the familiar approaching footsteps.

"Sorry it took so long. I had to go to the café for water. The well out back's dry."

"It's okay," Doc said, closing his bag, "I'm finished here for now. Why don't you leave it. Maybe Jess will want some, later. I see he has no water in here. Let's go buy Jess some clothes and let him rest. He needs it and we have a lot to do."

"I saw Ed White's rig down at the livery. Wasn't he supposed to be one of those witnesses?" Sean asked.

Doc Stone nodded. "There's a lot happening, Sean. We'd better let Jess get some rest while I fill you in."

There was a jangle of keys and a creaking chair. Blueson's heavy shadow darkened the cell like the spirit of doom. "Don't know why you bothered," he sneered. "He's just gonna hang."

Redness flashed up Sean's neck and the cords along his throat tightened as he tried desperately to suppress the rage within him. Catching himself, he strode rapidly down the hallway, followed closely by Doc and the raucous laughter of the marshal. As they paused in the office, where Sean picked up his revolver, their glances met over the short, heavy whip on Blueson's desk. Dried blood was caked on the lead tips and lash. Sean turned violently away and strode outside onto the boardwalk, suddenly needing clean air.

"That Blueson is inhuman!" Doc exploded as soon as they were out of hearing from the jail. "In all the years I've been a doctor, I've never seen a man so savagely beaten!"

"God, Doc, I know. When I went to get water, I got to thinking about Jess, back home, teasing Scotty...working in the hay with me...up looking at that old homestead at the head of the lake. Then that damned whip. Do you realize how hard he must have fought those handcuffs to cut his wrists up that bad?

"I couldn't get back right away. I couldn't stop throwing up." Sean sat down at the corner of the walk, his hands clasped, hanging between his legs. The street was quiet, with only a stray black dog wandering about aimlessly. "Hasn't he had enough, already? I feel so damn helpless!"

Doc Stone sat down next to him on the rough planking. "Sean. Did you notice that big, ugly bruise on his temple?" Sean nodded. "He didn't want you to know."

"What, Doc?" The catch in Doc's voice made Sean fear his next words.

"Sean…he's blind"

What could only be described as a choked roar of pain erupted from Sean, as he leaped to his feet and started back for the jail.

Doc followed and grabbed his arm in alarm. "No, Sean!"

"I'm going to kill that son of a bitch!"

"Sean! Stop. Think!"

Doc tried to hold Sean back, but the big man shook loose, sending him reeling up against the side of the building with a crash.

"Sean! You'll make it worse for Jess!"

Sean took two more steps before the truth of Doc's words sank in, curbing his rage. He slammed his fist helplessly into the wall. Lowering his head, he sighed, then turned back to Doc, feeling shame. "Are you alright?"

"Sure." Doc put his hand on Sean's shoulder. "Are you?"

"I could kill him! I don't know how I can stand being around Blueson without getting out of hand."

"You have to remember that he has Jess locked in there. Anything we do or say to rile him will only put Jess in danger."

"Yeah. I know." Sean breathed deeply in resignation.

"I hate to tell you right now, but Jess's trial is in three days."

"Three days!" Sean exclaimed in ragged panic. "My God! What can we do in three days?"

"We'll do what we need to," Doc replied calmly. "We just need to work faster. Now our witnesses are coming into town. I've seen Tad Wilkerson and Ed White's here. That leaves Jerry Tripp."

Sean looked up, past Doc, shook his head, and gestured down the rutted street. On a lathered red gelding, Tripp rode down to the saloon, sitting jaunty in the saddle, and yanked the horse to a stop, stepping off. Sean took a step toward him and was stopped by Doc's gentle grip on his arm. "No, Sean. Let's get Jess some clothes, then you ride back to Lawson and see what you can find out. Someone's bound to have seen what really happened that night. It was right in the middle of town and it wasn't late. Let me talk to those witnesses. I might get more out of them than you would. And Sean, see if John Jordan will come and defend Jess. He's good. I'm not sure who is available for an attorney, here...or even if there is one."

"Okay, Doc. I guess your way makes more sense. We don't have much time to waste."

Chapter 11

A day later, they had accomplished very little. The only attorney in Lawson flatly refused to defend Jess and the one they finally turned up in Carter City beat around the bush so badly they knew if he did take the case, he would do little to help.

Sean could turn up only bits of what people saw the night Walt Peterson was murdered and no one wanted to be involved. Only Clay Johnson may have seen something. He was the last to see Peterson alive. But he suddenly took the stage to Pinedale and wouldn't be back for three days or so.

Ed White only repeated the bare story the sheriff told, not wanting to go into detail and refusing any further questioning. Tad Wilkerson stuck tight to Jerry Tripp and both sarcastically bantered Doc's questions.

Night fell and down the dimly lit street, Jess waited. His whole being ached and the slightest movement caused stabs of torturing pain. There was little doubt in his mind he would hang. He wiped his head gingerly with his hand and sagged wearily. Sleep must have come to him, for again, in surprise, he saw her face; the dark, tragic eyes, the soft brown hair. And he knew she needed him to help her. He reached out his hand to her. In the background of the misty dream, he distinctly heard a baby crying. *A baby?*

Waking with a start, he heard the door to the jail office open, footsteps, then the door to his cell open. Jess tensed. Was it Blueson? The steps sounded different.

"Hazzard?" It was the young deputy's voice.

"Yeah?"

"Blueson's gone over to eat, so I brought you something. It's just stew but I reckon it's better than that slop he brought."

Jess struggled to straighten up, then said with a tight voice, "Lot of trouble to go to for a killer, ain't it?"

"If I thought you were, I wouldn't have brought it. I met your friend's little boy. He'd make a good defense lawyer," the deputy said quietly. "And Doc Stone brought me into this world...and he thinks a lot of you."

Jess heard the bowl being set next to him on the bunk, smelled the good, home-cooked stew, and heard the deputy turn to leave. "Deputy. Thank you."

"Let me know if you need anything else. There's coffee on the tray, too. Watch it. It's hot."

Later that night Sean and Doc Stone sat out in the cold night air, still trying to plan their best strategy. Scotty was in bed, but they didn't want their conversation to be overheard.

"Doc, what in the hell are we going to do about a lawyer? Try and find one in another town?"

"We don't have time. Even if we did, I don't know if we'd do any better than we already have. I'm going to ask Jess if he will let me defend him. I studied law in Pennsylvania before I decided to become a doctor."

"Why didn't you say something sooner? I was just about to go crazy trying to think of something!"

"Well, under the circumstances, I don't know how good a job I can do, but at least I'll try. I guess I was afraid of the responsibility...holding a friend's life in my hands."

Sean nodded. "But how can their lies stand up in court? There isn't one shred of evidence except for what they say they saw."

"They call them eyewitnesses. Before all this happened, I'd have said they didn't stand a chance of convicting Jess. Now, I'm not so sure." Doc shook his head sadly. "I just don't know what more we can do."

Chapter 12

Jess sat expressionless in the witness chair, waiting for the prosecuting attorney to begin. An hour earlier, the three 'witnesses' were called, in turn. They each recited their version of the murder that sounded very well-rehearsed and almost exactly matched what the sheriff said. But Prosecutor Downs had a knack for twisting what little they actually said into a great black fabric of guilt. The only sounds in the full courtroom were rustling papers and an occasional creak of a chair or cough from one of the onlookers.

There was a scrape of a heavy chair being moved and the prosecutor arose.

"Jess Hazzard," Downs said. "Is that your real name?"

Jess nodded slightly.

"Please answer. Yes or no," the judge instructed, sounding bored.

"Yes."

"Ah, but isn't it true you weren't born with that name? But were, in fact, born in an Apache village?" The prosecutor seemed very pleased with himself.

"Objection, Your Honor," Doc Stone rose. "Where he was born has nothing at all to do with this case!"

"If Your Honor pleases," Downs silky voice dripped. "I believe it has everything to do with it. And if you will permit me, I will proceed to show it."

"Objection overruled!"

Downs smiled. "Now, I repeat my question. Were you born in an Apache Indian village?"

"Yes."

Downs leaned closer. "Your mother?"

"Her name was Joanna Stuart," Jess answered quietly, waiting.

"Ah...a white woman? Just how did she come to live with Indians?"

"She was a survivor of a raid on a stagecoach."

"Survivor?" Downs asked abruptly. "Don't you mean captive?"

"She was a captive, but after a year, she married my father, became one..."

"A Christian white woman? Marry a savage? A heathen? Don't you mean he took her? Forced himself on her?" Downs shouted, pounding the desk.

"No," Jess bit off the word. "The Apache's morals are a lot better than most whites. They were married."

Jess heard Downs breathing angrily next to him.

"And then you came along. Just how long were you there? A half-breed, living as an Apache?"

"About fourteen years."

"And in that time, were you a prisoner in any way?"

"No."

"Then you were free to come and go as you pleased, and you chose to stay with those blood-thirsty savages?" he asked incredulously.

"They were my people," Jess said simply.

"Doc," Sean whispered urgently, "can't you do something? They're going to hang him on this alone!"

"I can't Sean! That judge won't let me get a word in. Maybe we can undo some of it later."

Downs continued persistently. "And, in that time, did you participate in any raids against whites?"

Jess was silent.

"Shall I repeat my question?" Downs sneered.

"I rode as a novice, not as a warrior." Jess clenched his jaw, waiting for the damnation that would surely follow. A loud murmur went through the crowd.

"Ah!" Downs exclaimed triumphantly. Turning to the jury, his voice grew louder, more dramatic. "You see, a man reared as a savage does not change! Just as the murdering Indians he was well trained by, with little regard for the life of one old white man, he stalked poor old Walt Peterson, stabbed him to death, and robbed his body!"

"Objection, Your Honor!" Doc leaped to his feet. "Mr. Downs is trying to sway the jury! If he wants to recite, let's put him on the witness stand."

There was a burst of laughter from the crowd. The judge rapped his gavel gruffly for silence. "Objection overruled!"

"You see what I mean, Sean?" Doc sat down, disgusted.

"And, to further my point," Downs smiled contemptuously, "where, exactly, did you spend the five years prior to coming to Lawson?"

Jess could feel the smile, the maliciousness in his voice. And he felt backed up against a cliff.

"In prison." Jess's voice held a bitter edge.

"May we ask why you were there?"

"My partner and a whore framed me."

"Let me restate my question. For what crime did they convict you?"

The cords in Jess's neck stood taut and white, as he remained silent.

"Were you not convicted for the robbery and rape of a young white woman?" he shouted.

Sean was jarred badly by Down's last accusation, and half expected Jess to explode.

"Your Honor," Downs continued, like a hound on a hot scent, "Please instruct the witness to answer."

"Answer the question." The judge leaned closer to hear the reply.

The courtroom was so still that one could hear the horses outside stomping impatiently.

"Come, now," Downs persisted. "It shouldn't be that hard to answer. Just a simple yes or no will do. Were you convicted of the robbery and rape of a young woman?"

Sean was appalled at the prosecutor's tactics. *My God! Don't do this to him! Jess could no more rape a woman than murder an old man.*

Jess's voice was hoarse. "I was, but I didn't..."

Downs cut him off and spun to face the jury. "You see, it all follows a pattern! Brutality and robbery! Always a helpless victim! You can't turn this beast loose on society! Next time it may be one of you! Or your wife or child!" His gaze went from face to face, to emphasize his point, before he turned back to Jess.

Jess felt hot, trembling as much from anger as weakness from his beating.

"Now, just where did you say you were, at the time of the murder?"

"Hunting."

"Was anyone with you?"

"No."

"Why were you hunting alone for two days?"

"We were out of fresh meat. There wasn't any sense of two of us going out. Someone had to do chores. There wasn't any game sign."

Jess drew a breath, realizing the worst was over.

"Well, did you bring back meat? A hide? Anything to show that you were hunting?"

"No. I never saw a deer or elk."

"I believe that will be all, Your Honor. I'm sure justice will be served today."

Sensing Jess's weariness, Doc Stone stood up slowly, feeling older than he had this morning. "Your Honor, this man has been beaten nearly to death by a man wearing a badge in this town. May I request an hour's recess, that he might rest, before continuing?"

The judge looked at Downs. "Do you have any objections, Mr. Downs?"

"Why no, Your Honor. But I fear that it will take longer than that to pull their flimsy case together!"

"This Court is adjourned until one o'clock." The judge rapped his gavel, looking bored.

Back in the jail, Sean and Doc stood opposite where Jess sat on his bunk.

"Here, you'd better eat this." Doc handed him a sandwich. "There's coffee, too."

Weary, Jess shook his head and said, "Not much of an appetite, Doc."

"Look, son, you've had a damn bad beating and if you're to stand up under all this, you have to eat something!"

Jess realized Doc was worried. Yielding, he took the plate, and ate the tasteless food.

"Now, we don't have much time. Jess, I know you'd rather not talk anymore, but there's a few things I've got to know if we're to stand a chance."

Jess nodded faintly, wishing they would just go away.

"Let's see. One of the parts that did the most damage was the part about those raids. Tell me, just exactly what a novice does in a raid?"

Sean listened, interested. There was no way he could believe Jess, living Apache or not, would outright murder anyone.

Jess gave a half smile, perhaps remembering the days of his youth.

"Well, he holds the horses, carries water...kind of a chore boy for the men. The novice is kind of between a boy and a man, until the men feel he's ready, able to be trusted in battle."

"Then you didn't do any actual fighting?"

"No." He smiled. "Not because I didn't think I was ready, though. The only raids I was on were to steal horses and cattle in Mexico. It was in the night and the men got thirty horses and fifteen head of cows from a ranch without waking up even a dog."

Doc nodded, satisfied. "What about that...about the woman," Doc asked gently. "We know it wasn't like they made it out. What really happened?"

Jess felt a sense of relief wash over him. Since old Elijah was killed, he had never had anyone believe in him, without question, until now.

"I had this partner and we spent the summer runnin' wild horses. We were supposed to split the money, fifty-fifty. I ended up doin' most of the work. Jed liked to gamble and spend time in the rooms over the saloon. But that wasn't so bad. I didn't like bein' around him much, anyway.

"We drove the horses in to the railhead, to sell. He took the check to the bank to get it cashed and I couldn't find him for two days after that. I wanted to pick up some supplies and clear out, so finally, I hunted him up.

"Like usual, he was in the saloon...upstairs in one of the girls' rooms. I found out the room number and walked in on them. He had this whore in bed.

"The money was on the table, next to the bed, with some other stuff outa his pants. I just walked over, counted out my share and started out.

"Then all hell broke loose. That girl started screamin'. Jed jumped up, grabbed his pants, knocked me down and ran out of the room. I fell against the bed and that whore grabbed my arm and started scratchin'.

"About then, the crowd from downstairs showed up...along with Jed in the lead. You can guess the rest. The only reason they didn't lynch me then was the girl disappeared, along with Jed, and there was no witness. Still, I was a 'breed with a reputation, and that bought me five years."

Jess leaned back against the wall, stiffly. "I don't think it'll help, Doc. They're out for blood. Nothin' you do will matter. But thanks, anyway."

"We have half an hour before we've got to be back in court. Here's another cup of coffee. We'll leave you alone, so you can get a little rest." Doc squeezed his forearm.

"You okay, Sean?" Jess asked. "You're too quiet."

"Yeah, Jess. This whole thing is just so damned rotten."

"It's okay. If I'd gone off somewhere else, instead of stayin' at your place, I wouldn't have had anything. This last year's been good...damn good."

"We better go now, Sean," Doc Stone said, standing.

Jess closed his eyes, unconsciously hoping to again see the woman's face, as if somehow she brought comfort to him. Seemingly, he had not slept, but hearing heavy steps approaching, he jerked awake, alert.

"Come on, you bastard." Blueson opened the cell door. "Time to get back to the courtroom. Maybe Judge Thomas'll quit this monkey business an' sentence you." He grabbed Jess's arm and roughly hauled him to his feet.

As if Blueson's words foretold the afternoon, the judge seemed in a hurry. Between the prosecutor and himself, they shot down Doc Stone's defense in minutes, point by point.

Repeatedly, Doc tried to bring the questioning into some semblance of fairness, but would be quickly stopped by Down's objections.

"Your Honor!" Doc finally rose angrily. "I demand the right to proceed with this defense in a normal manner!"

"You demand!" the judge retorted in disgust. "You don't have any rights! This is my courtroom, and you are taking up too much of my time!" The judge pounded his gavel to emphasize his point.

"Will the jury please rise!" The judge turned from the red-faced doctor, dismissing him. "You will now retire to make your decision. It is my hope that you will be fair...and speedy!"

"I don't believe that!" Doc Stone turned to Sean in total frustration. "This isn't a court of law!"

"It isn't, Doc. It isn't." Sean's mind was unclear and whirling. It was like a nightmare so unreal he knew he was dreaming, even while asleep. But this nightmare was no dream.

The jury only deliberated for ten minutes before the jury room door opened and they filed back into the courtroom. Sean felt like he was going to be sick. He turned to look at Jess, the brutal marshal on one side of him. There had to be something they could do! The foreman of the jury rose and faced the judge.

"Your Honor, we find the defendant, Jess Hazzard, guilty as charged."

Jess sat immobile, not giving any sign that he had heard the verdict. He had known from the start he would be found guilty. It was the white court's way. He just wished it would all end.

"Will the accused stand and face the bench!" The judge looked bored.

Jess felt for the edge of the table in front of him and rose to his feet without expression.

Mechanically, he droned, "Jess Hazzard, you have been found guilty by this court of robbery and murder. Tomorrow morning at dawn, you will be hanged by the neck until dead. And may God have mercy on your soul."

Jess heard Sean's footsteps as the big man stood and abruptly left the courtroom. Then the room hummed with dozens of voices, speaking at once. Drained of all feeling, he felt himself walking down the boardwalk, next to the young deputy, toward the jail.

Only minutes later, Doc and Sean were let in the cell with him.

"Jess," Sean began, "Jerry Tripp's left town, and I'm going to get the truth out of him, if I have to beat him within an inch of his miserable life." And Sean meant just that. "I know he's behind all of this and somehow, I'll prove it! I have a horse ready outside now."

"It won't do any good. Even if it did, I wouldn't want to live out my life, blind."

Sean could see Jess was totally resigned to his fate and it brought a painful catch in his throat.

"I'd better get going so I can catch up with Tripp. Doc, watch out for him, eh?" His voice was unsteady. Would he ever see Jess, alive, again?

Jess reached out and gripped Sean's hand strongly. "Thanks. You're a good friend."

Five minutes later, the echo of galloping hoof beats was all the company Jess had. "Adios, sheekasay," he whispered, unconsciously using the Apache word for brother. The medication Doc gave him allowed him to sleep for several hours, untroubled and without pain.

Whether the drug wore off, letting the pain again reach his consciousness, or some small noise troubled him, he stirred restlessly. Chilled, he moved away from the wall. With his hand, he swept the damp hair from his sightless eyes.

Again, he heard a sound, a light, hesitant step. A board creaked.

A small voice called out, just above a whisper, "Jess?"

Hazzard raised his head and listened. It came again.

"Scotty! What the devil are you doin' here?"

"I had to come." He sniffed and sounded like he'd been crying. "Don't make me go. Please?"

"But how'd you get in?"

"I snuck in past that ol' Marshal Blueson and the deputy said I could stay a few minutes." Scotty sniffed again.

"Here, you'd better blow your nose." Jess smiled a little and handed him a cloth Doc left. "There. That's better."

Jess could tell the boy was crying again. "Hey, that's no way to be," he said gently, reaching through the bars to touch the boy's warm, soft hair.

The sobbing boy reached through the bars and threw his arms around Jess. Hazzard held the boy to him, sharing his pain, wishing he was good with words. The boy was crying freely now, and Jess could feel the hot tears soaking into his shirt and he flinched uncontrollably, feeling his throat tighten painfully.

"Oh Jess! Why do they do these things to you? I hate all of them!"

Hazzard regained control of his voice. "Whoa, now. Don't do that. You get to hatin' people and you'll turn out worse than they are. Look what they're like now."

The boy hiccoughed. "But I heard them say they were going to hang you." A sob blotted out the rest of his words.

"Come on now, it's not all that bad. Why your Pa's on his way to get Jerry Tripp to tell the truth about what happened. I'll bet by mornin' he'll be back and they'll find out what really happened."

Calmer, now, the boy ceased crying.

"Do you really think so?" He hiccoughed again.

"Sure. Look, you'd better get outta here, now. And be careful. I promise things will be alright again, okay?" It was the first promise in his life he wouldn't be able to keep.

"Okay." The boy sounded more hopeful.

As Jess listened to the boy walk away, a stab went through his heart. "Sean, you've got a good boy there," Jess said to himself. "Help him get over this."

Chapter 13

Finding Jerry Tripp took longer than Sean expected. Trailing the two sets of prints, fresh on the trail, he dared not ride faster, for fear of losing them. Tad Wilkerson was with Jerry. You could almost bet on that. The boy was like a fawning shadow to Tripp.

The now-familiar tracks, set deeply in the spring-moist ground, turned off onto a faint trail a few miles south of the Tripp ranch. Dusk was overtaking Sean and he felt a panic grip him. *If I lose those tracks in the dark...*

Where are they headed? Trying to second-guess them was impossible, and would surely be fatal to Jess. Then, just as the last light faded into darkness, Sean spotted a pinpoint of light ahead. It was a small cabin, with a corral attached. Barely visible in the deep shadows were several horses.

Unsure of himself and what he was about to do, or even what he might be looking for, Sean tied his horse back, off the trail, in some dense brush. Then he crept stealthily toward the cabin, using every bit of cover available. The horses in the corral moved about as he passed. They were uneasy but not spooked. Suddenly, Sean recognized his own stolen gelding! Satan! Sean's thoughts spun. *Did these two not only frame Jess but are the ones who shot and robbed me?* His black whickered a welcoming, quiet greeting and moved closer to the fence. Sean laid a gentle hand on his silky neck then moved on toward the cabin, stopping to crouch beneath the small window on the side of the cabin.

From within, a voice Sean recognized Tad Wilkerson's said, "Call you and raise you ten."

There was the sound of cards being thrown on a table. "You goin' in for the hangin'?" Tad asked, collecting his winnings.

"You're damned right I am. I'm gonna stand there and watch Hazzard drop into hell!" Tripp exclaimed viciously.

"We gonna still keep robbin' folks after he's dead?"

Tripp snarled, "Now that would be stupid! Makin' those town people believe Hazzard was nippin' away at 'em, so they'd take care of him for me worked so well. If we kept it up, someone'll get to wondering and we wouldn't have a clear road any more. We've got enough here..." There was a heavy thud and a muffled jingle of heavy coins. "...to last awhile. And the Old Man will give me what I ask for." He mimicked his stern father. "If I stay out of trouble."

They both laughed. There was the sound of a bag being emptied on the table and Sean strained to peer into the window from the side, to avoid being seen. Tripp sat with his back to him and Tad was running his hands through a pile of bills and coins. The bag had the imprint of the Lawson National Bank!

The bank that had been robbed last year! And in the pile, were three worn wallets of different sizes and shapes, as well. But one drew Sean's riveting attention. One of those wallets was his! Suddenly the pieces all fit and he knew, without a doubt, who killed Walt Peterson. And why.

Sean quietly hammered back his rifle and kicked the door open wide. Stunned shock mirrored the faces within and Tripp's hand slipped, like a snake, toward his revolver.

"Go ahead. Save me some trouble!" Sean encouraged bluntly.

Wilting, Tripp dropped his gun on the table, out of reach.

"You too," Sean motioned to Wilkerson with the barrel of his Henry.

White-faced, Tad gingerly added his revolver to the pile.

"Now, which one is the old man's wallet?"

Neither made a move to answer, but Tad Wilkerson's eyes flew to a flat, worn billfold for a second. Cautiously watching the two, Sean reached for it. There were several papers inside, including a crumpled feed bill and a letter, both bearing the name of Walt Peterson.

"You'd better saddle up boys. We're going for a ride."

Sullenly, the pair stood and moved toward the door. Gathering the contents of the table into the canvas bank bag, Sean followed, his cocked rifle trained on the two ahead of him.

Outside, Sean watched as Tad Wilkerson followed his orders, switching his own saddle from the worn bay to his big, tireless black.

He stood a chance of reaching Carter City before dawn, now.

"Now get mounted." Sean waited until they were mounted, then tied their hands securely to their saddles and stepped onto his black. "Ride for Lawson, and make it as fast as those horses can go. We're going to pay the sheriff a visit."

"Won't do any good." Tripp replied sarcastically. "By the time you get back, the 'breed will be stretchin' hemp. An' I'll spit on his grave!"

"Jess should have killed you, when he had the chance. Ride!" Sean slapped Tripp's horse with the flat of his hand.

In Lawson, Sean pounded on the jail door. It was nearly three in the morning! It had taken him eight hours to make the rough thirty miles to Lawson and he had less than three to make it back. Again, impatiently, he pounded loudly on the door. A light went on and Syl Davis appeared at a window, lantern in hand. A look of surprise crossed his face and he disappeared from the window to unlock the door. Coming out onto the porch, he stood in his underwear, gazing in bewilderment at Tripp and Wilkerson.

"Sean! What the hell's goin' on? You know what time it is?"

"Yeah, Syl. Let us in and I'll explain."

Inside, Sean dumped the bag on the sheriff's desk and shoved Jerry Tripp into a cell, keeping Wilkerson with him. Stammering and sputtering, the sheriff walked back and forth in agitation.

"Look in that sack, Syl."

Half asleep, the sheriff put on his reading glasses and held the lantern close to his desktop. Impatiently, Sean shoved Wilkerson down in the chair next to the desk.

"These boys have been busy lately, Syl. They shot and robbed me, stole my horse, robbed the bank, and who knows how many other folks. And they killed Old Man Peterson!"

"Now wait a minute, Thursten," Tad exclaimed in a high-pitched, panic stricken voice. "It was Jerry! I didn't kill anybody!"

"Shut up, you fool!" Tripp snarled from the cell block. "Damn it, keep quiet!"

Wilkerson cringed in fear, then looked from the sheriff to Sean, knowing he had already said too much.

The sheriff shook his head in disbelief as he looked over the wallets and the large amount of money in the bag. "I don't know what to say, Sean. Guilty as egg-suckin' dogs. I thought for sure..."

"Yeah, so did a lot of other folks, it seems. Let's go to the telegraph office and send word to Carter City."

"Sean, we can't. They took down the lines to Carter City when the mines closed four years ago."

"No!" Sean pounded the desk in frustration. "Well, quick! Write out something for the marshal. I'll carry it horseback, then." Sean threw a wanted poster at the sheriff. "Hurry up, it's getting late!"

"You can't make it, Sean," the sheriff muttered, as he scrawled his message. "That's thirty miles of mighty rough country in less than three hours!" He handed the paper to the big man.

"I'll make it," Sean said with determination, jamming the folded paper into his pocket. Without looking back or closing the door, he yanked the reins free and swung onto the back of his big black.

Although Jess could not see the early rays of dawn, he knew it must be time when the Deputy opened the cell door.

"It's gettin' light," the deputy said quietly. "He wants you."

"Yeah." Jess stiffly got to his feet. His back would not allow him to straighten, but he forced himself upright and was soon able to follow the deputy's lead.

"I want you to know I'm sorry about all this. Wish there was something I could do. If there was any way I could get you out, I would."

Blueson interrupted by slamming the office door open. "Where the hell's the 'breed?" he roared impatiently. "Ah! I've waited a long time for this," he said with a coarse laugh.

Jess stumbled over the doorsill as the two men led him outside. Strangely enough, he felt nothing. His soul was numb from so many conflicts – his hatred for Blueson, bitterness toward the liars who had so easily sworn his life away, his affection for Scotty, great gratitude for Doc Stone's trust and kindness. And Sean. There were no words to describe his feelings toward the man who had become more than a brother to him.

And the woman's dark face. Jess sighed. *Maybe she's an angel I'll meet in the other world.* He smiled slightly, wryly. *Or just a foolish dream.*

Nowhere was there fear for himself. From birth, he was always but a step away from Death's door and came to regard it as something inescapable. To fear death was to fear life. Soldiers, gunmen, outlaws, "good" townspeople, and finally the badge of justice gone insane, they all tried to bring him fear and death and they all failed. Until now.

The ground was rubbery under two inches of new snow as Jess was led to the gallows. The air smelled fresh and invigorating. Somewhere close, a shutter flapped noisily in the cold morning wind and children played with a barking dog. As they walked down the street, he heard a low murmur ahead. Jess knew it was a crowd gathering around the gallows. They were the kind of people who get entertainment from death. And, today, there were more than an average number of these vultures crowded around the scaffolding, waiting. A church bell tolled mournfully, though Hazzard knew it was too early for church.

Ahead, Jess heard Blueson pause and there was the hollow sound of his heavy boot on a wooden step. There was the smell of newly cut pine. Were they there already?

"There's eight steps," the deputy said unsteadily.

Hazzard felt for the first one and stepped up. He cursed his blindness as he stumbled up the rough stairway. Then he stood on the platform and he could smell Blueson's hot breath on his face. The fetid smell sickened him.

"Shorten this rope up!" Blueson commanded. "This rope's too long. We don't want it to be easy on the 'breed by breakin' his neck, do we? Shorten her up so he'll kick!"

The rough rope was dropped over Jess's neck. Somehow, Jess found comfort in the deputy standing beside him. It would come soon, he knew, then, from somewhere in the darkness, a tearful voice came, cutting Jess to the heart, crumbling to dust his strength in the face of Death.

"Jess...." called Scotty. "Jess?"

"Scotty, go back!" he commanded hoarsely.

"But you didn't do anything!" the boy sobbed.

"Go on," Blueson ordered the hangman. "Finish it. We ain't got all day!"

"In the name of God, someone get that boy outa here!" Hazzard cried desperately, feeling every muscle in his body tighten, as if he could burst his bonds.

"Well, if you won't, I will!" Blueson shouted viciously.

Jess heard a step behind him and the floor beneath him fell abruptly away.

Sean was still five miles from Carson City and he held Satan to a steady pounding gallop. He glanced for the hundredth time at the horizon and spurred his black hard, for streaks of gray were beginning to show in the sky. The powerful black thoroughbred laid his ears back and lengthened his stride. Sean knew the horse could give no more speed. Already, gobs of white foam flew back into Sean's face from the gelding's sweat-soaked neck.

Down a ridge they charged, toward the wide stream near the abandoned mines two miles from town. Spray and ice crashed around them as the black leapt and churned through the water, throwing a curtain of silver spray into the air. There was no slack in his stride, but as he thundered up the far bank, Sean could feel the horse's hindquarters tremble with weakness as he scrambled desperately to keep his footing at that speed.

The big black was panting now, his nostrils flared and red. Never before had Sean misused a horse so badly, but he knew what the cost would be if he was too late.

The outskirts of town came into view. The black was weary now and his stride grew staggering, but still he ran on, teeth bared wildly and his nostrils open and red. He had outrun his stamina and was running on heart only, heart that would soon give out.

A crowd was gathered down the street ahead and Sean knew they were at the gallows. He could make out Jess standing there in the dim morning light and he shouted to get people's attention. The shout was unintelligible, a combination of rage, joy, and hope.

But suddenly that joy and hope were shattered as if they had been crystal for the trap of the gallows fell open and Jess dropped.

The crowd parted in panic as Satan thundered through, spraying mud and lather as he slid to a stop.

"Cut him down!" Sean shouted desperately to the men on the gallows, fearing he was too late. "I found out who really killed Peterson! Here's a letter from the sheriff!" Sean could only watch the rope, swinging back and forth.

The deputy desperately yanked his knife free and hacked the taut rope apart, not knowing what else to do. Blueson's mouth gaped open and for an instant, the deputy thought he was going to strike him down.

Sean flung himself off the big black and ran to where Jess lay in the shadows beneath the gallows. Was there any chance at all that he still lived? It didn't seem possible. A he knelt over Jess, he saw his son. The little boy's eyes were swollen and red, tears leaving their trail down his shining cheeks.

He had seen it all.

The boy stood so stricken by grief he could no longer cry. He just stood looking hopelessly.

Sean gently loosened the rope from Jess's raw neck. His neck had not been broken, but he was not breathing and his face was an ugly, mottled color. The big man numbly became aware of someone approaching, puffing from running. It was Doc.

Sean looked from Doc to Scotty, then staggered to his feet, feeling a great heaviness in his chest. There was no reality for him. Nothing. He was too late, he knew, as Doc rushed by him.

"Sean. Sean!" Doc called to him. "He's alive! His pulse is weak, but he's alive!" The doctor's voice shook with emotion he seldom let himself feel.

Jess drew a ragged, choking breath, his body convulsing with the effort. And another. Doc loosened his collar and threw the rope away.

"Leave him alone!" A mighty roar filled the air. "He was sentenced to hang, and by God he's gonna die!"

Sean was barely aware of Blueson's words, so numb was his mind. But when the marshal's whip sang across the big man's back, an unholy rage swelled his soul.

With an unintelligible roar, Sean spun like a great cat, to face Blueson unafraid.

As the marshal raised the quirt a second time, Sean sprang at him. The whip expertly cut a gash in Sean's muscular neck, but he never felt the blow.

Blueson was stepping back for a third blow when Sean's charge caught him and carried him backward. All his fury landed a terrible blow below Blueson's ribcage, nearly doubling the huge man. Breath exploding from him in a loud grunt, he fell to his back in the mud.

In his violent rage, Sean's only passion was to pound Blueson to death with his fists. When Blueson struck him in the face with a wicked blow, he never gave an inch, grabbing the huge man by the shirt front, hitting him square in the face with every ounce of strength he possessed.

Unable to stand back any longer, Scotty ran to Jess's side. *Please God. Don't let Jess be dead!* He grabbed at Hazzard's arm and pulled at it in desperation. "Jess! Get up. Please be okay!"

Through a clouded mind, Jess sensed the boy at his side, weakly reached out a hand, and squeezed Scotty's. Then, teetering on the edge of life, he began to hear sounds of the nearby struggle.

"What's goin' on?" he managed to whisper.

"What was bound to happen," replied Doc. "It's Sean and Blueson."

"No!" Jess cried in alarm. "Blueson'll cut him to pieces with that whip!"

"Don't misjudge Sean." The doctor laid a gentle restraining hand on Jess's shoulder. "He's doing just fine."

Again and again, Sean pounded Blueson, ripping the whip from his grasp and throwing it far into the crowd. His fists smashed blows to Blueson's face and body, and Sean felt an unholy satisfaction every time he felt flesh sink beneath is hands.

Unable to withstand the onslaught of Sean's rage, Blueson could only back up, stumbling, away, trying to escape those terrible, punishing fists. He had never been beaten before. When he finally slumped, nearly unconscious, blood running freely from his swollen, cut face, Sean grasped his shirt once again, yanked him to his feet, then hit him again and again in the face, leaving his features nearly indistinguishable.

It was a rage to kill and nothing short of sheer exhaustion brought Sean back to reality. In a final gathering of his last strength, he again dragged Blueson heavily to his feet, and with the last of his fury, he hurled him off his feet to crash against the gallows.

Exhausted, Sean fell to his hands and knees, fighting for breath. His shirt, soaked with sweat, blood, and mud, hung from his body in great, tatters.

"Doc, what's happened?" Jess heard nothing but silence and Sean's ragged gasps for breath.

"It's over, Jess," Doc replied with satisfaction. "Lay still. The day will never come when Blueson will use that whip on anyone again."

"Pa! Pa!" Scotty ran to Sean's side. "Pa, you beat him!"

Awareness filled Sean's glazed, empty eyes, and he staggered to his feet.

"Pa!" cried Scotty, trying to make his father, still drunk with exhaustion and grief, hear him. "Jess's alive! Jess is alright!"

Sean drew a wracking sob of breath and his face convulsed, instinctively raising upward, eyes closed in relief. "Thank you, God." Then, as sweat poured from his face, he hugged the boy to him and closed his eyes.

Chapter 14

It was one of those first spring days, when everything is right with the world. The bright sun and breeze quickly warmed and dried the ground and left a fresh earth smell floating in crisp air already fragrant with the smells of new aspen leaves, pine, and short green blades of grass pushing up through the stubble of last fall's turf. It was the kind of day that turned one's thoughts to planting seeds, and to newborn baby animals.

Though he was still sightless, Jess welcomed the new day. Earlier than usual, he sat up on his bed, listening to the first morning birds singing outside. He rubbed the corded scars on his upper back and shoulders. His wounds were almost healed, and the relief from constant pain added sweet comfort to the morning.

The day dawned sunny and bright. He put his hand to the window pane and felt the warming morning rays through the glass. The sun would feel good on his back. Naked to the waist, he silently opened the door. Bear greeted him with an eager whine and wagging tail.

By now the big dog knew where Jess went, and by going straight to the destination, generous praise or a bit of meat always fell his way. On the porch, Jess laid his hand on Bear's collar and without hesitation, they started for the barn.

As they walked, the cool air against his sun-warmed skin almost felt like a cold shower from a mountain waterfall. The mixture was exhilarating and just what he desperately needed to lift his spirits. It was only a short few weeks ago when, still sick and wracked by pain, he came close to ending it all. The prospect of the pain, and being blind for the rest of his life, were almost more than he could bear. But he clung stubbornly to life, and today, he was glad.

Jess smiled at Bear's eagerness to let him know they were at the barn. The dog, still much a puppy at heart, scratched at the door and whined in anticipation of his reward.

"Here you go, Bear." Jess reached into his pants pocket and tossed a bit of jerky to the big dog, which gulped down the tidbit, and happily followed Jess into the barn.

Chores were now a source of contentment to him. He knew exactly how many steps it took to reach each stall, the corral gate, feed bin, and manure pile. In only a little more time than when he had his sight, he could feed the stock, turn out the horses, and clean the stalls. At least he was not completely useless.

Taking extra time, he led his little stallion into the cross ties and began grooming him. Not because he needed it, but because of the pleasure it gave them both.

When the Morgan's dark coat shone like glass and felt like silk, Jess put the brush and currycomb away. Leaving the tack room, he brushed against his saddle and blanket. Running his hand reflectively over the leather, smoothed and polished by miles and years of hard riding, he felt a catch come into his chest. *Who ever heard of a blind man riding?*

Still, he tortured himself by carefully hefting its familiar weight, checking the cinch, and inhaling the satisfying, rich smell of mellow leather and horse sweat.

The stallion stamped impatiently in the aisle. Without thinking, Jess picked up the saddle and blanket off the rack and started down the aisle to the Morgan. Brushing his elbow lightly against the wall, he automatically counted out the steps to the horse.

Feeling carefully for the stallion with his left elbow, he laid the blanket on the horse's back and smoothed it lightly, and gently rocked the saddle into place. It all felt so natural. So right. After a lifetime with horses, it could not have been otherwise.

Would it be possible? Could I really ride the stallion again? Success would cut the bonds of his self-imposed imprisonment. But failure could destroy him.

What if I try and The Hawk throws me and gets loose? What if I can't balance without my sight? Can I stay in the saddle even with the stallion's play-bucking out of good spirits?

He gathered a handful of mane and felt for the stirrup. He felt a tightening in his chest. The stallion sidled away from him. *He's never been mounted in the cross ties. It has to be outside.* Bitterly, Jess began untying the cinch. It would not be today.

He put the saddle away, disappointed in himself and in his courage. Returning to the Hawk, who, as if in sympathy, let a low whicker rumble from his throat, Jess rubbed his long, silky neck and fastened the lead to his halter.

Outside, Jess felt the stallion puff himself up with pride as he searched the pasture for other horses. Mares. Thirty paces, then the gate. Bugling, the Morgan cried his virility to the world. Jess bumped the gate with his shoulder and felt the rough pine against his arm. Freeing the horse, he closed the gate securely and stepped back to the fence to listen to the horse explode in an exuberance that shook the earth. Leaping and pounding feet sounded on the hard packed earth near the gate, punctuated by squeals and snorts. Jess could envision the stallion sniffing the ground, as if to find just the right spot, then folding his knees and sinking to the ground to roll joyously. He heard the grunts of pleasure as the horse rolled over twice.

The sun was higher now and the warmth bathed Jess's back, bringing a soothing comfort better than any balm. He climbed onto the top rail of the pasture fence and sat absorbing sunlight, listening while his horse fell to grazing. He smelled the just torn green grass, then raised his head to listen.

He was amazed at the number of familiar small sounds he recognized, telling of insignificant activities going on all around him; the milk cow's bell jangling from down at the creek, bluebirds fighting for territory in the edge of the pasture, the scolding of red squirrels in the wood pile and the rip-rip-rip grazing sound, as the Hawk enjoyed the spring grass.

Jess rubbed his forehead with his hand. Damn. Maybe it was the spring weather. He felt like that stallion at times, ready to work, to bring in a bunch of horses and feel the surging leap of a fighting bronc under him. But he was imprisoned, not by a stall, but by his blindness. Or was it his lack of courage? Sean and Scotty had been understanding and supportive of his new limitations. But it was not enough. Somehow, he had to break away from these limitations and begin to live again.

He felt his forearm as he worked his hand and tightened his muscles. *I'm not an invalid. I can't spend the rest of my days on a porch somewhere, listening to the world go by. There has to be an answer somewhere.* He never felt stronger in his life. He spent the last year working hard and the ropy, lean muscles in his body showed it. Now they cried out for work. He longed to run, strain, sweat, and feel physical exhaustion once more.

When he was weak and sick from the savage beating he endured, the inactivity was easier to live with. It took all of his strength to simply live. But he could not endure his self-imposed limitations any longer. Overcoming the shame of being fearful, a splinter of an idea entered his mind.

After breakfast, Scotty and Bear set off to explore the creek, in search of the first tadpoles of the year. The men were left alone to enjoy their second cup of coffee in the warm sunlight flooding the cabin.

"Sean, do you have anything special planned for this mornin'?"

"No, why?"

"I want to try something and I need your help. You remember after you got bushwhacked up the valley. I ran alongside the old sorrel while you rode? I want to try it today. I want to get to know the trails. First the trail south of here. I want to get to know the feel of it, the sound of it, the smells of it. Sean, I've got to ride again."

"I was afraid it'd come to this. Jess...I don't know. A lot could happen. Maybe you'd better go slow." Jess heard the concern in his voice.

It was hard on Sean seeing Jess adjust to his blindness; the change in his fluid stride, stumbling over unseen objects, falling across chairs left away from the table.

"Damn it, Sean, I've *been* goin' slow and it's killin' me! I can't stand much more of this. I've got to get some of my life back. I can do chores, split wood, find the buildings, milk the cow, and strain the milk. But I think I can do a hell of a lot more, if I've got the guts to try. But with this one, I need your help."

The big man flinched under the directness of Jess's sightless eyes. "Sure Jess."

"Don't worry so much." Jess flashed him a boyish smile. "We're only goin' runnin'."

Late that morning, Jess felt a thrill of anticipation as he sat on a rock in the barnyard, untying the soft bundle that held his moccasins. He untied the thongs, feeling the softness of the velvet leather with his fingertips. The heavy smell of sweet leather was pungent in the air as they unfolded in his lap.

"I've got Old Sorrel saddled, in the barn," Jess told Sean. "You want to get him, while I get these on?"

"Why don't I ride Satan? I feel a little heavy to be riding Sorrel."

"No, Sean. If this is going to work, it has to be him at first. There's only two horses on the ranch I really know, Sorrel and the Hawk. I'm goin' to have to start with Sorrel. I've got to know how his feet sound on every foot of that trail until I know it as well as this yard."

Sean could see Jess put a lot of careful thought into his plan, and prayed it would pay off.

With Sean mounted on Sorrel, Jess took hold of the left stirrup and nodded. "Let's try a jog, until we see how this'll work."

The big man felt a stab of compassion as he watched Jess's first awkward mile. He often stumbled, catching himself by his grip on the stirrup. But slowly, his gait improved, lengthened, and became more fluid as his feet became educated to feeling the ground beneath them without the aid of his sight. Bit by bit, his stride lengthened until it was almost as smooth as it was a year ago.

After three miles, they paused to let Jess catch his breath. The tenseness was gone from his face, replaced by a look of exhilaration. Sweat dripped from his hair and glistened on his bare shoulders. He fought for breath with a huge smile on his face.

"It's going to work, Sean! It's going to work!"

"You want to go back now?"

"Hell no! Just let me blow for a while. I want to go as far as the west fork. After that, the trail gets a little brushy."

"You sure you're alright?" Sean's voice sounded worried again.

"I just wish I could tell you how good this feels! I need to run 'till I can't run anymore, 'till I flop down like a hound that's run all night."

The next three miles went faster, as Jess's gait improved, and running became easier for him.

Sounds and smells drifted to him, sometimes one at a time, sometimes in concert with others – the clunk of rocks hitting each other beneath Sorrel's feet near the rock slide, the smell of dampness and decayed vegetation coupled with coolness and a spongy quietness when they passed the big spring on the hillside, the loud whisper of pines and the smell of moist, sun-warmed pine needles, the shaking rush of the aspens, and finally, the harder ground as they reached the fork in the trail. Ahead, Jess could hear the rushing sound of the river as it boiled over the rocky bottom in the narrows just before the west fork. He slowed to a walk.

Listening carefully, he brushed the grass with his fingertips, feeling his way down to the bank of the river. He sat down and pulled off his moccasins. While Sean watered the Sorrel, Jess waded into the icy river, up to his knees, feeling the slippery, mossy rocks underfoot. Splashing the icy water over his head and shoulders, he gasped with the exhilarating shock as the water cascaded down his back and chest. Then he turned back toward the bank where he heard Sean walking with Old Sorrel. He slipped on the rocks and fell, catching himself with his hand. Quickly regaining his feet, Jess climbed on the bank.

"Can't always be sure-footed!" he said with a wry grimace, but Sean could hear a new smile in his voice. "Damn, that water's cold!"

Sean laughed. "It was snow and ice, just a few miles upstream. You going to run back, too?"

Jess nodded. "Yeah. I've got to if I'm going to learn. I'll have to do this every day until I'm sure of where I am, all the time. I can't feel turned around."

Chapter 15

Julie nervously paced the floor, wondering what she was doing leaving the security of her hometown and nearby parents, to take a job clear across the country, across the wild west, in California! Nearly a year ago, she wrote a shirt-tail cousin in San Francisco, asking if he might know of a position available as a bookkeeper. It was the only marketable skill she possessed. She was afraid for her life and wanted to run away, far away from the beatings, shouting, and threats, where he would never find her.

Her husband, Garth, was a handsome, successful businessman who her parents had pushed her into marrying. They said she would have a good life and not want for anything. They were wrong. She longed for gentleness, kindness, and most of all, love. She had none of them, only a lavishly furnished home that turned into a prison, complete with regular physical abuse. A week ago, she received a letter back from San Francisco. The bank her cousin worked for desperately needed an honest, dependable clerk and bookkeeper. If she could get there by fall, the job was hers. But the job would not wait longer than that. If she didn't take the position, they would be forced to hire someone else. As it was, they had two people working part time, just to fill in.

She was able to talk her favorite uncle and aunt into letting her join them in their wagon. They were also moving to California to homestead, and even now, were packing a large wagon with their things.

What was she thinking? Her hand unconsciously stroked her

abdomen protectively. Here she was, so far along and she was getting ready to ride off into the wilderness. She would be having the baby in the wagon, right along the pioneer trail! No doctors and who knows what could happen. Savagely, she plunged her favorite small things into her traveling bag. No! She was doing the right thing. No more would she have to listen to her parents ask what she had done to make him angry enough to beat her. No more would she lie awake at night, fearing every small sound, fearing he would return home and take up where he left off that morning. She would never forget him slamming her into the wall and stalking out the door the very night she told him she was carrying his child.

She desperately needed to get away from him, this house, this city, and these fears. And if she needed to ride across the wilderness and bear her child in a wagon, by God, that's just what she would do. After all, many pioneering women before her gave birth along that trail. She was young and strong. She needed a new life, both for herself and her unborn babe. Somehow, somewhere, way out there, she believed she would have it.

Chapter 16

Every day for a week, Sean and Jess made the same run to the west fork and Sean marveled to himself over how his friend was regaining his old confidence, becoming more the old Jess he knew. Not only was he running as easily as he did before, with his sight, but he could accurately place himself on the trail, within a few feet. Maybe riding wasn't just a wishful hope for him after all.

During the afternoons, Jess began riding Sorrel in the corral. It wasn't much at the start, but Jess was surprised to feel how natural it was. He did have trouble, at first, learning where the fences were and what direction he was going. Then he thought of using the breeze and the sun's warmth as guides. When he mounted at the gate, he took notice of the breeze on his face and the direction from which the sun's warmth shone upon him. Then he began to ride by the direction of the sun and wind. There was also a slightly different sound of the horse's hoof beats as he neared the outside track, just before the fence, as the ground was packed harder there.

But it would be different on the outside. The landmarks would be less easily distinguished and getting turned around and confused would be much easier. Could he do it? He was going to have to put a lot of trust in his horse.

All night the thoughts and doubts troubled him, until, rising early, he decided he had to do it today or go crazy. Fifteen minutes later, Old Sorrel stood saddled in front of the barn.

Sean stood in the doorway of the cabin, in his stocking feet, feeling a knot of apprehension. But he knew Jess was one man you didn't coddle. Reaching for the stirrup, Jess slipped into the saddle, lacking none of his old grace.

He clucked to the sorrel and the horse started across the yard and down the trail to the south. Keeping the horse at a steady jog, Jess strained to maintain contact with his location.

The rockslide. The spring. The pines. He reached the widest part of the trail where he hesitated, not quite sure of himself and his courage. Then he touched the sorrel lightly with his spurs, urging him into a lope. It felt good! His balance was unaffected and he realized he used to ride by feel more than he knew.

After an easy mile down the trail, he slowed the horse to a walk. He heard the aspens whisper in the light breeze, and a small flock of ducks quacking as they took off from the river. He was nearing the fork in the trail.

He urged the sorrel ahead again, hearing the roar of water from the west fork. It rained during the night, and water rushing down out of a steep canyon in the mountains turned the mild, smooth-running stream that crossed that fork turned into a treacherous, often dangerous boiling river. But Jess knew without more rain, it would tame down in two days and again be a clear, tranquil, gentle stream.

He reined the gelding around, feeling him perk up a bit as they headed toward the ranch. Jess laughed. There weren't many horses that went away from home as enthusiastically as they returned! He knew if he should get turned around in the wrong direction, he could give the sorrel free rein and soon be heading for the ranch.

The next two days, Jess only rode as far as the west fork, as he knew riding across the ford in the creek would be dangerous until the waters tamed down. He felt a growing confidence, despite nearly being thrown when some animal spooked the sorrel, which spun around and danced in fear for an instant. As he regained his seat, he was surprised and pleased at how quickly he regained his bearings and picked up the sound of a buck deer snorting in panic as it bounded away up the mountainside. When all was again quiet, Jess could hear the big pine whisper softly to his left and knew he was once again facing north, toward home.

Heavy rain caused Jess to miss two days' riding, so when the sun came out bright the next morning, he was up early, eager to get on the trail. He wanted to get in his ride so he could return and cut some firewood. He desperately wanted to be doing something to help on the place. Scotty was both his eyes and an extra pair of hands, choosing each length of firewood and helping to get it onto the sawbuck.

As he saddled up, the wind brought the scent of freshly harrowed earth and he knew Sean was out in the ten acres they cleared, scattering seed among the clods. The big man raised his head as Jess rode by, feeling a sense of gladness. Jess was returning to himself. It was a good thing, indeed.

The ride to the west fork went faster than before. Perhaps it was because the brightness of the day, the mellow, earthy smells, and springtime sounds all about him made Jess's senses feel alive and fine-tuned. Soon, they reached the fork in the trail and the old gelding, fat from little use and good care, danced playfully, tossing his forelock.

It was about time to try his stallion. Only the Hawk felt as natural to him as the old sorrel did. His every movement felt right before Jess lost his sight, and now he felt he and the stallion could once again be one.

Old Sorrel stopped abruptly and snorted. Jess could feel the horse's muscles tense under him. He strained to catch a sound, a smell, anything to tell him what Sorrel was spooked by. The horse may be old, but he still retained the alertness of a wild mustang. There was something out there, for the horse did not act out of the foolishness of youth. A bear? Jess doubted it. Few grizzlies came down into the valley so early in the season. A black bear, maybe, or a wolf?

Then, with a change in the wind, Jess could hear it – a thin, wavering wail. It came from somewhere on the main trail, down toward the ford across the river. Jess reined Sorrel around and followed the sound. Suddenly Jess knew what spooked the old horse, for he caught the unmistakable scent of death in the air. His heart pounded. The cry grew louder and the gelding became harder to urge forward. Still, he could not place the sound. A bear cub? No. He strained his memory to recall the sound. Suddenly he knew what it was. The sound was that of a weak and starved baby, one he remembered well, from long ago. As a boy with the Apache, soldiers discovered their hidden camp and attacked, burning everything and killing as many of the People as they could, men, women, and children. When he and the others who managed to escape came back, he saw and heard those pitiful babies. Half starved, they cried and whimpered for mothers who could no longer hear them. He would never forget it as long as he lived.

But a baby? Here? Miles from a main trail or town? He was very close now. He strained for any sounds of activity – of horses stamping, of people, anything – but there was just the rushing, angry gurgle of the roaring river, the sweet, cloying smell of death, and the incessant cries of the baby.

Jess hesitated, not knowing what he was walking into, but finally dismounted. *What happened here?* He silently damned his blindness.

"Hello the camp," he called, tense for any response. There was no answer save the buzzing of death flies, the cheerful singing of a meadow lark nearby, and the weak wail of the baby.

The sorrel pulled back against the reins in Jess's hand. Not violently, but firmly. He did not want to go on. Jess suddenly stumbled against something. He bent down to find out what it was. He recoiled in shock as his fingers closed on the leg of a dead man!

Forcing himself on, though he felt like fleeing, his searching hand felt the roughness of wood – an overturned wagon. The roaring river was close-by now. The wagon was half in, half out of the water. He followed the wagon forward, to find the front dropped deep into the swiftly boiling water. There was no sign of a team.

"Anyone here?" Jess called, wondering if anyone else was still alive, perhaps hurt and lying close by, in desperate need of help. Again he cursed his blindness. If he could only see! There was no answer. Only the baby crying.

Stumbling back through the brush, he searched for the child with his fingers. He found it, lying behind the wagon, slightly under the cover. Other than being in sad need of having its diaper and clothes changed and being half-starved, it seemed to be unharmed.

Jess gingerly undressed the baby and laid him on the sun-warmed grass of the ground. After cleaning him up the best he could with a piece of soft cloth he found on the ground, Jess wrapped him in his shirt for warmth. The child's cries stopped as he grabbed Jess's hand for comfort. His fingers felt so tiny as he pulled Jess's hand to his mouth and began sucking with loud, smacking noises.

He smiled at the insistence of the grasp. "You'll have to wait a while for that."

After carefully bundling the baby in his shirt, Jess mounted Old Sorrel. With the child cradled gingerly in front of him, he got his bearings and urged the gelding into a canter toward the ranch, worried there could still be someone he could not find lying there hurt.

Sean was still seeding when Jess rode down the hill and into the clearing. He smiled to see him lope into the yard, as natural as could be. But he frowned in puzzlement, trying to see why Jess was bare to the waist and what he held in front of him. He walked to the trail to intercept him.

"Sean?" Jess called. "Hey, Sean!"

"Over here, Jess. What've you got?"

"You ain't gonna believe this." Jess gently pulled the shirt away to reveal the baby's tiny, pink face. "There's been some kind of accident down by the west fork. Wagon overturned and a man's dead under it. You'd better go take a look. There may be someone else hurt out there."

He stepped off and held the baby out to Sean. "This little fella must have got dumped out in the accident. Is he okay?"

"Well, I'll be." Sean unwrapped the shirt and examined the child, which proceeded to send a stream of urine over his shoulder. "Plumbing works anyway," he chuckled. "Seems okay to me. I'd better ride down there and look. Can you manage with this little guy?"

"I guess so. I feel like he's gonna break." Jess took the infant.

Sean smiled as Jess tentatively tried to hold the baby. "They're tougher than they look. I'll get saddled and ride out there. Think you can handle things till I get back?"

"Sure, Sean."

Dropping Old Sorrel's reins over the hitching rail next to the cabin, Jess felt for the porch step with his toe, opened the door, and lay the baby on his bed. Then, raising the window, he called Scotty, knowing the boy would be just about half done cleaning the hen house.

He heard the boy coming on the run, probably anxious for any excuse to get out of the chore. "What Jess? Where are you?"

"In here," he replied as the boy came through the front door. "There's been an accident at the west fork ford. A man was killed and I brought back a pretty hungry baby. Is there a bottle or something we can feed him with?"

Scotty's eyes grew big as he took it all in. "Wow!"

Jess smiled. "Well? Is there?"

"Uh...Sure. There's a couple of old bottles and baby things in the chest, up in the attic. From when I was little, I guess."

"Well, crawl up there an' see what you can find. We can use anything up there for him. I'll warm some water and heat some milk."

Jess went in to check the baby for the third time since he put a pint of milk on to warm. The little thing was awake and whining pitifully, as if the very effort of crying was too much for his weakened condition.

"I brought all the baby stuff down," Scotty said "There's a couple of bottles, diapers an' clothes an' stuff. Here's the bottles. I washed 'em out good."

"Good boy. Now pour some of this milk into one."

Jess gently picked up the baby and sat down on his bed. Taking the warm bottle in his hand, he guided the nipple toward the small, puckered mouth. "You be good to me, kid. I'm not very good at this."

At first, the baby seemed too weak to be able to suck. But Jess squeezed several drops of rich milk into his mouth and his lips began to make sucking sounds. The next time the nipple touched his mouth, he grasped the bottle firmly with both tiny hands and began sucking in earnest.

A few minutes after finishing the milk, the baby began to fall asleep. This time, he slept without hunger, without fear. As Jess sat, holding child in his arms, he wondered if a man who had killed so many men had a right to touch anything so innocent.

Two hours later, Sean returned home.

"I buried the man. There was a woman too, drowned, downstream a little. Buried her, too, with him. There wasn't anyone else. They must have tried to cross the ford when it started to flood. They sure weren't from around here to try that! I better ride on into town and tell Syl. I have the man's strongbox. There's papers in there, so maybe he can find out about them and notify kin. You think you can handle things here?"

"I reckon. Any idea who they were?"

"No. Greenhorns. It looked like they were homesteaders by the looks of what was in the wagon. Headed for Oregon or California, I'd guess. But what they were doing way over here and by themselves, I couldn't guess. By the looks of the river, they didn't stand a chance of making it across. Maybe before I go, you and I should take the team there and right the wagon. It doesn't look like anything's broken and if there's another rain, it's likely to be torn up and everything in it carried away, down river."

The roaring stream was down to a loud gurgle and seemed so innocent of the wreck and destruction it so recently wrought. Only the mud, debris, torn wagon cover, and fresh graves told of the savage wrath of which it was capable.

It took Jess driving the team and Sean on his powerful black with a rope to right the heavily laden wagon. The first tries rocked the wagon substantially and on the fourth try, Jess shouted to the team as he heard a creak and groan from the wagon. With a lunging pull, the sounds of creaking wood, pounding feet and snorting, laboring horses, told of the wagon tipping back upright.

The wagon settled on its wheels with a loud sigh. Mud splashed and water sprayed into the air.

"They really had it loaded!" Sean exclaimed, looking over the wagon's interior as Jess stood by holding the team. "I guess we better bring it on home, in case there's any kin. We can't just leave it here."

"I can take it home," Jess said. "You go on to town, seein's you're this far now."

There were times Sean nearly forgot Jess's blindness now. Like when he was handling the team, pulling the wagon upright.

"Are you sure?"

"Yeah, Sean. The team's tired and I know the trail. It'll be okay. You go on. But first, you want to look underneath. I don't want the reach to be broke or an axle cracked."

"Looks fine to me," Sean answered, peering under the wagon.

They hooked the team up and got the wagon started back up the bank, toward the ranch. Jess tied the sorrel to the back and climbed up onto the seat.

"I'll be back as soon as I can," Sean said, mounting his black. "There must be someone who wants that baby."

In the weeks that followed, there was no word about any relatives. Syl sent a telegram back east, where the couple came from, but there was no reply. And the letters sent to addresses on the letters in the couple's box remained unanswered. It seemed Jess had himself a baby.

Weeks turned into months and the baby remained with them. Sean felt a warm smile inside when he saw Jess with the baby. They needed each other and the need was fulfilled. Wherever Jess was, the baby was not far away, be it in the sweet smelling hay in the barn, the dappled sunlight of the pines, or tucked gently against his side in the bunk at night.

The baby gave Jess a purpose, a reason to live, and compensation for his tragic loss of sight. He paid his debt in full with love and tenderness, belying his image as a hardened gunman and killer.

Chapter 17

Summer lengthened and the Morgan stallion once again wore Jess's saddle. Slowly at first, Jess began to trust him, just as the horse once learned to trust Jess. Somehow the Hawk knew of his rider's limitations and changed his ways. The stallion's light feet still danced with every step and his neck arched with pride, as he tossed his glossy, long mane in waves. But gone were the bucking and violent sudden leaps of joy. The two were truly one again.

Haying started and while Sean was in the field, cutting the luxuriant stands of grasses and clover, Jess managed the chores. They were making lunch when Bear ran barking out toward the trail.

"Scotty, see who's coming," Jess said, the old clammy feeling once again in his chest. He wiped his hands and thought to where he hung his pistol.

Scotty ran in, excited, and cried, "It's Doc Stone and Martha!"

Jess shook his head ruefully. When would he ever get over that feeling within him every time someone rode in? It was the same feeling he used to have when someone shouted his name in challenge in some dusty, no-name town.

Jess met Doc on the porch with a warm grasp.

Doc smiled as he looked Jess over with satisfaction, from calloused hands to his deeply tanned face, showing the long hours of work outdoors he put in this summer. "Jess, you're looking good! How are things going? I hear you're a family man now."

"Seems that way." Jess flushed. "Come on in. Dinner's about ready. Sean'll be here in a few minutes." He turned toward the buggy, hearing a light creak, and held out his hand to help Martha down. "Ma'am."

He felt her slight, smooth hand in his, a gentle, dove-soft weight, and felt her step down beside him.

"Jess, you're going to spoil me." She gathered her skirt and kept hold of his arm until they were inside the cabin. "Where's the baby? I couldn't stand being this close and not come to see him!"

The baby lay sleeping in a soft deerskin hammock that was stretched out in the corner of the kitchen. The Stones were used to seeing babies covered, pale and white, protected from every ray of sunlight, so it came as a surprise to see the baby golden tan. He was so brown, so sturdy, that he almost looked like an Indian baby with his dark, straight hair.

"Oh, he's gorgeous!" Martha sighed quietly.

As if in answer, the baby's eyes opened and he waved his fists in a contented stretch.

"Jess, I'm afraid we woke him. Can I hold him?" Martha asked.

Scotty giggled. "I don't think he'll let you. Me'n Jess are the only ones he'll let hold him," he said with some pride.

"Go ahead, Ma'am. Maybe he won't be strange with you," Jess invited quietly.

Martha reached gently for the baby, but by the time she had him securely in her arms, he was fussing in protest. Not crying yet, but protesting.

"You were right, Scotty," Martha laughed. "Here, Jess. See if you have better luck."

Jess smiled, self-consciously, and reached for the baby. At his familiar touch, the child stopped fussing and smiled widely.

"Look Simon! He smiled! Did you see that?" Martha exclaimed in amazement.

"Scotty, why don't you fix him a bottle and I'll go call your pa. Dinner's about ready," Jess said, laying the baby down in his hammock and giving it a gentle swing.

On the porch, Jess could feel the dry hotness of the summer sun. Good haying weather. He raised his head to feel the sun, warm on his face. It was still strange to him to see the velvety blackness and know the day was clear and bright.

Suddenly, an excruciating stab of pain shot through his head. It was all he could do to keep from crying out. Another struck and he pressed his hand tightly against his forehead and sagged heavily against the porch railing. Another and still another wave of searing pain shot through Jess's head, forcing him to his knees.

"Jess!" Sean's voice came from close by. "Jess, what is it?"

"I don't know," he gasped. "My head." His voice was tight with unbearable pain.

"Doc!" Sean shouted, helplessly.

Jess stirred. He was no longer in the throes of pain on the porch, but in bed. Someone was sitting close by. He could hear the breathing.

"Well, Jess," Doc said kindly, "are you feeling better?"

"Yeah. It's gone. But what the hell happened?"

"I don't quite know how to tell you, but I believe there's a good chance you're going to regain your sight."

"What?" Jess asked hoarsely.

"Now, I don't want to raise any false hopes, but I've seen something like this happen before. I worked ringside with fighters back east for several years and treated a lot of serious head injuries, including a few that resulted in blindness, from a blow.

"I'm not sure why, but those headaches often precede the return of sight. Maybe it's the beginning of function of injured nerves, but I think it's a good sign. Or maybe you got too much direct sunlight."

"How long?" Jess fought the surge of hope as he swung his feet onto the floor.

"I'm not sure. Please understand me. Your sight may never return. But we need to have hope and those migraines give us a base for that. It could happen tomorrow, without warning, or return to some extent over a period of time. We'll have to wait. I can give you a powder to take in some water, in case you have any more pain, like today," Doc said, his head shaking. "I hate to raise your hopes when I'm not sure."

"It's okay, Doc. I didn't think I had a chance of seeing before, so if it doesn't work out, I haven't lost anything."

Even as he spoke, Jess knew how painfully dashed his new hopes could be. He felt a torrent of mixed emotions, as though someone might give him back his life, anticipation for that great day, and fear it would not come.

Chapter 18

A week passed. And another. There was no more encouragement for Jess other than another severe headache, controlled by the powder Doc left. Out of self-preservation, he put away the thought of rcgaining his sight, and tried to live through one day at a time and let the future take care of itself.

While Sean and Scotty mowed the last of the hay, he again worked the Hawk. The powerful little stallion circled the corral beneath Jess as he worked to fine-tune the Morgan. He wanted to make him as responsive as he knew he could be. With the grace of a cougar, the Hawk loped, spun, dropped to a walk, then at a slight squeeze, leapt into a lope. He circled, stopped, backed, reversed, and traveled straight along the fence. The horse was responding to the slightest touch and shift of Jess's weight. He felt as if the Morgan could read his mind and they were finally of one body.

Suddenly, Jess could feel the stallion stepping lighter and more tensely. A whicker escaped the Morgan's throat. A whicker of welcome to a strange horse. The feeling of being trapped flooded Jess for an instant. He let the Hawk go toward the fence, toward the oncoming horse.

Then Jess could hear the buggy wheels and relaxed a little. Sheriffs and gunfighters seldom used a buggy! The trotting hoof beats halted close and the buggy horse whickered to his stallion. He pressed his spurs to the Morgan's sides and the Hawk again became obedient and did not answer. A slight trace of fresh soap and perfume drifted through the air and he heard a light footstep as the buggy creaked.

Dismounting, Jess waited.

"Would you be Jess Hazzard?" a woman's soft voice asked hesitantly, almost fearfully.

"Yes Ma'am," he replied, touching the brim of his hat. *Who is she? Should I shake her hand?*

"They tell me you have the baby you saved after an accident. My baby."

Taken completely off guard, the wound was more painful. Stunned, he did not want to believe her words. "Yours?"

"Yes. My aunt and uncle were bringing him to me when they were killed in that accident." Her voice caught and he heard the rustle of paper, a letter being pulled from an envelope. "I was in San Francisco. The mails were slow. I have the letter Sheriff Davis sent me at my old address so long ago." Jess could not deny her sincerity.

Numbly, he tied the Hawk to the corral fence and walked to where the baby lay in the cool shade of a small pine. He felt the child's soft hands close on his as he picked him up, heard the child's squeal of happiness, and a knot of loss tore at his chest and made fire run up his throat into his eyes. He carefully tucked the blanket around the baby's moccasin-clad feet, then held him for her to see.

The woman gazed in wonderment at his bronzed skin and growth. She would not have been able to pick out her own son from a group of other babies! The last time she saw him, he was so small.

Reluctantly, Jess allowed her to take the baby from him and with immense relief, she held her son closely.

Jess spent his life fighting with his hands, knives and guns, but there was no fighting against this. A mother's love was going to kill him.

"His things are in the house," he said, trying to control his voice.

"No. I've brought things."

"You have nothing to fear, from me," Jess said, catching the unmistakable tremble in her voice. A far-off roll of thunder broke the silence of the hot, still day. "Did your husband come with you, Ma'am?" The echoing rumble from the high country died in the valley.

"No. He left me before Keith was born. I came alone." She sounded defensive.

"I'm sorry, Ma'am. What I mean is the trail can get pretty bad in stormy weather. That little branch of the river you crossed is dangerous with rain in the high country. Maybe you'd better wait awhile and see how bad it's goin' to rain." Jess's mind swam as the baby began to cry. *For me.*

"I think I best go now," she answered, feeling awkward.

"At least let me ride as far as the river with you." he struggled, not wanting to let go.

"No! No." she said, regretting the fear in her voice, but remembering what she had heard about this man. "I'll make it alright." She saw the twitch of his jaw as the baby continued to cry and unwillingly felt his pain. Confused, she just wanted her child and to be away from this man, this place.

Jess heard the baby's cry fade as she carried him to the buggy, heard the creak as she stepped in, and could not stand to listen to them leave. He turned abruptly back to the corral and the stallion. His mind was totally numb and instead of leading the Morgan back to the barn, he stood next to him, perhaps for the comfort of another living thing, and leaned heavily across the top rail of the corral.

He was still there when Sean came in from the meadow with the team. Driving them past, he called out to Jess. There was no answer, no sign Jess even heard him. Sensing there was something seriously wrong, the big man tied the team, walked to Jess, and saw the pain on his face.

"Jess. Jess! What is it?" Sean touched his shoulder.

With an ominous fury, a pelting rain began falling, but Jess turned to Sean, unmindful of it.

His voice was hoarse and cracked as he said, "She took the baby."

"What?" Sean felt a stab of compassion, for he well knew what that small baby meant to his friend. "Who?"

"His mother. She had the letter. She…I…"

"Come on," Sean put his arm around Jess's shoulder. "Let's put the Hawk up and go to the house. It's raining."

It took two cups of black coffee to drive the numbness from Jess's mind, to make him realize the baby was really gone. His baby. His son for all these months.

A great boom of thunder shook the cabin, rattling the windows, telling of the building wrath of the storm as wind drove great sheets of rain against the window next to him. Standing abruptly, he set his cup on the table. "Damn it, Sean, I'm goin' as far as the west fork. I've got to know she made it!"

"You'll get drowned out there. It's pouring."

"Yeah. Just the same, I've got to go." Jess reached for his slicker. "I'll be back in awhile."

"Just a minute. I'll go with you." Sean stood up.

"No. Not much use in both of us gettin' soaked. Besides, who'll stay with Scotty?"

"Look Jess, riding in decent weather's alright, but anything could happen out there tonight."

"To a blind man, you mean? Sean, I'll be okay. Maybe I just need to work this out." Then he smiled briefly. "Look, Sean, I ain't gonna melt. And the Hawk'll bring me home."

"Alright. But...

"Jess," Scotty said, stopping him at the door. "Please be careful."

He smiled at the boy and affectionately squeezed the back of his neck. "Sure I will." Then he disappeared into the driving sheets of rain.

For what seemed like hours, Jess rode the stallion through the storm and gummy clay mud. The trees whipped around them and the going got rougher and more treacherous with each passing mile. As they rode, Jess found the familiar trail, with its sounds and smells totally obscured by the crashing thunder and pouring rain, felt unfamiliar. He felt lost and confused as he strained to hear the slightest sound that would orient him. It seemed they surely should have reached the west fork by now.

But he knew there would be no missing it today. The small branch of the river would be swollen deep enough to swim a horse in by now, if a man was that crazy. He hoped to God they made it across before it rose.

The Hawk slipped and scrambled under him. Where the hell were they? The wind swirled and whipped about, making telling directions impossible.

Then, ahead, Jess could hear the roar of the fast, angry water, and he felt a sigh go through him. At least he knew where he was. But that feeling was instantly replaced by fear as he realized that the flooded river could have already carried the woman and baby – his baby – away.

The Morgan stopped dead and threw his head up erect. Jess could feel a tremble go through the stallion. Keeping his heels into the Hawk's sides, he held him from spinning away. What was it? Fear clutched his insides. Pictures of another deadly wreck struck his heart.

The Hawk gave a whickering bugle to another horse. A mare. From the distance, above the crashing roar of the flood waters, Jess heard a frightened voice call to him.

"Oh, Mr. Hazzard, I'm so glad you came! The buggy's stuck in the river and the water is rising fast. I tried and tried, but I can't move it." She sounded on the verge of tears and panic.

"Where's the baby?" Jess asked quickly.

"In the buggy. It's the only dry place."

"Get him out of there!" Jess said, cursing his blindness.

Hearing splashing ahead of him, he knew she was following his command. He dismounted and worked his way down the shafts to the mare. The icy water tugged and swirled about his waist. The buggy wheels were hopelessly entangled in debris but maybe he could get the mare loose in time. Drawing his knife, he slashed through the traces and wrap straps, feeling the urgency of the rising waters.

With the mare free of the buggy, he shouted to her and slapped her rump hard with the lines. She floundered, struggling valiantly, but was too mired in the mud and debris to free herself. Jess could hear her puff and snort, panicked that she was trapped.

He waded back to the Hawk, keeping one hand on the buggy. *If I should lose contact with it...* The water was numbing his legs and he didn't know if he could mount. *If I fall into that water, I'll die.* With the water pulling at him, weighing him down, he clawed his way into the saddle.

He shook out his rope and let the stallion move toward the mare. Grabbing for a line, Jess felt his way to her head, keeping his spurs into the stallion's sides firmly, demanding him to put aside his instincts. He quickly slipped a loop over the mare's head.

"Hurry! There's a big tree coming!" the woman shouted with urgency.

He spurred the stallion and spun him back toward the bank. The little Morgan strained against the rope, floundering and lunging mightily. At first, the mare fought the rope. But then with a mighty groan, she lunged forward with a great splash and followed the stallion to solid ground.

Close behind him, Jess heard a rending crash and he knew the buggy was splintered like kindling. *If the baby had still been in there...*

Shaking with exertion and chill, he dismounted and slid his hand down the rope to the mare. He tugged at the rope and could feel her come toward him, her head bobbing at every step. Lame, but alive. He unharnessed her and turned her free. She would find her way to the ranch, sooner or later.

He heard footsteps splash in the mud behind him and turned the Hawk so his body would afford some shelter against the driving rain.

"Come over here, Ma'am."

As they stood in the lee of the Hawk's body, Jess quickly pulled off his slicker. "Here, put this on. It'll help break the wind." He stripped off his flannel shirt. "And wrap the baby in this. Try to keep him dry.

"Now take off your petticoats. They're too wet and heavy. I've never had anyone ride double on the Hawk an' I don't want the extra weight to cause trouble with the baby aboard." He could feel her hesitate. "I won't see anything."

"But..."

"No time to argue. We've got to get that baby back to the ranch where it's warm."

Jess heard a rustle of wet cloth as he mounted the stallion. "Now hand me the baby."

With the child held securely against his chest, he held out his hand to the woman. Her hand gripped his, she slid her foot in the stirrup, and he swung her up behind him. The Morgan squatted in fear, but Jess held him, calming him with quiet words in Apache. He felt the stallion dance forward a few quick steps, humping his back. Then the Hawk settled down. The battle was over as quickly as it had started.

Jess breathed a silent thank you and sighed. "Here, slip the baby under the slicker and hold him tight. Put your other arm around me and hang on. It's gonna be pretty rough goin' back."

He squeezed the stallion forward and let him choose his way back to the ranch. Behind them, he could hear the mare hesitate and follow.

A great sheet of lightning lit up the night and she saw the great scars that roped Jess's back, left as a reminder of Blueson's beating. It was all she could do to force herself to touch those horrible white ridges, right there in front of her face. But soon she found herself clinging tightly as the stallion slipped and lurched through the slick mud. Half an hour later, she was glad to huddle close, her cheek touching Jess's back, as the chill of the night wind closed in on them. At least he was warm. Her revulsion to his scarred back passed.

The going got worse with the unmerciful rain. Under the double load, the stallion was soon lathered and steaming in the cold night, despite the downpour. Jess stopped the horse and slid to the ground.

"He's about done in," he said, patting the stallion's lathered neck gently. "I'll walk awhile. You slip up into the saddle. It'll be more comfortable. Let me know if I go wrong."

Suddenly the woman realized Jess was blind! She knew there was something odd about him, his gaze, but had not realized what it was. Terror gripped her. She and her infant son were out in this wilderness, in this violent storm, led by a blind man!

He untied the mecate, the horsehair rope on the hackamore, leaving her the reins, and began walking, leading the stallion, but letting him pick his own way. At each step, Jess sank past his ankles and despite the cold rain driving against his bare skin, he was soon sweating. There was no footing and he clung to the horse's long mane for support. More than once, unseen branches, blown by the wind, slapped him cruelly across the face. Unseen ruts and stones tripped him. But he led them on. The woman's terror was replaced by great compassion. He was blind, but he was a man, a good man!

Time became endless to Jess. In the lee of a small, rocky outcropping, he paused and turned to the woman. A flash of lightning lit his face.

"You alright, Ma'am?"

"Yes. We could rest here. You're awfully tired."

Jess smiled. "Been tired before. We've only got two more miles." He hesitated, his voice catching. "How's the little fella?"

"Just fine. He's fast asleep." She reached out and touched his hand. "Mr. Hazzard, thank you."

He raised his head, wishing that he could see her face, her eyes. Then, swallowing hard, he smiled. "We better get goin'"

Jess turned from the shelter, from the voice that seemed strangely familiar, the voice that left him strangely weak, but uplifted at the same time.

Once again, he trudged through the mire and storm with his head bowed into the wind. His mind filled with thoughts of her until thunder crashed about him and brought him back to reality. *Don't be a fool. She's only glad you came after them and they're not out here alone in this storm.*

Suddenly, his feet shot out from under him, and he slammed to the mire and out into nothingness. The bank, weakened and eroded by the flooding, had crumbled into a mud slide beneath his weight, carrying him over the edge of the trail toward the river far below in the darkness. Desperately clinging to the mecate, he heard the woman's scream over the storm as his feet clawed for a foothold but found none on the steep cliff.

He felt a yank on the rough hair rope in his hands and called up to the Hawk. "Back! Back!"

The rope jerked again and pulled. Fighting the muddy bank with his feet, he climbed as the little stallion backed against the pull. He heard the woman call to him, then felt her hand on the rope, helping the horse pull him.

Finally, he crawled to his knees in the mud, his chest heaving for breath. A minute later, regaining his feet, he clutched the Hawk's mane as she leaned over and gripped his arm.

"Oh, Jess! I thought we lost you!" Carefully, her hand never leaving his arm, she dismounted.

A great sheet of lightning, accompanied by an explosion of thunder, lit up the trail like daylight. And there, in the midst of the violent storm, he could see! It was not the fuzzy half-sight he imagined it would be, but was as if someone yanked off a blindfold! Jess looked into the face before him and, for the first time in his life, he was in love.

"I can see," he whispered. "I can see!"

Their eyes held, and despite the storm raging around them, neither moved, her hand still on his bare arm.

"I've always believed in miracles," she said.

Her quiet words and soft expression made Jess understand she no longer feared, but admired him. The storm raging around them faded from his consciousness as he stood hypnotized by the sweet, trusting soul he saw deep within her eyes.

"So have I," Jess replied, unable to shake the feeling he knew her, knew her face and voice. But could he trust his new sight? *Could she truly be the woman in my dreams, the woman who's frightened, tragic face has haunted me for so long?*

He covered the hand on his arm with his other hand and gently drew her forward. Relief coursed through him when he saw her smile and lean until their faces were but inches apart. *Can this be real? Or did I fall to my death and am in an afterlife?* There was only one way to know for sure.

He closed the remaining inches and gently pressed his lips to hers. She met him, returned his passion, then encircled his neck with her arm, never wanting to let go. The storm roared and crashed about them, but it took a small mew of displeasure to end their embrace, as pressed between them, under her slicker, the baby voiced his opinion about still being out in the weather.

Jess leaned back and smiled. "We'd best get both of you to the cabin and a good warm fire." He squeezed her hand. "We aren't far now."

"Only if you'll ride with me," she said shyly.

Jess nodded. "The Hawk's rested now."

He tightened the cinch, stepped into the saddle, and held out his hand to her. He helped her up, behind him, feeling a leap in his chest as she snuggled against him, her one arm holding the baby, her other around his waist. His hand found hers and gently cupped around it as he started the Morgan toward home.

The going was still difficult, but now Jess knew where they were by the brilliant flashes of lightning. The little stallion gamely forged on through the storm until, he suddenly came to a stop. Jess started to urge him on when he heard a dog bark. Raising his weary head, he saw they reached the yard.

Weary beyond words, he urged the Hawk toward the cabin. He was shaking now, both from the cold rain and the exhaustion that threatened to claim him. As he neared the cabin, the door opened, flooding the porch with lantern light as Sean strode out.

"Thank God you're back!" he exclaimed, coming through the rain toward them.

Jess turned to the woman who clung to him, half dazed. "Can you slide off the horse? Sean'll help you." He felt her nod. Numbly, she released her hold on him and slid down, nearly falling.

He slid off the stallion and stiffly followed them toward the porch. Then he thought of his steaming, tired horse, stepping obediently beside him. Turning back toward the barn, he felt Sean's hand on his arm.

"I'll put the Hawk away," the big man said.

Jess turned to Sean, gratefully handing him the reins. "I've got my sight back," he said, almost as an afterthought. "I can see again."

Sean's head snapped up, looking into his friend's eyes. He saw it was true and words failed him. Only a grateful sigh escaped as he squeezed Jess's arm and nodded. "You help the lady into the house and I'll take good care of the Hawk."

Jess nodded, and guided the woman and her precious bundle into the warmth of the cabin.

As she warmed and dried the baby, Jess sat near the fire in a dry wool shirt, clinging to a cup of hot coffee, trying to drive the fatigue and chill from his body and mind. Steam rose from his drenched, muddy Levis but his hands would not stop shaking.

The baby was soon lulled to sleep by a full stomach and the warm, cozy dry blankets of his familiar spot in Jess's bunk. The fire crackled, and comforting warmth began to soak into Jess's body.

He was unaware of anything else until Sean lay his hand gently on his shoulder. "Jess? Why don't you turn in. The Hawk's been rubbed down and fed and the lady's changing her things in my room."

"Yeah...okay," Jess sighed. Thanks."

Jess's head scarcely touched his bunk after drawing the sleeping baby to his warm wool shirt in comforting closeness before he was asleep. Even the mud and rain-soaked Levis did not hamper his sleep, for he was far too exhausted to notice them.

Sean poured a cup of coffee for the woman, who sat, warming herself by the fire, in a dry pair of Jess's Levis and one of his wool shirts. "Here. I guess a little more coffee wouldn't hurt. Are you warm enough yet?"

"Yes. I didn't really get that wet. Jess...Mr. Hazzard, gave me his raincoat. He was so cold, so tired."

Sean nodded. "Been a tough day for him." He glanced at her. "Especially losing that baby." He saw her start to protest and raised a hand. "Whoa. We know he's yours and you have every right to him. But you have to understand. Jess saved his life, brought him home, and raised him better than most men would raise their own son."

"I know that, now," she said with a slight nod as she looked up at Sean with troubled eyes. "Oh why couldn't things have been as simple as I thought they would be? I don't know what I expected him to be like. You must know the kind of stories they tell in town about him. Killer. Half-breed. Ex-convict. I guess I never stopped to think he might have any feelings. And I was afraid of him. Then, what he did for us today…" Her voice caught, perhaps remembering the way he held her and kissed her.

"Sean, what happened? Those terrible scars, I mean."

He glanced quizzically at her. "They didn't tell you in town?" The big man paused and sighed. "No, I guess they wouldn't have." He tossed another log on the fire and settled into a chair. "This spring, a man was murdered in town and some witnesses said Jess did it. Sheriff took him in and they were so anxious to hang him they sent him to Carter City with a marshal. An insane marshall. Jess was handcuffed to a tree and the marshal cut him to ribbons with a whip."

Sean shook his head, remembering the horror of it all. "I've never seen anything like it and hope I never do again. That left those scars...and took his sight." Sean tossed his coffee grounds into the fire and continued.

"Turned out to be one of the witnesses killed that man, just to see Jess hang. By the time I found out and got back to Carter City, we had to cut Jess down off the gallows. Maybe you noticed the rope scar on his neck.

"It just about broke Jess to lose his sight. Then when he found the baby and no one turned up to claim him, it somehow made up for it. He seemed to come back alive...be the old Jess again." He looked up at her. "Maybe getting his sight back will help some, now."

There were tears in her eyes and she bit her lip to keep from breaking down and crying.

"You'd better get some sleep," Sean said kindly. "It's been a long day. You'll sleep in my room and I'll keep the fire going and sleep out on the couch."

Despite how tired she was, sleep was evasive. She lay on the bed, wearing Jess's soft wool shirt so her dress could dry by the fire. She closed her eyes, smelling the mixture of the fresh, sun-dried shirt and his faint body scent. Her mind returned to the awful journey they made that night and the desperate, yet tender way he looked at her, held her, and kissed her. *Jess Hazzard. Only a name and shadowed rumors before. A man, flesh and blood, now. A man I love!* Though it made no sense, she felt a lump in her throat and a strange joy in her breast. She heard of love at first sight, but never in her wildest dreams would she have ever have believed it could happen to her. She found herself wishing her husband had been more like this half-breed, so-called, killer. And she realized that never before in her life had she truly been in love.

Stroking the softness of the shirt, she closed her eyes, wishing he was here with her now so she could curl up in his protective arms. A soft sigh escaped as she drifted off to sleep, knowing he would never allow harm to come to her, or her small son.

Chapter 19

Morning dawned clear and bright. Droplets of rain still dripped off the cottonwood tree next to the window. The fiery sunlight woke Jess as it struck his face. Through closed eyelids accustomed to blindness, the light was stunning. After waking so long in velvet darkness, it was good to see the golden rays of a soft dawn creeping into the gray sky over the eastern mountains.

Eager to be outside, he quickly slipped on a clean pair of Levis, socks, and his boots. Pausing to gently pull back the light blanket, he gazed in awe at the small face he was seeing for the first time. The baby slept with a contented smile. Jess closed his eyes and gently touched the boy's soft cheek. It still felt the same, but now he had the image to keep, too. He felt his eyes suddenly sting. *How can I bear this loss? Why does life have to be so hard?*

In the past year, he had been shot, beaten, blinded, and nearly hung twice. His lips curled into a wry smile. Long ago, his father told him a man is very close to death three times in his life before he is taken by it. *If that's true, I'm overdue and what kind of gift is that for a baby? It's better his mother came to take him to raise, that the child...Keith...his name is Keith. It's better he grow up never to know me.*

He loved Keith fiercely, like a son. Indeed, he had become his son in the last months, as the bond strengthened between them. But what did he have to offer the child? Or his mother? Painful bitterness flooded Jess's soul. Nothing. Nothing but himself and the shadows that followed him everywhere. Half-breed. Gunman. Ex-con.

With a sharp pang, he remembered the minutes he let his guard down, allowed his feelings to show, allowed himself to kiss her and hold her in his arms for long minutes. A flood of unfamiliar emotions tore through him. *I am such a fool!*

Like any man, he dreamt of finding the right woman, of building their own place, maybe even having kids, but for a man like him, he knew dreams were all they could be.

He could never bring the degradation of marrying a half-breed gunfighter to a woman, especially not a woman like her, a woman he knew he loved. *I can only bring pain to her...pain, danger, and hatred. It can never be allowed to begin. For both our sakes.*

Jess turned toward the sun, now above the mountain peaks, as if in prayer. An ache came to his throat as he thought of how it might have been if only his father was white. But the thought was fleeting, replaced by great guilt. His father may have been a Chiricahua Apache, but he was a good man, a good father, and patient teacher. Even today, Jess felt more Apache in his heart, than white. *Why does that have to be so bad? Are humans really so different, after all?*

He turned away and walked quietly outside, not wanting to awaken anyone else. He needed time alone, to control the pain, to think of what he could say to her.

He was amazed at all the small things he overlooked before – the bird nest under the barn eaves, the little blue flowers growing near the corral fence, the axe marks on the rails. Beyond the fence, the glass-coated Morgan raised his head and whickered a greeting. It was magic to see the fluttering of his nostrils, the trust in the stallion's dark eyes.

Flooded with emotion, Jess vaulted the fence, walked quickly to the stallion, and grabbing a handful of mane, swung onto his back. He squeezed the Hawk into a run. Once around the corral they flew, the grass and trees a mad blur of color. Then Jess swung him around by leg pressure and weight alone, like some great war horse, and turned him toward the corral fence. The little horse picked up Jess's excitement and threw his ears forward in anticipation. As one, they sailed over the poles, then up the trail, hoof beats splashing loudly in the wet, still morning.

Swooping across the edge of the hayfield, they crashed through the shallow creek, leaping the piles of saw logs at the edge of the clearing. Then, feeling the Hawk begin to puff beneath him, Jess turned him back to the barn and coaxed him into a gentle, dancing jog.

The bright greens, blues, yellows, and rich browns of the fields and trees were almost painfully clear. Coupled with the scents and sounds that were his guides in his dark world, they became as a banquet to him in the light.

With a sigh, he slipped off the glossy black stallion and led him into the barn by a handful of his long mane. The other horses began to whicker for feed. After putting the Hawk in his stall and rubbing him down, Jess began chores. As he dipped out oats for the team, he took note of the axe marks on the logs around the window, carefully done to square the frame.

His thoughts drifted wildly. He wondered how it would be to start with a few logs, the right woman – her – and build a home, a true home. He glanced at his hands and flexed his fingers. He knew he could do it.

But again reality invaded his dreams. There was his Indian blood and his past filled with dead men standing between him and this woman who suddenly would not leave his thoughts, or his heart.

His head dropped in despair. Then he heard her footsteps behind him, striking a small panic within him. He felt like running.

"Jess?"

He turned around, wondering if he could control his feelings, and saw she looked into his soul the way she had in his dreams, again sad, asking him to help. And he could not.

"What's wrong?" she asked, her voice quiet, hesitant, as if afraid of his answer.

He drew a slow, painful breath, still looking into her eyes. "I don't even know your name," he heard his voice say, against his will.

"My name is Julie," she said simply, still waiting.

Jess swallowed hard, trying to escape her eyes. "I'm sorry."

"What for? What could you possibly be sorry about after saving our lives last night?"

"You could never understand," he choked out.

"Please. Let me try."

"I'm afraid. For you...for any chance we could ever have," he began, unsure of her feelings for him. "You know I'm half Indian. And I've lived with that all my life...or tried to live it down. The more I fought it, the more trouble it brought. When I was not much more than a kid, I learned I had a fast hand with a gun. And I thought that would even things up with other men. It didn't. It just made things worse. Folks think the only thing worse than a 'breed is a 'breed with a fast gun. You must have seen that when you were in town. But I guess I've got feelings, just like any other man, no matter what they say. It can't go beyond this."

"Can't?" she asked quietly, the fear back in her voice and eyes.

Jess drew a deep breath, letting it out in a ragged, hopeless sigh. "I could never bring that kind of degradation to you. That kind of pain. If you and I were together, made a start for ourselves, people...those *good* people in town, would never forget you're white and I'm a half-breed." Bitter, he spat out the hated word. "All their hate for me would spill over onto you. And it's ugly, so ugly. No matter where you go, it's the same. There's no running from it...no fighting it. It's what put me in prison and nearly got me hung."

The pain of the past filled his face, startling her.

"And if a new baby was born later? What if it had the look of an Indian? It could, you know. Could a white woman...could you look on it as your own? I know of one woman that ended up killin' herself over it." Jess drew another ragged breath. "A family, a home...just won't happen for me. Don't you understand?"

"No," she replied simply. "I don't. But at least I understand how you feel." She dropped her eyes in an instant of pain that mirrored his. "I was afraid you just decided I wasn't what you wanted in a woman." Turning away, so he could not see her distress, she spoke in a trembling voice. "You know, I've been alone, too. Maybe it wasn't as bad as it's been for you. But it hurt. My husband left me for another woman the day I told him I was carrying his child. Just left, without a word. Slapped me across the face, shoved me to the floor, and walked out, slamming the door." The pain cut her voice into little pieces.

"Oh, he was white, rich, and respected in Southport. But that didn't make him a man. He left me without a penny and nowhere to go. Just old bruises from the times he hit me. Word came that he was killed in a saloon brawl a week later. I was not sorry.

"For so long, I felt cheap and lost. I kept asking myself why it happened. Why he left me...for her. What I did or didn't do to make him happy. I never found the answer.

"Most people in town, including my parents and his, liked and respected Garth. But they never saw the other side of him, the wild, savage side without mercy of any kind...especially when he had been drinking. They blamed me for his disgrace.

"I didn't know how to change it, but I had to get away from it, from him! I just had to, even though I knew I would be giving birth to my child on some desolate wagon trail. Aunt Elsie and Uncle Zeke were going to California and I begged them to let me go with them. I had an offer of a good job in San Francisco.

"When we reached Denver, I had to go on ahead, without Keith. We were late and time was running out. I had to be in San Francisco by September first or lose the job. Our future depended on it. Keith had a touch of cholera he picked up from some of the people on the wagon train and wasn't strong enough yet to travel by stagecoach, with me. I hated to leave him, but didn't know what else to do!

"I took the stagecoach, then a train, and got there in time to begin my new job and find us a place to live. I was so worried about Keith." She looked at him, her eyes filled with sadness. "There were a few men who asked me to dinner or to take a buggy ride with them. But when they learned I had Keith, they stopped calling." Her voice tightened as she fought back tears of rejection.

Jess laid his hand on her shoulder in a futile effort to comfort her, longing to take her into his arms again. "Don't Julie. Any man would be proud to have you and Keith both."

She looked at him, her eyes hard, trying to make him understand. "No. Not both of us, and I would never give Keith away. I've tried to forget the pain and rejection, to put it behind me. It hurts too much to dwell on. I know you understand."

"Yeah," he said through a wry smile. "I do. But there's times you do remember. I wake up in a cold sweat sometimes. Dead men are hard to forget. The blood in the street washes away in time, but the sight of it never does and haunts me at night.

"It's been better, since I've been here with Sean and Scotty, away from the old ways. But still, there's nights..." The look in his shadowed eyes told of his torture. "God, Julie, I wish it could be different."

"Can't it?" she asked. "Can't things change?" Her voice was shaking again.

"Some things. For you, they will. I know things'll work out for you and the baby. They can't help but work out." Jess found his eyes burning and chest aching, as even a bullet had not hurt. "But there's always going to be someone tryin' to prove himself against me. Someday I may have to stand against one of them again. I know it's not over, no matter how much I wish it was. It won't be over until I'm dead."

She turned away as she felt tears spring to her eyes. "Sean said the road dries quickly. I'll start for town as soon as I can."

Gently, Jess turned her back and enfolding her in his arms, cut deeply by her tears. Her heart beat against his chest, like a frightened bird beating against a window, trying to escape. "Please, Julie. Please don't cry. It just can't be any different. I can't do that to you."

Chapter 20

The hot afternoon sun's rays drove the last dampness from the soil as Jess bored the holes for the new gate. Working hard, he could almost force his mind away from that morning. And her.

The hinges were set firmly and the gate was ready to hang. The heavy plank gate would be stronger and more dependable than the old poles. Easier to open, too. *What is she doing? Is she thinking of me, too?* The way his heart seemed to be tearing within him, begging him to relent, forced him to shake his head and hit the pole.

"Wait a minute," Sean called from the barn. "I'll help you hang that. I just went out to check the hayfield. It's going to take a few more days before it's ready to cut again. It seemed dry enough, but the team's feet cut into the ground pretty bad."

While Sean talked, he lifted the gate, waiting for Jess to slip the hinges over the hinge pins. Jess smiled, shaking his head. That gate must weigh a hundred and fifty pounds; sixteen feet of two inch planks, five feet high, and Sean lifted it like it was a kitchen chair. He'd hate to be on the wrong side of him, as Blueson had been.

Nodding to Sean the gate was in place, Jess scanned it, gratified it hung level.

"Not bad!" Sean exclaimed. "Let that old mare try to crawl through that gate!"

Jess stooped to pick up his tools.

"Say Jess, what's this about Julie planning to leave in the morning? I haven't seen much of either of you. I kinda figured there might be a romance brewing." Along with the question in his voice was a touch of tease.

Jess passed the big man wordlessly and dropped the tools into the bin by the door. Were there any answers? He wasn't sure.

Sean waited, leaning on the corral rails. A breeze picked up, sending a whisper-like sigh through the pines. Tomorrow morning would be hard, for everyone.

Then Jess joined him, also listening to the trees murmur. They stood in silence like that for several minutes.

"Can you take her to town?" Jess asked at last. "I don't think I could do it."

"Yeah. Sure. But I kind of figured you might be asking her to stay." Sean picked up a blade of grass and thoughtfully chewed on it.

"I couldn't do that to her...or the baby. You know how it would be for her. There's always going to be another Jerry Tripp or Blueson. It wouldn't be fair to either of them."

"Fair? You three belong together and you know it. What about you? Are you going to tell me you don't have feelings for her?"

"No," Jess answered quietly. "But a half-breed doesn't ask a woman like her to share his life."

"Jess, don't be a fool! You have to bury that half-breed bullshit. There isn't anyone who knows you that even thinks about it. Unless maybe they're wondering at how you can train an outlaw horse, track a deer across rock, or know what pool the trout are laying up in.

"There'll always be ignorant people. But don't lose a woman like her because of them. A man's lucky to get one chance like you have in his life." Sean's green eyes clouded, remembering his wife. "Don't throw it away."

Jess was quiet a long time, perhaps searching the whispers of the pines for answers. "Sean, I'm afraid for her. For both of them. If they go, they'll end up in San Francisco and live a normal life. If...if I did ask her to stay, maybe she could live with the hate. But what if some gunman came? How could I kill him in front of them? She's not used to that kind of violence. And what if he was faster...and he sure could be. There's always someone faster. She's too fine a woman to leave a widow. I haven't hardly touched my gun in months. I sure don't miss it, but I'm not kiddin' myself. I'll lose my edge. It's dangerous to get too comfortable."

Jess bleakly shook his head. "No. It's better they go. I'll watch things for you here. Take Scotty with you. He'll like the trip." His jaw convulsed. His voice was rough. "Make goodbyes for me, will you. I'll be goin' out huntin' first thing. It'll be better for everyone that way."

Sean shook his head. "You are a stubborn son-of-a-bitch, aren't you." His voice softened with understanding. "Okay, but think about what you're doing."

Jess smiled faintly. "I will. It's goin' to be a long night."

He agonized over his decision a hundred times that endless night, knowing soon they would be gone from his life forever. But he remembered, with much pain, the many years gone by and remained sure he was doing the right thing for them.

Night seemed to last longer than usual, but finally the birds began twittering in the pre-dawn light. When the rooster crowed, Jess quietly dressed, walked into the kitchen, and pulled his carbine down from the wall, hurrying to load it. He had to be away from there before there was the slightest chance of anyone else waking. He could not face talking to anyone.

The darkness outside brought back the familiar feeling of blindness. For a second, he felt constricted by it. But the feeling evaporated as the horses whickered a low greeting in the barn and the milk cow lowed softly, clanging her bell. He lit no lantern. After months of blindness, he did not need it. A sense of urgency gripped him as he quickly saddled the Hawk. The sky was lightening and the birds outside were becoming more noisy. The Morgan danced lightly as the cinch was drawn up, picking up Jess's mood.

Outside, Jess swung up onto the stallion and felt his body go tense with expectation. Turning him north, Jess let the horse out into a mile-eating lope. Already there was lamplight in the cabin. A sense of shame gripped his insides. *Am I a coward?* He knew if he saw her again, he could never let her go.

Then he thought of her tear-filled eyes and a wave of pain hit him hard. No. He couldn't be there and watch the little things before the trip. Packing. Hooking the team. Readying the baby. Everyone under strain. He couldn't cause her any more pain. Nor could he take any more, himself. He was only human.

The morning dawned cool and bright. A heavy dew spoke of autumn, soon to come. Three miles from the cabin, a big buck stepped majestically onto the trail in front of the Hawk. Jess reined the stallion in. For a full three minutes, it stood there in the clear, velvet antlers sparkling with dew drops. It snorted, sending plumes of steam into the cool air. Then he stamped one forefoot in a challenge.

Jess never moved his hand toward his carbine. That morning, he wasn't hunting. He was running. He squeezed the Hawk's sides and they moved closer to the buck. Finally, only yards from the puzzled animal, it broke and bounced away, in mule deer fashion, disappearing into the underbrush.

Are they gone yet? He knew Sean liked to leave very early for the trip into town. The thought struck him with great finality. At the top of a hill, he glanced at the ever-advancing sun, nearly to the mountain peaks. *Soon now, if they haven't already gone.* Agony ripped through him.

He squeezed the Morgan with his spurs and they galloped down the hill. A mile farther, he slowed the stallion again, ashamed of his lack of control. They neared the wide valley of the upper river and Jess felt the Morgan bunch up and step lighter. He scented horses. Cresting the rise, Jess saw a small bunch of mustangs grazing in the clearing, led by a big, rawboned sorrel stallion. Under him, the Hawk half-reared and uttered a whicker of desire, then a bugle of challenge. His wild days were not entirely forgotten.

Normally, Jess would have enjoyed the wild ones. But today his mind was not in this valley. It was back at the ranch, watching the woman and child he loved leave his life forever. *Because you chose it. You sent them away.* The thought of never seeing them again became too painful to bear. *I have to go after them!*

Wheeling around the dancing stallion, Jess sent him into a run. The near-panic gripping him quickly passed and he slowed the stallion into a long-reaching lope. Sean would be driving the heavy team on the wagon and he knew he could easily overtake them. *But what if she won't stay? She had all night to think, too.*

Ahead, a small herd of elk melted into the trees at their clattering approach. The north fence of the pasture caught his sight and again, pulled by the same sense of urgency, he decided to cut a mile off his ride. The fence was strong and tight but Jess knew the little Morgan could jump. He could fly!

The top rail skimmed by under them and they galloped across the familiar meadow. The buildings loomed over the rise and Jess headed the Hawk for the new gate. He intended to stop to open it but felt a thrill as the stallion pointed his ears to the gate and bunched his hindquarters for the leap. Giving him a word of encouragement, Jess leaned forward and let him go. The heavy five-foot gate disappeared as the Hawk rose into the air.

Then Jess was in the vacant yard. The emptiness struck him hard. They were gone. Glancing to the ground, he saw the tracks of the team and the wagon, heading south, toward town. And there in the soft dirt near the porch, he saw her tracks. The Morgan danced, pulling on the reins, eager to run and Jess let him go.

He lost track of time as the Morgan splashed through the overflow by the hillside spring, clattered over the loose rocks of the rockslide and thudded noiselessly in the deeply carpeted pine needles beneath the huge pines. He was one with the stallion, alone on the trail. *Where are they?* On went the tracks before them.

Then the Hawk lowered his head as he ran, scenting like a hound, and Jess knew they were close now. The stallion was following the team of mares with the wild instincts of a herd sire.

Despondent, Julie sat on the seat next to Sean as the wagon lurched through the west fork. The stream was still heavily swollen, but passable with the team of strong mares and the big man's knowledge of the ford. Turning parallel to the river, they again headed toward town, many miles away. She glanced at the baby, sleeping peacefully in a basket beneath her feet, and thought of the past few days. It seemed impossible she fell in love in so short a time! Again she felt the pain of finding Jess gone that morning, but maybe it would have been harder of he had been there when they left. Tears stung her eyes and she turned her head toward the hills so Sean would not see. She was probably a fool!

Then she became aware of a sound behind them, from somewhere across the creek. A rhythmic drumming. Hollow sounding. A horse?

"Pa!" Scotty exclaimed, turning to watch the trail behind them. "Someone's comin'!"

Sean reined in the team and looked at Julie, who was watching the trail, half afraid to hope. He smiled at her as she looked back to him, as if in question. "I wondered how long he could hold out," he laughed.

The black Morgan burst into sight through the trees, sliding down the river bank. But instead of going back on the trail, to the ford, Jess sent him leaping into the water, opposite them. The roiling water was deep and swift. Deep enough the Hawk had to swim and fight being carried downstream. But it was not far and the stallion was a powerful swimmer. Soon he lunged into the shallows, sending plumes of spray high in the cool air.

At first, Julie was unsure, frightened by the strength of her hope. But as she saw his face, she knew. Glancing back to Sean, who nodded, smiling in encouragement, she jumped down from the wagon, gathered her skirt, and ran to meet him.

Jess was off the Hawk, catching her in his arms, holding her as tightly as she clung to him, kissing her to drown the fear, to tell her how he felt. When they both stopped shaking, he held her out at arm's length, gently.

"Stay? Marry me?"

She met his eyes and nodded, afraid to trust her voice.

"I hope you're never sorry," he said softly, his eyes smiling into hers. Gently kissing her, he sealed the reality of the moment.

Then, remembering they had an audience, Jess flushed and pulled away. "Come on. We're keeping folks waitin'." He mounted the Hawk and held his hand out to her.

Feeling sixteen again, Julie slipped her toe into the stirrup, gathered her skirts and laughed as she pulled herself up behind the man she loved. The Morgan danced lightly sideways and she held onto Jess tighter than she needed to. Then they headed toward the waiting wagon.

Puzzled, Scotty turned to his smiling father. "Does this mean we're not goin' to town?"

Sean rumpled the boy's hair in affection. "Not today. But I have an idea we will be, real soon." He turned to Jess as they rode up. "I'm glad you finally got some sense. We're goin' back?"

Jess smiled, grateful for Sean's understanding. "Yeah. We're goin' back."

Sean wheeled the team around in the trail. "We'll go on ahead. I expect you'll have a few things to talk about." He chuckled, slapping the broad rumps of the team with the lines.

"How come, Pa."

"You'll find out, when you're about ten years older. You come up here and watch that baby, you hear?"

The wagon jolted back down the trail and through the ford again, disappearing into the trees. The stallion danced under them, pulling to follow the wagon, but Jess turned him toward the river where they dismounted on the sunny bank. He let the stallion drink, then tied him to a nearby tree.

Julie stood close to Jess, feeling the joy of her hand in his, watching the river flow in front of them.

"There's a place up the valley," Jess began, "at the head of the river. Pretty, clear, green lake, pines, a nice meadow. Good spring water and even an old barn. It's kind of wild, but maybe no one would bother us there. A fire went through there years ago and took the cabin. The fire killed a lot of big pines, but the wood's still sound and good. There's enough for a pretty-good-sized cabin, lookin' out on the lake."

She heard the question in his voice and sighed. "It sounds perfect. I've always wanted to live in the mountains."

"The first year's liable to be rough. This is a hell of a time to be startin' out, a couple of months before the snow flies. But we can do it," Jess said, almost to himself.

"We'll just have to work faster!" Julie answered with spirit. "When can I see it?"

"How about tomorrow morning? If we go early enough, we can get back before afternoon. Sean kinda wants to get the rest of the hay up and one more day should finish it. He can use the help.

"It's pretty remote, up there. We'll be snowed in for six months of the year. No chance of goin' to town then. Can you handle that?"

"Can I have a garden?" she smiled.

"Sure, but remember the cold. You'll have to grow things that can stand the cold and ripen fast."

"It's a deal, Mr. Hazzard." She laughed, kissing him lightly. "If you keep me warm."

In return, he took her in his arms, and showed her how much he loved her.

Jess lay on a sunlit hill of grass, overlooking the clear, emerald green lake, listening to the pines over his head moan in the shifting late summer breeze. He watched a pair of eagles sweep through the skies above him. They had a nest on the north side of the lake and were raising a family. Soon he and Julie would be joining them. For it was here, on this spot, they would build the cabin, their new home. A thrill ran though him. The sun shone brightly and the morning was warm.

He stretched, feeling lazy, as he heard stealthy steps behind him.

"How do you like your new home?" he asked with a smile in his voice. "Think it'll do?"

She laughed. "And I thought I could sneak up on you! I love it! It's the most beautiful spot in the world. And, to be able to see it every day of our lives!" She lay the baby down on the soft grass and pine needles, then sat down next to Jess, holding her knees in front of her, as a small girl might. She snuggled close to his warmth as she, too, looked out across the lake, then up to the eagles, marveling at the intense beauty of the spot.

It's so strange. Back home, I'd be worried at being alone with a man I've known for so short a time. But here I am, next to a man I know to be half Indian, a gunman who's killed men, has even been in prison on the charge of an unspeakable crime. Yet I feel safe and trust him completely. This gentle man is not the man the townspeople think he is.

Here, fifty miles from the nearest town, she was totally at ease, wholly in love.

She felt him stir next to her. Sitting up, his lips brushed her hair softly. She felt a tinge of shame. She believed those horrid people when she first came here. Believed them until he stumbled blindly through the savage storm, leading her upon his great horse. She held him close, burying her face against his shoulder, hoping he would never know.

"We really better get goin," Jess said, helping her to her feet.

"I know. The hay will be drying," she said, teasing.

"That, too." Jess smiled with the look of a mischievous boy. "Any more of this and I'll forget we aren't married yet."

"I trust you," she replied, cocking her head at him. "You're the first real gentleman I've ever met."

He laughed aloud, stooping to pick up the baby, who was quickly learning to roll onto his knees. "That's one thing I've never been accused of!"

She smiled, taking the baby from him. "You know, Jess, I'll be coming to you with somewhat of a dowry." A smile crept into her voice at the puzzled look on his face.

"Well, it isn't really that much. My aunt and uncle had no children, no family. When we left on our journey, we all made out a will, just in case something happened to one of us. They were in their strongbox. They left what little they had to Keith and me." Shadows passed through her eyes at the pain of remembering their death.

"Everything they owned was in that wagon. Except for their box, I was going to have Sean sell it and the contents. But I think we'd better save it. Uncle Zeke was going to homestead and there's all sorts of tools, household things, even seeds, if they didn't get ruined in the accident." Her spirits rose a bit, thinking of the things that would make starting easier for them. "There are quilts, pillows, dishes, and quite a bit of food, too."

"Are you sure it's okay," Jess asked hesitantly.

"Yes. I am. I'm positive that my aunt and uncle would be very happy to see us use the things they treasured so much. They didn't get a chance to build a new life. But we do." She squeezed his hand.

He put his arm around her shoulders and for a second, felt his throat constrict, knowing how lucky he was to have them, to have this chance so late in life. "You know I love you," he whispered, gently touching her face with one finger.

Chapter 21

A long four days later, they arrived at Doc Stone's home to get ready for the wedding. With Jess and Julie left in Martha's capable, but bustling hands, Sean went to take care of the team. Doc was gone on a call and all that fluttering about, taking in one of Doc's suits for Jess, talking to the minister, and pressing Julie's dress was too much for him.

As he went into the barn, Sean noticed Scotty, the boy who never was still a moment, sitting on the water trough. He was still there when he came back, making aimless ripples on the surface of the water with a small stick.

"What's the matter, son?"

"Nothin'."

He smiled, understanding. "Nothing?"

The boy was silent for several minutes. Then he looked up at Sean. "Does he have to go away, Pa?" He choked, as though fighting tears.

"He's not going far. Just up to the lake. It's close enough we can ride over there in an hour or so. You can ride over yourself when you get a little older. Any time you want."

"What's he have to go'n get married for, anyway? I wish she'd never of come!" The boy threw away the stick.

"Thinking like that isn't fair to Jess, Scotty."

"Why Pa? Wasn't he happy with us? What's he gotta have *her* for, anyway?"

"It may be hard for you to understand, until you're older. You know, there's all kinds of love. Love of the country where we live, the mountains, the river. My love for you. A boy for his dog or a man, his friends. But until a man knows the love of a good woman, there's something missing in him. He may not even know it. But when he meets the right woman, he finds out. It was that way with your mother and me.

"But with us, it was easier than it's been for Jess. You know things have been pretty rough for him in the past. Maybe that's why it's so important to him that Julie loves him and will stick by him, no matter what. He can finally make a start, get out from under a bad name and build something good, find the kind of happiness I had with your mother. Does that make sense?"

"Yeah. I guess so. But..." He heaved an adult-sized sigh.

Sean smiled and put his arm around the boy's shoulders. "Yeah. I know. We'll both miss him. But we'll go up and help him build. And he'll be back. Often. It won't be like he's really gone. Now take off that long sheep face and come into the house."

The boy kicked at his father, but smiled and followed him toward the back door.

Chapter 22

The new day dawned hot and dry, with the whirring song of grasshoppers blending in with roosters crowing. Inside the house, Martha hovered back and forth between the men and Julie, trying to get everyone dressed perfectly and started on time. Confined by the black suit, Jess felt uncomfortable, even though it fit him like he was born in it. But it was a discomfort that was easily borne. For her.

Eight o'clock came and Julie was spirited away by Doc, Martha, and Scotty in the buggy. A few minutes later, Sean and Jess followed on their horses.

For the first time in his life Jess was unarmed in a town and it rested uneasily upon him. However, he had strong feelings against wearing a Colt to his wedding.

The horses' feet clopped loudly on the dry, hard-packed street. An ominous silence followed them through town as they rode toward the white church at the end of the street. Every eye turned toward the handsome pair of black-suited men, riding equally dark, light-stepping horses. Somewhere, a dog barked and the sound seemed out of place. Jess's muscles corded, expecting trouble. He waited for the challenge, the shot. Faces peered from windows, some curious, others dark with hate. Still, he waited. The powerful stallion under him walked steadily onward, neck arched, long, shining mane flowing. Jess glanced to Sean, sitting tall and proud, eyes fixed ahead. It was a good feeling.

He turned and looked away, letting his eyes scan the buildings ahead, the alleys, the doorways. They were nearing the church now.

Jess saw the buggy tied in front and people on the steps. Still no sound broke the icy silence of the town. They finally stopped at the hitching rail next to the church.

An immense sense of relief touched Jess as he stepped off the Hawk and tied him. It was the first time he ever rode into a town without trouble of any kind. Half an hour spun by, the brief ceremony was over and Jess found himself outside being congratulated. Julie stood aside with Martha, who noticed, even as Jess shook the Reverend Saunder's hand, he glanced down the street, alert for trouble.

On impulse, she squeezed the younger woman's hand and spoke in almost a whisper. "Give him happiness. He's had so little of it!"

Julie looked at her, then to Jess, standing with the men at the foot of the steps, waiting for them. "I will." She almost choked on the tightness in her throat.

Jess's eyes met hers and smiled. For the rest of his life, he would hold the memory of her in her simple, but beautiful, dark green dress with a bit of white lace at the throat, standing at that alter with him.

They returned to the Stone's house to find a strange team of shiny, well-muscled matching gray Percheron mares tied to the hitching rail. No wagon. No buckboard. Just the harnessed team.

"I see Cyrus was here while we were gone," Doc said.

"What?" Jess asked.

Doc chuckled and raised his eyebrows. "You'll have to ask your wife."

Julie laughed. "They were my last fling as a free woman. I traded my train ticket to San Francisco for them. Mr. Wells even threw in the harness. I wasn't going to need the ticket and thought we might need a team to pull aunt and uncle's wagon. He wanted to move by his son, in 'Frisco. What do you think of them?" Her eyes twinkled.

"They're a good team." Jess shook his head and laughed. "But I never figured I was marryin' a lady horse trader."

"I kind of helped out a little," Doc said. "I knew Cyrus really wanted to live closer to his only son and didn't have any money for the trip. And I knew he had a good young team of mares. We worked from there. Even traded his wagon to Al Grey for the wrecked buggy Julie rented, so everybody's happy with the deal."

They spent a pleasant day and evening visiting with Doc and Martha. Al unexpectedly dropped by, contributing a fifty pound keg of nails to the newly married couple.

The next morning, they bought supplies, packed Sean's wagon and left town with the team of dapple gray mares tied to the back.

They stopped at the Miller's, and by the time they left, a crate of laying hens and a rooster was added to the full wagon, a wedding gift from Jenny Miller.

Despite the heat of the day, Jess felt the urgency of approaching winter and was glad when they finally arrived at the ranch. There was so much planning and work to do.

He and Sean decided to take both teams and wagons up to the lake the following morning. The old barn was large and in good repair, so Jess and Julie decided they would live in one end until the cabin was finished. They could store tools, household goods, and supplies in the rest of it to keep them safe from the weather. Jess's head spun, trying to see to every necessary detail. Lucky for him, Sean went through the same thing himself and was able to provide invaluable advice and help along with encouragement and enthusiasm.

They had not yet gone through the contents of Uncle Zeke's wagon, so that night they loaded Sean's wagon with every possible tool they might need. They wanted the building to go as smoothly and quickly as possible. By lantern light, they lashed the load down.

Sean laughed at Jess, fussing over every detail. "You'll live through this, you know."

Jess smiled back, looking so much younger than he did a year ago. "Yeah. I know. I guess I just need to get working, be doing something."

"Oh. I just remembered. Doc's sending up a couple of wagon loads of lumber for the floor of your house. A wedding present. He didn't want to tell you, so you couldn't argue about it. They should get up here from the mill about Friday."

Jess shook his head in wonder at Doc's generosity. "You know, Sean, this all scares me. It's too good too fast."

"Things work out that way, sometimes. Maybe it's just making up for last year." The big man blew out the lantern. "Come on. We'd better get on up to the house or your wife's going to send out the troops, wondering what's keeping us."

Wife. The word sounds so strange. Strange and very good. He grinned and followed Sean.

Early the next morning, Sean and Jess harnessed both teams and hooked them to the wagons. Jess tied the Hawk behind their wagon while Sean tied his black and Old Sorrel behind his.

Helping Julie into the wagon, Jess smiled at her. Their eyes met and she knew what he was thinking. The greatest adventure in their lives was beginning. They were on their way up into the mountains to build their home.

The heavily laden wagons creaked and groaned. As they slowly headed up the river trail, Jess wondered if they would ever get there. It was so much faster on horseback. He knew the load was heavy, but gave a half-hearted flip of the lines on the wide rumps of the mares, wanting to hurry them. They completely ignored him.

Sean smiled at Jess's impatience. It had been the same with him. He remembered how long it took from Lawson, up over the pass – fifty incredibly slow miles.

Finally, after two hours, Jess spotted the tops of the towering pines and knew they were almost there. But, as his wagon topped the rise, he pulled the team up. Something was not right. First, just a feeling, then the faint smell of wood smoke! His right hand dropped to touch the carbine under the seat. Julie looked at him with frightened eyes, then down below. A horse was standing hobbled, grazing in the clearing. Then a man limped to his horse with a pail. Ernie! Breathing again, Jess urged the mares ahead, down the slope.

Hearing the rumble of the wagons, Ernie came to meet them, grumbling good-naturedly, "About time you showed up! Half the day's gone!" He eyed Julie appraisingly, knowing if Jess's judgment in women was as good as his judgment of horses, she must be special, indeed.

"You must be the new Missus." At her nod, he tipped his hat. "Ma'am."

"I almost shot you, sneakin' around the place like that," Jess admonished with a smile. "What're you doin' here?"

"Humph! I heard there was gonna be a house-raisin' startin' today an' I thought to myself, Ernie, you'd better go keep an eye on them young bucks. Make sure things are done right. Well? Are we goin' to work, or what?" He turned and slapped his hat back on, then turned back, took it off again, and waved it toward the baby. "There's somethin' in the barn, Missus, for you an' that little fella there." Then the old man set his hat back on his head and turned to Jess and

Sean. "You boys comin'?"

A smile flickered across Jess's face as he started the mares down toward the barn.

Almost in a whisper, Julie asked, "Jess, who is that?"

Jess laughed, remembering how stunned he was when he first met the old man. "That's Ernie. He might be a bit odd, but he's a good friend and he ain't half as rough as he seems."

"What did he mean about something in the barn?"

"Darned if I know. Maybe it's a pet skunk. He has one, you know. Maybe he thought you needed one, too."

She shot him a panicked look. Then, at a lowing sound, she jumped. "Oh, Jess! It's a milk cow!"

Tied in a freshly bedded stall was a liver roan cow with a pink, silky udder and a set of delicately curved horns. Julie moved forward and patted the cow's side with great appreciation, for here was milk for the baby, cream, butter, and cheese for them. It seemed too good to be true. She hurried outside to thank Ernie but he was already busy, staking out the cabin site.

Jess unhooked his team and drove them up beside Sean's big bays, tying them to the side of the wagon.

"Come over here, Jess," Ernie called, "and step off the walls. I 'spect you got everything figured out pretty well. I've got corner stones located. Let's get this house up! How'd the Missus like the cow?" The old man cocked his head, pausing from his work for an instant.

"She liked her real well, Ernie. Thanks. Couldn't have been a nicer present."

Once the foundation was set, work seemed to go quicker. All afternoon, the stillness of the little valley was punctuated by the crack and groan of trees falling. Tree after tree was selected, cut and measured for length. The big pines were well seasoned and had no bark, standing dead for years. Light and strong, they were hauled two by two, down to the cabin site where Sean carefully hollowed out a cupped grove on the bottom of each log, to fit precisely on the log below with no gap. It was the Swedish way of log building he learned as a young man in Minnesota. The house would be snug and warm, with little chinking needed.

Ernie cut the notches, not seeming to work quickly, but each notch was perfectly cut and when the three men rolled a log into place, it squeaked into place tightly the first time. The old man was a master log builder, an artist with logs.

At six o'clock, they stopped work and gathered to eat the meal Julie prepared for them. The walls were well started! As tired as he was, Jess wished they could work longer, but he knew Ernie and Sean both had long rides home, to get back for their chores.

As they left, Jess took the team down to the lake to water them. While they drank, he watched a flock of ducks on the water feeding. Trout were beginning to make ripples and way out, a big one leaped high. *This is going to be a good place to live.*

He worked another two hours, cutting and hauling more logs down to the cabin site, then cared for the mares and staked them out to graze in the lush grass beyond the barn. Glancing back, he marveled at the progress they made on the cabin and at the big pile of logs waiting for the next day.

When Jess walked over to take one last look at the house, he saw he was not the only one with those thoughts. Julie stood looking into the doorway, logs standing as high as her waist.

Quietly, he stepped behind her and put his arms around her shoulders, drawing her close to him.

"Oh! Jess!"

"Is it alright?"

"It's much bigger than I thought it would be. Oh, Jess, it's going to be so nice!" She turned, filled with joy, and kissed him. Then she tugged at his hand. "Come see what I did in the barn."

Jess saw she emptied half of her aunt and uncle's heavily laden wagon and sorted the contents. Some, mostly clothing and books that were soaked in the accident and then molded, would have to be discarded, but there were axes, mauls, wedges, saws, hammers – tools of every kind – as well as pails, pots, pans, tinware, a scrub board and tub, quilts, blankets, pillows and more.

Past the array of tools and household goods, he saw their temporary living quarters, neatly swept with a tick of fresh meadow hay laid out for a bed. Already, a contented Keith lay sleeping to one side in his familiar hammock. Jess smiled at her keeping the old ways, instead of insisting he sleep in a white man's cradle.

He put his arms around her, drawing her close. "You are a wonder. I didn't expect you to work so hard."

"Why? You were. It's the least I could do. And I pulled a big pile of dry moss from below the spring, where Sean and Scotty were getting it so they won't have to, tomorrow. Scotty showed me how. Now it's all ready for them to lay between the logs so it'll go even faster in the morning."

He shook his head in wonder. "Tired?"

"No." She looked deep into his eyes to the gentleness there, the love and desire, and allowed herself to be led to the waiting softness of the quilts over the sun-dried grasses. It was their first night alone.

Chapter 23

A week later, Jess harnessed the gray mares in the faint light of the new day. Already the area looked better, with the stark, dead trees gone. *Funny how much better they look in the cabin walls!* A fog lay low on the lake as the sun tried to break through. The lake was noisy with water birds waking to the new day.

Trees began loudly cracking as they fell in the morning stillness, but the moose, standing in the lake below, paid it no mind as he dipped his great, antlered head to browse below the surface.

They would be working on the rafters for the roof today and if he could have a good lot cut before Sean and Ernie came, the roof would go up quickly. He cut smaller trees for rafters, and soon had twenty in a pile, neatly limbed and cut to length. The sun was heating up and rivulets of sweat trickled down Jess's face and back. He was hungry. Tying four poles together, he headed the mares down the ridge, toward the cabin.

Ernie, Sean, and Scotty arrived minutes earlier and were surveying the cabin, as it stood.

"You've been out early," Ernie grinned, nodding at the poles.

"Got to be, to keep ahead of you! There's sixteen more, just like these, ready to bring in."

"Sean kin bring 'em in. You better get some grub in you. We got some boards comin'. I passed the freight wagons, about six miles back."

Less than two hours later, the poles were all dragged in. Ernie sat astride the top log, measuring and cutting notches. Then, swinging down, he began cutting angles on the tops of each rafter. They would meet, without a ridgepole, forming a steep enough slope to shed heavy snows and to provide a loft for storage, or more children. Ernie chuckled to himself at the thought.

By the time the freight wagons arrived, piled high with one-inch boards, they had four pairs of rafters set in place. Two days later, the rafters were all set.

"Say, Jess," Ernie began as he was getting ready to leave for the evening. "I counted out the boards in the wagons, and we've got enough for both the roof and the floor! Using boards for the roof will make a stronger, tighter roof than poles and shakes."

"Doc must have misfigured," Jess said, puzzled.

"Oh, I doubt that." Sean laughed. "He probably had it figured out, real well! By the way, I brought you four windows I had in the barn loft at home. They're in the wagon, between some boards so they didn't get broken. You'd better ask Julie where she wants to put them. It'll take some thought."

"Thanks." Jess shook his head in amazement. "We'll beat the snow, yet." He reached out and gripped his friend's hand.

After all were gone, Jess split some ends and pieces for Julie to use for the cook fire and carried what he could up to the barn, away from the dew, where they would stay drier.

"Hello!" Julie said, looking up from where she sat with the baby. "I just finished changing Keith. Would you like a cup of coffee?"

"Not now. Come on. Walk with me. The lake's beautiful tonight. I think I heard an elk bugle. First one of the year." He held out his hand.

Together, they walked down to the emerald lake, which reflected the sunset like a huge mirror. Across, on a wooded shore, a doe and big twin fawns appeared and came to drink. Far away, a loon sang its eerie, laughing cry. Another picked it up, echoing the cry. Then a distinct, full, flute-like bugle joined them in concert.

"That's an elk. A big bull by the sound of him," Jess said, trying to catch a glimpse of the faraway monarch.

"The mountains have music," Julie sighed. "It's beautiful."

They looked at one another, eyes saying what words could not. For a long while, they stood at the edge of the lake until there were only a few graying streaks remaining of the day. The deer were gone and from somewhere closer, another bull elk bugled the approach of fall.

Jess put his arm around her, drawing her closer. "Come on Julie, it's time we were goin' home. It's past our son's bedtime."

She looked up at him, eyes filling with tears.

"What's the matter?" he asked gently.

"Oh Jess, I'm so happy. I have Keith and you...all of this. Sometimes I think it's more than I can stand."

"I know. I've never had anything but what I could pack on my horse. Now, all this. And you." He kissed her softly.

The baby stretched, partly waking. Jess reached out and took him from her. Keith was getting heavy.

She squeezed his hand and walked close to him back toward their camp. Her heart and mind filled with the quiet serenity. *He loves us. He really loves us.*

Chapter 24

A few days later, the roof boards on, the men began working on the fireplace and chimney. Jess had built a stone boat and hauled load after load of smooth stone up from the river and lakeshore. Sean and Ernie kidded him about not just finding good rock for working material, but searching for beautiful stone. As the fireplace slowly went together, the result was not just functional, but a thing of true beauty, dominating the end of the house.

Not to be outdone by the men, Julie and Scotty kept mortar mixed, hauled building debris away, and kept a good supply of wash water available. As she peered out the barn window, she saw the chimney was through the roof now. Her new home was nearly finished.

She watched as Jess helped Sean lift the heavy stone onto the roof. He wouldn't settle for using small rock up high, but wanted to use as large a stone as the two men could lift, just for the beauty of it. She flushed.

She was so proud of her new home, with its fresh new window glass shining in the sun. Back East, where everyone had big, splendid houses, each larger and more ornate than the next, such a modest cabin would have been laughed at. But this really was going to be a home, not just an empty-feeling house, and would fit perfectly in its setting, just above the lake, blending like it was there forever. It was part of the earth – part log, part stone, and part of each of them going into every square inch.

Two days later, with the floor joists laid and the chimney finished,

Jess insisted Sean and Ernie leave the rest to him. They both had work of their own to do before winter and it was too much extra work for them to come miles to help him each day.

But it was hard to say goodbye.

"First freezing weather, I'll get an elk and bring you a quarter," Jess promised Ernie as the old man mounted his horse for the final time.

"That'd sure be nice. I sure do like elk steak but my ole bones don't cotton to stalkin' elk through the snow."

Jess shook his hand. "We really appreciate your help."

The old man heard the sincerity in his voice but just harrumphed deep in his throat, waving to Julie. "You come see me. Man gets tired of his own company." Then he turned his horse, letting it break into a jog downriver.

Scotty stood quietly next to Sean, who shook hands with Jess and mounted. Then Jess turned to the boy.

"I'm gonna miss you, Jess." He seemed to be on the verge of tears.

Jess's jaw twitched as he hugged the boy to him. "I'll miss you too, Scotty. You've been a real help around here, workin' like a man." His words and warm smile pleased the boy. "You pester your pa to come up here an' visit."

"I will."

Swinging the boy lightly into the saddle, Jess handed him the reins, and looked at Sean. Neither said a thing, just nodded, words being unnecessary between them.

The newlyweds waved and watched them leave. Jess felt a knot in his throat, but the knot loosened as Julie squeezed his hand. Grateful, he turned and put his arm around her. From the ridge, Scotty, Sean and Ernie paused, waving a final farewell before they disappeared from sight.

Sensing his need to be alone with his work, Julie kissed him and went back to the barn with Keith. There was still much sorting to do in their wagon.

Jess worked hard until dusk, cutting, planing, and pegging a heavy door for the cabin. They were deep in grizzly country and he would feel better about the times he had to leave Julie and Keith alone, knowing a big bear smelling food would have a hard time breaking into the cabin. So would any other predator, including man. He would soon fashion similar shutters for the windows that could be closed, if necessary, from inside.

Finally tired, with his feelings worked through, Jess lay his tools up and walked to the barn, their temporary camp. It would not be long before they could move into their new home.

In the dim, yellow lantern light, Julie sat, her back to him, studying an old photo album. Hearing him close the door, she turned to him without rising.

"I'm glad you finally came in. You work too hard. I worry about you." She motioned to the pot over to one side of the fire. "There's fresh coffee."

He filled his cup and sat close to her.

"I finished cleaning out the wagon today and found a small trunk with some of Uncle Zeke and Aunt Elsie's personal things in it. These pictures were in it. The water didn't spoil them." She slowly turned the pages. "This is Uncle Zeke and Aunt Elsie on their wedding day. Oh! This is the front of the house where I grew up. See that little window up there? That was above my bed when I was a little girl. I used to stand up on my bed and peek out at the people passing on the street." She pointed to a yellowing tin type. "And that's my Grandma and Grandpa Gibson. They were my mother's parents. They were from New England. Oh! I didn't know this existed! That's Mother and Father. They must be holding me when I was about Keith's age." The stern photograph was mellowed by the wide-eyed, smiling baby, wearing a white, lace-trimmed dress. Jess smiled. He could see her eyes, even in the baby picture.

She turned the page, adventuring through old memories, and stopped short to stare at another, larger picture she did not expect to find. She paled slightly as Jess bent to look. It was Julie in a lacy white wedding gown, standing next to a hard-eyed, well-dressed, handsome man with a dark mustache. Her eyes in the picture haunted Jess. They held the look of confusion or, perhaps, fear. They were the eyes he saw so many times, in his dreams.

"Your husband?" he asked quietly.

She nodded, carefully closed the book, and put it away. "He was a violent man. Hard-hearted and cruel. He acted so nice to other people. Even though he's dead, I'm still afraid of him."

Small wonder, Jess thought. He knew men with eyes like those before. Gunmen. Killers. Then, with a start, he realized Jerry Tripp had those eyes. Hard. Vicious.

The lonely sound of the loons drifted into the barn, crying a farewell to the sun's last rays as she drew closer to him for comfort. The night was warm but he felt her tremble. He leaned back against a post, drawing her head down into his lap. "I'll never let anyone hurt you again."

For a long time, they stayed there, Jess softly stroking her hair. He thought she was asleep but finally, she stirred and sat up.

"What was it like...your growing up?" she asked, feeling like a sad little girl asking for a bedtime story. Settling back into his lap, she gazed into his eyes for an answer.

Jess leaned back again, trying to find the words. "I guess when I was little, I didn't understand a lot of things. I didn't know there was a difference between white and Apache. The older kids would tease me...call me names. I learned later my mother was taken captive on a raid. Apaches don't believe in rape, but I guess that's the way she thought of her marriage to my father. She had the choice of remaining a slave or accepting marriage and joining the tribe. She chose marriage.

"When I was born she tried to keep me white, raising me as much like a white baby as she could. When I learned to talk, she taught me English. But I learned Apache from my father and everyone else in camp. I became Chiricahua, even to her, and I think she hated me for it.

"My father loved her but could never understand her or the way she treated me, so he took me with him, hunting and riding, even when I was little. He was a good father. A good man. From him, I learned to understand what the deer, wolf, and horse said, where the snake finds shade in the summer heat, where to find water when there is none in the desert. I learned to run for miles across the desert with no water, and how to fast and pray to find myself. By the time I was ten, I could read sign as well as any man and I could draw my father's heavy bow and shoot his rifle at eleven.

"I was smaller than most boys my age....and half white. I had to run faster, shoot straighter, and ride better than any of them, just to keep from being picked on. We played on desert that white soldiers were afraid to cross. My name then was Blue-Eyes-Wolf.

"By the time I was twelve, I learned to hate the bluecoats. I saw our camp hit by the cavalry. Turncoat Mescalero scouts led them in and they killed as many men, women and children as they could...my aunt, little cousins...boys I played with...even tiny babies. I'll never forget the smoke from the burned wickiups...and the crying babies." His words sounded hollow and strained.

"After that, my father grew serious and my mother grew hopeful of rescue. There were no more hunting trips, lessons, or funny stories at night. The soldiers were coming more often into Apacheria and the camp slept light.

"Then, one morning, they came again. We were fewer and even the women and children had to fight. Except my mother. She welcomed them! My father tried to hold them off at the entrance of the camp until the others reached the rocks. I found a rifle and ran to help him but there were too many soldiers. He was shot through the chest and leg. The rifle I picked up was old and the shell jammed. I stood there with that useless gun and watched them kill him like a dog.

"I remember pulling out my knife to at least die with one of them. Then a horse hit me from behind and a soldier clubbed me in the face with the butt of his carbine.

"When I woke up I was tied, laying in a wagon bed. My mother was there and three soldiers. 'They rescued us,' she told me." His voice grew bitter. "Rescued us! Killed my father, relatives, and friends! She told me if I would promise not to run off or fight, they would untie me. We were going home to Georgia. I told her, in no uncertain terms, that I'd rather die than live white.

"We ended up in Georgia, alright, but it wasn't long before I got loose and ran. I didn't know where I was or where to go. I ran west for three days until I got bit by a water moccasin." He sighed and seemed ready to stop his story.

"What did you do?" Julie asked, not sure if she wanted him to finish.

"An old man, a runaway slave, found me an' nursed me through it. I stayed with Elijah until he was killed. Maybe I felt safe with him because he was black, not white. He was a good man and taught me how to get along in the white world.

"Anyway, the War Between the States broke out. I wasn't for either side. Didn't have the slightest idea of what it was all about. But I guess I was still fightin' bluecoats. Only this time, there were Rebs in gray coats instead of Apaches fightin' beside me.

"In those years, I guess I got enough of killin' bluecoats. I just wanted go home. After the war, I headed back west but things weren't the same. I didn't fit anywhere. Not in Apacheria and not in the white man's world. I guess I tried to even things up with a fast gun.

"I drifted everywhere from Mexico to Canada in those days. I didn't know if I was runnin' or looking for something. I didn't know until I came here, and found you." He hugged her, embarrassed he talked so long.

Late that night, Julie woke to find Jess sitting on the edge of their pallet, so as not to wake her. In the moonlight, she could see his hair was wet and beads of sweat shone on his bare back.

Concerned, she asked, "Jess, what is it?"

He started, then turned and gave her a quick smile of reassurance. "Just a nightmare. Old ghosts. I didn't mean to wake you."

She held out her hand and drew him back into bed. Kissing him, she buried her head in his chest. Julie was still holding him tightly when the sun's early rays brightened the barn. It was to be the last night the drams would visit him. The ghosts were buried.

Chapter 25

Dew still clung to the grass as Jess hung the heavy door on the cabin, adjusting the latch and bar to fit perfectly. The day would be hot and dry, one of the few like that he knew were left. It was a good day to cut hay. They had the team, the milk cow, and the Hawk to feed over winter. There was good pasture now but soon winter's snows would begin falling, and there would be no feed. There was much hay to put up. Looking out over the meadow, he was thankful Sean and Ernie insisted he use the horse-drawn mower. They bought it together, sharing it each summer. He was added to the list of sharing neighbors and knew he would be helping make their hay in years to come, in repayment, and out of gratitude.

He hitched the team and began mowing, listening to the comforting whir of the sickle as it flashed back and forth, laying down the tall meadow grass. He laughed as he made the first round of the clearing. *I feel like a farmer...a far cry from a bronc stomper and gunman!*

As the grass was cut and lay neatly flat on the ground, he felt a growing satisfaction and confidence about the coming winter. The grasses were thick and it wouldn't take much more than a few rounds to fill the wagon.

The sun rose higher, heating the ground, making the air so still it was nearly stifling. His shirt was soon soaked with sweat but he didn't mind. The heat would make the hay cure quickly. He watched the rumps of the gray mares march down the meadow, never slowing, never out of step. Their corners were true and not a blade of grass was uncut. They were a good team, trained well by someone who gave them good care. They made the hardest work easier.

Jess glanced toward the cool, rippling surface of the lake and it beckoned him. He cast off the temptation. *Later. First the hay must be cut.* His attention turned back to watching for rocks that could knock out sections of the mower.

The one round turned to three as the mowing, the easy part, went smoothly. Then it had to be gathered by hand and pitched onto the wagon, then stacked. *Best not get too much down at once. I don't have Sean to help me now.*

When he finished the fourth pass, he stopped and unhitched the team. *Funny. They're doing all the pulling and I'm sweating harder than they are.* Patiently, they stood for him to hook the trace chains onto the hip straps. Driving them back on foot, across the drying grass, Jess noticed it was already beginning to rustle under their feet. Big grasshoppers, the heralds of fall, buzzed loudly from the drying grass. Good trout bait, he thought.

He pulled the harness off the mares, watered them, and turned them out to graze. They had earned a rest. He became aware someone was behind him as he stood watching the horses and milk cow grazing peacefully in the clearing.

She put her arms around him. "You got a lot done this morning. I was moving us into the cabin."

Jess smiled, then kissed her. "I'm goin' down to the lake for a swim to clean up. Why don't you come along?"

She blushed. "I don't have anything to swim in."

He laughed. "You were born in all you need. Who's to see? Didn't you ever swim like that, before?"

The redness deepened in her face. "No." She could just imagine swimming naked in Southport!

"Come on," he teased.

"Alright. I'll get Keith and put him where we can watch him. I'll be right back." Her voice gained enthusiasm. She spent the morning baking while she moved so the day's unseasonable heat was doubled for her.

They lay Keith under a small pine, away from the gentle lake bank, and having just eaten, he fell asleep almost at once.

Jess quickly stripped off his boots and clothes and, without hesitation, plunged into the icy water off the largest boulder jutting out from the rocky point. The water was clear and he dove deeply, feeling the sweat, dust and hay seed wash from his body. Surfacing, he shook the hair out of his eyes. Julie was shyly unpinning her hair at the water's edge, stalling.

"Come on in," Jess called, "It's not bad."

She waded gingerly, up to her knees. "It's cold!"

Jess laughed, treading water. "Come on in, or I'll drag you in!"

"You'd have to catch me first!"

"And you think I can't?" Jess swam strongly toward her with swift, sure strokes.

"No!" She turned and sprinted along the lakeshore, hearing splashing behind her, as Jess reached the gravelly shore.

Like a pair of deer, they raced down the grassy beach. Julie was laughing so much she could hardly run and was little surprised to hear Jess closing in on her. Up into the pines they ran, through the soft pine needle carpet, until Jess caught her. Kicking and laughing, she was carried back to the water where they started. He waded determinedly in, slipping and sliding on the rounded rocks beneath his bare feet, carrying her above the water's icy reach. Then, when he was above his waist, he let go.

She screamed as the water closed over her head, then came up, choking and laughing. "It's still cold, Jess Hazzard!" she exclaimed, splashing to keep warm.

A look passed between them before Jess's soft kiss brushed her lips, her bare shoulder, then trailed to her breast. The water did not seem as cold now.

Later, as they lay together on the soft grass letting the warm sun dry them, Julie saw Jess was asleep. He looks so at peace, she thought. Oh, let it be this way, always! She kissed him softly, careful not to wake him. This man of hers! One minute a boy, one minute a passionate lover. But gentle, always treating her like she was some priceless treasure. Life was so good!

Chapter 26

This new life of theirs was a strange mixture of many things. The hellish heat of late fall that stifled Jess as he worked feverishly to get hay in and cut firewood changed into icy winds as winter set in. In the mountains, winter comes fast and early.

Jess saw Julie's hands become work-roughened and her beautiful chestnut hair, bleached by the sun as she worked beside him, but she was happy, there was no denying that. But there were lonely times, too.

Jess started a trap line around the lake and up the river, to the smaller lake beyond and even farther. At times he would be gone several days, working his traps. Each time, he hated to leave, but come spring, they would need supplies, and the pelts would provide them. In the shed was a growing pile of stretched beaver, mink, marten, lynx, and wolf pelts. Already, their spring supplies were assured, but more pelts would allow them to buy other necessities, and maybe some frills.

Julie worried about being left alone with little Keith in the cabin. She couldn't help it. Winter winds cut through the trees, bringing icy sleet, and more blowing snow. What if something should happen to him so far from home?

Despite the worry, she knew it was good for him to be out there. He was changing. Perhaps he was finding himself. She saw it in his face. The tenseness and hardness that was always beneath every expression was fading and in its place, she saw peace.

A storm had blown for two days and Jess was anxious to be out on the trapline. He disliked leaving it unchecked for more than a day. Not only did trapped animals suffer needlessly, but it left the traps open to robbery by coyotes and other predators.

Morning dawned clear and still, with the snow bright and lightly drifted. He glanced out and saw the lake was frozen solid. He readied a light pack and slipped on heavy wool socks and moccasins. Julie felt the familiar shiver course through her as he made ready to leave. Keith was beginning to creep about and Jess took the time to swing him high above his head. Laughing with glee, the baby struggled away from him, crawling with speed. Jess pretended to chase him, then stopped to face his wife.

"Will you be okay?" he asked quietly, already feeling the loneliness. He hated to be away from them, even for a day. He worried about Julie and the baby being alone while he was gone as much as she worried about him.

"Yes, of course I will. I have Keith. He keeps me busy, these days." She tried to hide the tightness in her throat as he stepped toward the door. "I love you."

He heard the quaver in her voice and turned back to hold her once again. "I don't know what I'd do without you," he said, almost in a whisper, before kissing her hard.

As she watched him go outside and slip into his snowshoes, she quietly said, "Be careful." It was almost a prayer.

The morning passed uneventfully. He located trap after trap. Some were empty and simply needed resetting or new bait. One or two sprang from the heavy new snow, a blown stick or fallen branch. But there was some success. On the edge of the lake, near where the river flowed into it, he pulled out a fine beaver. Farther up the trail, in the pines, a dark, silky-coated marten.

As he followed the river up into the bosom of the Wind Rivers, he came to the log where a set had been. It was gone. Puzzled, he searched, knowing he fastened it securely, not wanting any animal to escape with a snare on it. He brushed away the snow on the log to find frozen specks of blood and hair.

It wasn't the first time he had a trap robbed, but for some reason, he began to get a feeling of uneasiness. He brushed the snow from his knees and reached into his pack for another snare. Setting it carefully, he backed away and started off for the next set.

The snare by the downed pine was sprung, the bait gone and

empty. All the marks of an expert trap robber. A wolf? Coyote? There was nothing to do but set it again and hope the robber was either caught or left the area.

He felt a quick lift of elation as he neared the next trap. There was a dark pelt showing in the loose snow. Snowshoeing closer, he felt anger well up within him. There was a lynx in the snare, but something had ripped the carcass up, eating only the midsection. Disgusted with the waste, he pulled the ruined carcass from the snare and carefully reset the trap.

Casting for any sign, he spotted some partial tracks under some low spruce. They were large, and at first he thought they were wolf or lynx, but on closer inspection, he felt a shiver go up his back. That was no wolf. It was Carcajou! The northern Indian tribes called him Devil Bear, believing him to be the incarnation of all that is evil. He could kill a grown moose or elk, fight a grizzly or wolf pack off a kill, and bring ruin to a trapper. What he did not eat, he would tear, mutilate, or defile, taking almost supernatural care to escape the traps himself.

Jess never before experienced a wolverine, but just hearing stories about them from Canadian trappers and the Cree, he felt a prickle of danger invade the peaceful afternoon. He never heard of them attacking man, but he had another six miles of trapline to run and had no reason to think the animal just struck and left the area. One trapper told him he just pulled up stakes and left the area when a carcajou began raiding his traps.

"He is the Devil," he told Jess. "There is no man alive that can trap Carcajou! Not Indian. Not white. Once the Stink Devil, he follow me to my cabin. When I'm not home, he break in an' eat an' eat. What food he did not eat, he stink up so I could not stand to touch! He even break into my cache an' ruin all winter furs. No. Better to leave the woods to Carcajou!"

John Beaupre trapped all his life. He did not fear the grizzly or Blackfoot. But he ran from the carcajou, a forty pound, low-slung cousin of the weasel, and just as bloodthirsty.

Jess found himself hurrying from trap to trap all afternoon, hoping against hope, to find one untouched. Or, better yet, to find Carcajou in one of them. But a gradual fear overtook him like the mist forming on the river at night. *What if Carcajou followed me, trap to trap, back to the cabin? Julie and Keith are alone.*

He ate a quick handful of jerky and boiled a cup of coffee to give him strength for the trip home. He would leave his traps to be sure they were safe. The sun was going down fast and he had two miles to travel, across the lake and through the woods, to reach them.

The silence of the dusky evening settled over the lake's frozen surface. It was extremely dangerous, he knew, to chance crossing the lake so soon after it had frozen. There might be places that were only skinned over with thin ice. But his weight was widely distributed by the snowshoes and he knew it would take an extra hour, going around the lakeshore. An hour he could not risk, would not risk. The only sounds were the far-off call of an owl. It sent shivers down his back, for the owl was the Apache's herald of death. Partway across the lake, the silence was broken only by the squeak of Jess's snowshoes and the puff of his breath. His legs ached from pushing on so hard. He already covered ten miles since morning, and felt himself nearly breaking into a run. The ice suddenly felt bad in the center of the lake, still a mile from home. Slowing carefully, he kept on in a smooth pace, straight for home. But he carefully watched the ice ahead. A plunge through the ice would kill him. It was twenty below and falling. The ice got better and he felt himself pushing on faster until, half a mile from home, he regained the lakeshore trail. But the relief he felt was short lived. There were fresh tracks in the moonlight ahead of him. He stooped to examine them. He had cut the fresh trail of Carcajou! And it was heading southwest, toward the cabin, running back along Jess's own morning snowshoe tracks!

He yanked the carbine off his back and while hurrying toward home, he checked the load. The temperature was dropping as the night fell. At thirty below, his breath plumed in front of him, freezing on his eyebrows and hat, creating a small snow shower before him. The icy night air made his lungs ache as he jogged on harder, faster, as the beast's tracks became fresher.

Then through the still night air, he could hear the challenging bugle of the Hawk, in the barn. The sound of crashing, kicking. The thing was in the barn! He could see the buildings now and the straight plume of smoke coming from the cabin. Both lamps must be lit, as the cabin window nearest the barn shone brightly. He felt the grip of fear. The others were shuttered tightly, as they never had been before.

He met Julie at the cabin door. She had his loaded .44 in her hand and was shaking with fear.

"Jess! Thank God you came home! There's something awful here! I think it's in the barn! I was going to try to kill it."

"Get in the house and lock the door!" He kicked out of his snowshoes and ran for the barn, rifle ready.

A sickening musky smell struck him as he swung open the barn door. With Winchester in hand, he carefully lit the lantern. Nerves on edge, he searched the barn, lantern held high. The Hawk had broken out of his box stall and stood guard, lathered, sweating, and eyes rolling wildly by the gray mares. Even the milk cow was crowded in behind him, as if for protection.

The stallion blew a challenging snort, looking toward the back door. Carefully, Jess searched until he found the ripped boards that told of the carcajou's entrance. Outside, he found two sets of tracks, the warm ones, leaving the barn, running across the yard, down to the lakeshore.

Jess quickly tied the Hawk and milk cow, then blew out the lantern. Running across the yard, he knocked on the cabin door. "Julie. It's me. Are you alright?" he panted.

The door swung open quickly and he stepped inside.

"God, Jess what was it?" Julie clasped him. "It was awful! I looked out the window, where that bit of tallow I hung to feed the birds is. It was out there! It looked right at me, only inches away from the window. And it snarled! Was it a bear?"

His breathing was returning to normal. "No. It was a carcajou...a wolverine. Not so big, but vicious. He's been into my traps. Really tore them up."

He thought of it returning to the cabin again when he was gone, and the thought sickened him. "I've got to go after it. Now. Before it gets too far ahead of me. I don't want it to come back. Ever," Jess said, grabbing a handful of jerky strips and stuffing them into his pack.

She shuddered. "It was so ugly! It wasn't the least bit afraid of me. It just gulped down the tallow and snarled at me!"

He glanced at Keith, still sleeping peacefully. "It won't be back, Julie. It may take me a day or two. They're cunning." He reached onto the shelf and took out a box of shells for his rifle as he remembered John Beaupre's words. *No man can catch the Carcajou! Not Indian. Not white!*

"Jess, be careful." She was frightened, remembering the bear-like head, the snarling teeth, and the glimmering red eyes.

Nodding, he kissed her briefly and stepped out into the frigid night, shutting the cabin door behind him. Luckily, there was a good tracking moon and the wolverine's tracks were big, dark holes in the light, fresh snow. Onto the lake and back up near the lakeshore trail, they led. Through heavy spruce and pine, then up the river bank, toward the upper lake, always keeping to the rough woods. Jess tracked quickly, but carefully. He did not want to chance losing the trail or having to backtrack. Carcajou would not again invade his home.

The wolverine cleverly climbed trees, leaping to others, in trying to keep his trail secret. But minute scraps of bark, laying on the fresh snow, gave his tricks away to the experienced tracker following him. Slowly, the tracks grew fresher until Jess could see the depressions in the snow where Carcajou's body had lain as his pause for a rest melted the snow. And the moisture was not yet frozen. The imprint was still wet, at thirty below. He had to be close.

With senses straining, Jess tracked more slowly now, taking greater care to move without a sound. There was no wind, no breeze to carry his scent to the wily Devil, but sound would carry far in the icy stillness.

Here, the beast made a mighty leap, leaving a space of more than fourteen feet with no tracks. Had it heard him, sensed his presence?

A ways off, a pack of wolves sang, baying a deer or elk. Normally, he would have paused to listen to the story the sounds told. But tonight the sounds were distracting and he prayed for silence. He needed every edge he could get. *No man can catch Carcajou.*

Ahead, a dry branch snapped and he slowly reached for the rifle on his back. Was it Carcajou? He knew he would only have time for one shot, and that if he was lucky. He shut out all else, save that spot four hundred feet away, straining for the slightest sound or movement in the shadowed trees ahead.

Suddenly, he became aware of the rapidly approaching crashing of the hunting wolf pack. Damn! They were coming from the east, right toward him.

He could hear the puffing grunts of the hunted animal as it leaped through the snow in terror. An old elk cow crashed out through the trees, followed closely by her last-spring's calf, eyes rolling in fear. They were crossing the wolverine's trail, just in front of him! A scant minute behind them came a dozen big wolves. They weren't running hard but were running in a mile-eating lope, good for many hours yet. They were patient and they would eat tonight. He almost admired them. Then he remembered Carcajou. The elk and wolf pack crossed the trail, covering it with newly kicked up snow and hundreds of deep tracks!

Then the wolves scented Jess or spotted him and left the elk. Stopping as one, they turned to search for him, ears pricked from nervousness. As he moved on to search for the tracks of the wolverine among the tangled maze of prints ahead, they recognized man and leaped away in terror.

Carcajou took advantage of the mass of torn tracks, stepping carefully into wolf tracks, cleverly covering his trail.

He must know he is being followed. No wonder the Indians call him Devil. It took an hour before Jess again found a clear trail. After being so close, he felt a surge of disappointment as he took up the now-old trail once again.

He lost track of time and hardly realized it when the night turned to day. He only saw the big round tracks, the long claws, and the drag marks of the bushy tail. Somehow, the wolverine was staying ahead of him. They wound all through the woods, now and again crossing the familiar trapline trail. Carcajou was not leaving. He was just toying with Jess and it angered him.

Doubling his effort, he found himself pounding through the snow, trying to close the distance between them. If it had been any other animal, Jess would have circled, trying to cut the trail closer to the beast, or intercept it. But he dare not with Carcajou, the Devil that thought like a man.

He did not stop to make coffee. Only chew a bit of jerky as he jogged on, squatting occasionally to drink from a spring, the river, or a creek to quench his thirst. It was maddening. The wolverine had stopped long enough to gorge itself on a cougar-killed deer, but still shuffled on ahead of him.

It circled around again, coming back to the maze of tracks that gained it an hour last night. But this time, a light frost gave Jess easy tracking. The Devil did not lose him again there.

So many hours later, the sun was setting and the moon was climbing into a cloudy sky. Jess had to get closer or risk losing the trail when darkness overtook him. There would not be good tracking tonight. It would be dark.

He hung his pack in a pine to lighten his load, quickly checked his rifle, and started out again, jogging after Carcajou.

He winced as a spike of pain struck his head; the old familiar headache from his blindness. Damn it! Not now. He still got them, from time to time, usually when he had been in the sun a long while. Or strained his eyes. It would pass, he knew, but he did not want to be hampered by anything.

With dogged determination, he pushed on, always watching those tracks. His muscles ached from the punishment of the last two days but he swung forward faster, noticing a cloud bank coming in, soon to cover the moon.

He was panting now but felt satisfaction as he saw the tracks becoming fresh. The edges of the tracks were sharp and no flakes of snow had fallen into them. He was gaining! Did it know he was getting close? All of a sudden it was heading for hilly ground, spotted with heavy pine cover.

He found himself praying as he nearly ran. He knew he couldn't last much longer at this pace. If he didn't get to Carcajou before the moon went under the clouds, he would lose him, perhaps until morning. Too big a lead! It must be now!

The moonlight became spotty, as the cloud cover came closer, making tracking more difficult, lending an unreal quality to the still night. As the tracks became warm, Jess slowed his pace, using more caution. Carcajou was not used to giving ground to any animal, including man. The strong claws and powerful jaws that could bring down an elk must be respected.

Then, in a small, tight clearing, bordered by small shrubby pines, he could smell Carcajou. It was the same musky odor he had smelled in the barn.

Suddenly, not giving Jess a chance to think, a dark shape hurled itself at him from the deep shadows under the trees. Stumbling backward in his snowshoes, Jess's hand snatched his knife from the sheath, his other, fending off the forty pounds of snarling beast, clinging to his shoulder by teeth and claws. It had missed Jess's throat by only inches.

The wolverine's face was close to Jess's and he looked, for an instant, into the creature's hate-filled red eyes as it chewed like a bulldog for a better hold on his shoulder. The pain was unbelievable for an animal of that size.

With an instinctive thrust, Jess buried his knife into the beast's side and thrust it away from him. Hissing a savage challenge, Carcajou landed on its feet ten feet in front of Jess. Champing its jaws and stamping its feet in rage, it savagely shook its head, throwing froth from its gaping mouth.

Slowly, so as not to initiate another attack, Jess reached for his carbine, which had dropped to the snow. Was it plugged? Carcajou made a short rush at him, snarling and hissing, snapping his jaws, not unlike an enraged grizzly. Jess levered a shell quietly into the chamber as Carcajou crouched to spring. The sound made the wolverine leap to the side and, in a flashing bound, it was in the edge of the shadowed trees. Instinctively, without aiming, Jess snapped off a shot, running forward. If he could only get one clear shot! He had not seriously wounded the animal with his knife.

Then he saw a dark spot on the snow. Blood! Had his shot been true? Did he hit Carcajou? Or was it just blood from the knife? He stooped to examine the blood and tracks when he heard a bloodcurdling snarl. Looking up, he stared, face to face with the Devil, only five feet away!

Without thinking, he yanked another shell into the chamber as, without further warning, the enraged beast leaped for him. A single shot rang out, echoing through the silent night. And all was still.

Julie managed to keep busy with some sort of normal life the first night and the bright, sunny day that followed. After all, she tried to convince her heart, Jess was raised Apache. He knew about wild animals, knew these mountains day or night, and was a good shot.

She did the normal chores, although admittedly quickly and nervously, and carried Jess's revolver with her wherever she went. Each strange sound brought a jump and tightening in her chest. Shutting the cabin door the second evening, she felt as though something was following her and she yanked the bar into place. Then, feeling foolish, she put more wood into the fire and began to cook supper. If only he would come back.

Keith laughed and played on the floor next to her, unmindful of her fears, too young to know worry. She put him to bed early that night, adding an extra log to the fire, leaving one lamp burning low and all windows tightly shuttered. She looked to Jess's .44 in the holster which hung from the end of the mantle. *What if it came back?*

She squeezed her eyes shut and prayed for him to be alright and come home to them soon. She needed him now. Drawing a chair close to the lamp, she tried to do some mending, but found her thoughts out in the dark mountains, with him, and gave up her sewing in despair.

Finally, near exhaustion, she checked the fire and added big logs to keep it going. Maybe he would be home in the morning. She heard wolves howling mournfully in the distance and she shivered. He told her that wolves would not attack a person. *But what if something happened to him out there? Would they attack an injured man?*

Sleep came hard to her that night, as she sat up in her chair, her shawl wrapped snuggly around her shoulders. When she finally slept, her dreams were filled with horrors that were not curbed by her restraint. Somewhere in the snowy woods, she searched for him. So cold! Winds howled, as ghosts and wolves wailed of doom. It was dark, even though daytime. She knew not how long she searched, never finding him. Then, for an instant, it was lighter. She felt such relief.

What was that up ahead? Something in the snow. Something dark and still. She drifted closer, buoyed by hope. Puzzled, she bent over. It looked like Jess, but it didn't. Pulling at his shoulder, she rolled him over. Something had ripped out his throat. Oh God! It had gorged itself on his midsection, leaving nothing but a cavern, dripping with blood and gore.

"Oh no!" she screamed, "No! No!" She screamed again and again until Keith's frightened cries saved her from seeing more. She awoke sobbing, but even with the realization it was only a nightmare, she could not stop crying. She went to Keith, picked him up, and rocked him for comfort. Exhausted but deathly afraid to fall back to sleep, Julie hummed a nameless tune, fighting the sleep she earlier prayed for.

She could hear his voice calling to her from far away. Then she felt his soft kiss, his arm around her, holding her close. She shook free. Why wouldn't this torture stop?

"Julie...Julie," he said softly. "I'm home. It's alright."

There was a brief minute, between sleep and consciousness, that she stared at him, not comprehending, fearing another cruel trick of her imagination. She reached out, hesitating to touch him. Then, finding him truly there, she grasped him to her in desperate relief. He was cold from the bitter night air, but even so, it felt wonderful to bury her head against his chest in comfort.

Minutes later, realizing how tired and cold he must be, she broke from the embrace. "Let me put some coffee on for you. Fix you something to eat." She looked from his lined, pale, tired face, darkened with unshaven beard to the long rips and teeth marks on his coat, feeling a stab of fear. Had her dream been that close to the truth, or was it more than just a dream?

He took the sleeping child from her and gently slipped him into the warm bed. Watching Julie go about building up the fire, picking up the coffee pot, rustling in her dishes, he sighed. *Damn! It feels good to be home!* As the coffee pot sent droplets of water out, hissing into the fire, he took her hand, leading her to the door.

"Come here. There's something I have for you." When he swung open the door open, the first silver rays of the winter dawn shone on the dark, glossy mahogany pelt of Carcajou.

Julie never again felt the intense fear when he was out on the trapline. He would be gone, but he would return. And when he came back, he would lay his new pelts in the shed to stretch, next to the ever-growing pile of furs, hang up his snowshoes, and brush off the snow of the trip. Nights like that gave them a time of quiet togetherness as they sat in front of the fire. For a long while, they would just sit close together, neither speaking, as the wet snow melted from Jess's moccasins. Julie glowed with relief her husband was once again home, safe, while Jess enjoyed having a time of rest from all physical discomfort and a chance to be alone with his wife.

It was on such an evening, early in the spring, that Julie told him she was with child.

Chapter 27

The heavy, fluffy snow fell silently all day. Sitting with Keith in front of the fire, Julie mended a pair of Jess's worn, woolen socks. He was again working his trapline but should be home soon. Secretly, she was proud of him and the way he trapped. He told her this area was nearly trapped out in the forties and fifties and he was being careful to maintain the abundance that lived here now. When trapping beaver, he would only take one or two animals from an area, letting the others alone to replenish. Likewise, he was constantly moving his traplines so the mink, marten, lynx, and bobcat would remain bountiful. It meant many more miles of snowshoeing, but he believed it was worth every step. Today, he was moving a short line, east of the lake.

She baked some bread and had a pot of beans cooking over the fire, knowing he would come home hungry.

Jess hated trapping as much as she did, but it was a way for them to have an income until he could build up a small horse herd and buy cattle. Even though the furs were not worth what they were years ago, they would bring in a goodly sum, come spring.

Jess hoped to eventually buy the range next to them, over the mountain. Sean told him it could be had and he knew owning that land, as well as their own, would protect them from ever being closed in by others. Wilderness is fragile, he said and won't last forever. The only way they could keep that special area and the life they loved was to keep it wilderness, free of those who would do it harm. Their horses and cattle could pasture those mountain slopes and valleys during the summer and return to the valley come fall to be fed hay over the winter. It was not the big ranchers' way of doing things, but it would work fine for them. They had no great needs and were happy living simply.

Julie stood and walked to the east window. Wiping a small spot clear, she peered out into the snow-laden pines, hoping to catch a glimpse of his dark figure coming home. It was getting dark earlier this evening because of the snow. Chores needed doing if Jess was going to be late. Besides, he would be tired and the crisp, cold evening air would feel good to her after the heat and humidity of the cabin.

"Come on, Keith. We'd better get your clothes on. It's time to feed the stock." While she dressed the toddler, she glanced out the window. The snow had turned to sleet. She was glad all the animals could be in the warm barn with plenty of hay overhead.

With the child held by a mittened hand, she opened the door and stepped outside into the icy wind. Looking down to help the boy as they walked, she almost ran into the side of a big black horse. She glanced up, startled, and a gasp of fear escaped her. The rider pulled away the scarf over his face. Scotty! The boy had grown so tall and wore a big, heavy coat. Julie hardly recognized him. But what was he doing out here on a stormy winter night like this? And on his father's horse?

"Where's Jess?" Scotty asked urgently. "Pa's had a tree fall on him an' I can't get it off him. He's hurt!"

"He's on his trapline," Julie answered, as the gravity of the situation enveloped her. "You put your horse in the barn. Then come up to the house to warm up. I'll see if I can get Jess in."

Julie turned back to the cabin, carrying Keith, so she could hurry. Quickly and gingerly she carried the revolver outdoors. Pointing the gun at the ground in front of her, she closed her eyes, held the grip tightly, and fired three shots. The echo of the shots crashed in the stillness of the valley and rumbled across the lake. He taught her to shoot the guns and that three shots, fired in close succession, meant trouble. If he could hear the shots, he would come. But in the sleet and driving rain and snow that was falling, how far would the sound carry?

She got Scotty in, standing him in front of the fire to warm himself and dry his damp clothing. It seemed like only minutes later when the door burst open. Worry stood out on Jess's face as he quickly glanced around the room. Scotty! He knew at a glance something happened to Sean.

"What's wrong?"

Scotty hurried around, making ready to ride back. "Pa's hurt. A tree fell on him. He cut it an' it kicked back. I couldn't get him out an' he said to take Satan and come get you."

"Let's go," he said to Scotty. "Julie, I may have to stay a day or so. Will you be okay?" He paused in the doorway to kiss her.

"Yes. Please hurry. But be careful. It's so icy."

The horses were ready in minutes and Jess helped Scotty mount the big black.

The Hawk snorted and danced. It had been days since he was ridden and he was fresh and eager to go.

"Scotty, I'll ride ahead of you. If you see the Hawk slip on the ice, slow down." Jess turned to go.

"Do you think he'll be okay?" the boy asked in a small voice. "It's so cold and the tree is real big."

He looked at Scotty and smiled. "Sure. Your pa's strong as a bull." Urging the Hawk down the trail, he wished he felt so confident, inside.

The driving sleet blew straight into their faces, burning and stinging like needles, the icy rain feeling like knives. Jess turned up his collar and urged the Morgan faster. It was going to be a cold night. Glancing back, he saw Satan behind, fighting the bit, trying to go faster. But the boy held him in doggedly.

The ice built up and became glassy with the freezing rain until the Hawk slipped to his knees, scrambling up a gully. Beneath a giant pine, Jess stopped and waited for Scotty. In his haste to get to Sean, he nearly forgot he had a young boy behind him, barely big enough to control the big gelding. Knuckles white as he gripped the fork of his saddle, Jess watched. Would the black go down with the boy?

The gelding was nearly to the top when his legs shot out to the side. He fell, sliding to the bottom on his side. Jess jumped off the stallion and stood helplessly as the black scrambled to regain his feet on the ice. Slipping and snorting with the effort, Satan lurched forward and kept coming up the slope. Miraculously, Scotty clung to him like a burr.

"You okay, boy?" Jess asked, somewhat shaken.

Scotty nodded, biting his lip. He was a bit pale and his eyes were big, but he was game.

As they rode, Jess pressed a gloved hand to his cheek. His face was nearly numb. How long had Sean been out in this? If the tree hadn't crushed him fatally, the cold could finish him in a short time.

A grove of young pines marked the far corner of the hayfield.

Maybe a mile farther. The ice crust was nearly thick enough now to bear the horses' weight. Nearly. But they broke through often, the crust scraping the backs of their fetlocks. Jess and Scotty were forced to slow the horses to a slow trot or risk making them lame.

The woodlot, finally! Jess touched his spurs to the stallion's sides as he saw a slight movement in the trees. Barking, at first protectively, then in greeting, Bear ran toward him. Jess looked to where the dog had been laying. A big downed pine and freshly cut.

"Sean!" he called, stepping off the Morgan, "Sean!"

"Jess?" Sean's voice was weak, strained. "Over here."

Jess knelt beside Sean. The butt of the tree across his chest pinned him fast to the snow-covered ground. The only thing that saved him were the heavy branches higher up the tree trunk. The butt could not drop entirely to the ground, but enough to trap a man, maybe crush him.

Scotty had laid a tarp over the trunk, making a lean-to over his father, trying to keep the sleet and rain off and brought a blanket from the cabin to cover him as best he could.

"How bad are you hurt?" Jess asked, trying to decide the safest way to free Sean.

"I don't know. I don't think it's too bad but I'm so numb I can't tell."

"Come here, boy," Jess called Scotty. "When I tell you, you get hold of your pa and help him pull away. Pull on his coat, in case he has broken ribs."

Jess got to his feet and picked up the axe. He quickly limbed the branches off a straight pole, six inches thick and twelve feet long. He slipped the pole under the tree and lifted, trying the weight. The trunk moved slightly.

"You think you can move, if I can get the tree up off you a little?" he asked, crouching by his friend, removing the blanket so it would not hinder Sean's escape.

"Yeah, I think so." He grimaced. "Don't care to spend the night under here."

Taking a good hold, Jess set his shoulder under the pole, straining to lift. The trunk shifted and rose an inch, then two. Muscles corded in his neck and back as he held it there, not daring to let it drop. Then he groaned and lifted it another inch.

"Now, Scotty!" he gasped. "Get him out!" Sweat beaded on his face as he fought to hold what he gained. He wouldn't be able to get it that high again, and it would be too dangerous, using a horse. He saw Sean struggling to draw himself free, Scotty frantically pulling on his coat with all his might. Jess closed his eyes against the strain. He couldn't hold it much longer. His arms began to shake and the tree trunk sank half an inch.

"Okay, Jess!" Sean called. "Let it go!"

With a tremendous shudder of relief, Jess let the tree settle back to the ground. Sean was in the clear. For a moment, Jess staggered, leaning against the rough-barked pine trunk. Then, recovering his breath, he squatted by his friend's side. Despite the shelter of the tarp, he was wet, and his clothes were covered with a crust of ice.

Numb with pain and cold, the big man struggled to sit up.

"You think you can stand, if I help you? Walk back to the cabin?" Jess looked for signs of serious injury to his friend's back and legs.

"Yeah. I think I have a couple of cracked ribs, but everything else feels okay." He grimaced again as he rose, helped by Jess's shoulder under his arm. "Watch the ribs, eh?"

"Scotty," Jess said, "go ahead and get a fire built. He's going to have to thaw out."

Watching the boy leave, they slowly made their way across the woodlot to the barn. They paused there in the shelter for Sean to rest and catch his breath while Jess quickly unsaddled, watered, and put the horses in their stalls.

"I sure as hell was glad to see you!" Sean exclaimed, managing to stand, unaided.

While Sean got out of his icy, wet clothes, Jess went out into the shed and sliced off thick steaks from a venison haunch. As the cabin quickly warmed, he put on a pot of coffee and began frying up a pan of potatoes and venison. The big man was shaking now, even though he sat in front of a roaring fire, wrapped in two thick blankets. The coffee would help drive the chill out.

"What about you, boy?" Jess asked, noticing the steam rising from Scotty's clothes. "You'd better get into some dry clothes, too."

"Aw, I'm not too wet," Scotty stalled, not wanting to leave the heat of the fire.

Jess squeezed water from the boy's shirt sleeve. "Call that dry? Go change. You were a real man today. You probably saved your pa's life with all you did. You oughta be proud."

The boy blushed red and smiled at the praise, then left to get into dry clothes.

Jess turned to Sean. "You warmin' up any?" he asked.

"Not really." Sean sipped the boiling coffee cautiously. "I'm colder now than I was out there under that tree!"

"It's just gettin' to you. After you drink a couple of cups of coffee and eat supper, you'll quit shakin'" Jess dished out the meat, potatoes and fried bannock. "Let's see those ribs."

Sean leaned carefully back, opening his shirt, revealing a large, blotchy, ugly blue bruise halfway down his rib cage. Bending down, Jess examined the area gently. With relief, he decided that there weren't any broken ribs, but Sean would be pretty sore for weeks. *If that tree had dropped another few inches...* Jess shook his head, wincing at the thought.

"You were lucky. Better watch those big trees. They kick back." Jess's eyes twinkled with a smile. Sean was the one to always warn him of the very same thing.

"I stepped back onto a branch and tripped," Sean smiled sheepishly. "What've you been doing with yourself?" he asked, wanting to change the subject.

Jess told him of his trapline, and of Carcajou.

"No fooling!" Sean exclaimed. "I've heard about them, but never did see one."

"I hadn't either, until that one. Got a real close look at him." Jess touched the neatly patched tears in his sheepskin coat. Then he opened his shirt to reveal the yellowish purple bruise. "He did that through my coat. Got ahold of my shoulder with his teeth. Has real powerful jaws. I was sure glad for that old sheepskin coat!"

Scotty's eyes went big. "Did he attack you?"

Jess nodded. "I guess he about had it with me followin' him for two days and nights."

"You were lucky to get him," Sean said. "I've heard stories about how they think like a man." He stretched out, finally feeling the heat of the fire. "Could you save the skin?"

"All but the head and one front foot. First shot I got was a snap shot an' I guess it took off the foot. He jumped at me again and I had just long enough to aim." Jess thought back to that night and shuddered.

"I hear a wolverine pelt's worth quite a bit. You might be paid pretty well. How's Julie and Keith?"

"They're fine. Keith's walkin' now." Jess shook his head, looking up with a half-shy, boyish smile. "An we're expectin' a baby along about July."

Sean let out a whoop that made him wince with pain.

"Good for you!" he boomed. "Must be that married life's agreeing with both of you." He chuckled at the redness creeping up Jess's neck and face. "I'm glad things are finally working out for you. It's been a long time coming."

Chapter 28

The wagon creaked and lurched as Jess urged the team through the ruts made by the everyday spring traffic in Lawson.

"You alright?" Jess asked Julie in a concerned voice.

"I'm fine. Don't worry so much! After all, women have been having babies for centuries." She laughed, clutching the wagon seat with one hand and Keith with the other. "It's not nearly as bad here as where you sold your furs!"

He pulled the team of gray mares to a stop. "You'd better get out now and walk," he said, setting the brake. "By the looks of that pothole in front of the saloon, it's gettin' worse. I'll be back as soon as the team's put up."

"Oh, there's Martha!" Julie exclaimed, excited to see her friend.

Martha rushed to meet them, holding her skirts up out of the dirt. "Why Jess! Julie! My gracious, this can't be Keith? My how he's grown!"

Jess carefully helped Julie, who was now big and awkward, down onto the boardwalk. Then he lifted Keith down beside her. "Doc in town?" he asked, preparing to step back up onto the wagon.

"Yes. He is. He just got back from Fred Watkins' place a few minutes ago. I think he's home now. At least he was when I left." Martha laughed merrily.

"I'll put the team up an' see you ladies later." Jess tipped his hat and smiled. The horses leaned into their collars and the wagon lurched on down the main street toward the livery barn.

Funny how I don't feel so naked without my .44 now. His carbine was next to the seat, but he left his Colt at home. *Maybe it's like Sean said. It'll take time, but people will get used to having me around and leave me alone.*

The town was crowded. It was the first warm, dry week in late May and the first chance since winter a lot of ranchers from outlying spreads had to get into Lawson. Like them, people ran low of supplies and were planting, building, and fixing fences. And they just needed to be around others for a few days.

Al Grey was just finishing shoeing a big bay work horse out in front of the open, double doors of the livery barn. The big man wiped the sweat from his face and bald head as he tossed his tools into the tool box. Hearing the wagon approach, he looked up, and, recognizing Jess, he smiled a broad smile, showing a missing front tooth knocked out by a rank horse in the past.

"Well, hello there! Glad to see you stuck around." He wiped off his hand and offered it to Jess.

"You have room for these two?" Jess asked, meeting his grip.

"Sure! Pull your wagon around back and unhook. Be with you after I get this one put up."

Jess just started to unharness the mares when Al returned to help him and put the mares away.

"Have you still got that outlaw stud?" he asked.

Jess nodded. "I left him with Sean, this trip. I had my wife and son with me in the wagon and figured he'd be too much trouble to bring."

"You wouldn't be interested in breedin' some mares to him this season, would you? There's gettin' to be a real market around here for good, strong, light drivin' teams...somethin' a little better than common broncs. I've got six mares at home, mostly thoroughbred, that I'd really like to breed to that little Morgan. I'll bet their foals would really trot!"

"If you bring them up, we could work something out," Jess smiled. "I've got a twenty acre pasture about fenced in." He hesitated, a somber cloud drifting through his thoughts. "Say Al, whatever happened about Jerry Tripp?"

"Aw, his pa got the trial postponed, then they got some fancy Eastern lawyer on it. They're still dinkin' around with trials back in Laramie, now."

Jess shook his head, remembering how quickly they stood him on the gallows after his arrest.

"I guess you can't really blame his pa. The old man's had it rough, losin' his first son in an accident, when he was only twenty. Then his wife a couple of years later. With Jerry, he was so scared of losin' him that he spoiled him too much. And Jerry always was a rotten egg. But Matt couldn't see it. The kid was all he had. I guess no one want's to see their boy hung."

"I guess," Jess agreed quietly. "Well, I better go find my wife."

"Say," Al exclaimed, slapping his leg. "You should get over to the stockyard this afternoon. They're havin' a rodeo. I remember how you got that wild stud. Think you can still ride a bronc?" He laughed.

"Maybe." Jess smiled, feeling a spark of interest. *It would be good to feel the surge of a fighting bronc rising under me again.*

"Think on it. They're offerin' a hundred dollars, gold, prize money. That would sure sweeten the spring!'

"Just might, at that," Jess replied, turning to leave. "I'll be over at Doc's. See you later." He turned back. "Say Al, the seat of your pants is ripped out." Jess smiled a mischievous grin, watching the huge man reach to check. He'd been standing on Main Street all morning, bent over that bay, with the rear seam split widely out, grandly showing the whole world his red long johns!

Al broke into a loud roar of laughter, slapping his thigh. "No wonder Granny Goodnight didn't stop to talk to me! Haaa haaa haa!"

Julie and Martha visited briefly on the boardwalk. Then, taking Keith by the hand, Julie followed the older woman into the mercantile. She made a careful list of all the things she needed and ran out of during the winter. *It's funny. Back home I never thought about all the small things when I could walk a few blocks any time I needed them. But here, I had to learn to be more careful and think far ahead!* Such small things as a spool of thread or tin of black pepper could not be forgotten when they were only able to come to town a few times a year, and it was a two day trip, each way.

"They have some of the nicest material, just in!" Martha exclaimed. "There are two bolts that would be just right for baby clothes," she smiled. "It looks as if you may need some things in a little while. I'm so happy for you and Jess!" She squeezed Julie's hand.

The two women were alone in the store and they talked buoyantly for some time as Julie went about shopping for the things on her list and picking up a few things she forgot. Although Jess received a good price for his furs, she was careful of her purchases. She knew he hoped to get a start for them with some cattle and some good brood mares to breed to the Hawk, and she shared his dream of someday buying the range next to their place.

But, oh, it was so good to be here with Martha. Such small purchases as a few yards of material, a paper of needles, a yard of lace, some yarn and ten pounds of white sugar became treasures to her. Of course, they still needed to buy flour and other staples, but Jess would help her with that later on.

Two women entered the store and when they saw her, their pleasant visiting stopped. When they reached the far side of the store, they began animated conversation, staring at Julie and one even pointed at her.

Later, when Martha and Julie finished with their purchases and went to the counter, they had to pass close to them. Julie knew women like these before. Gossips. Vicious, pinched faced gossips. Suddenly, she wished she was somewhere else.

The boldest, a short, nondescript woman with her hair done in a severe bun in the back of her head, wire glasses perched on her nose, cocked her head at Julie.

"So, you're the one? His woman. We've all heard so much about you. You poor thing. Of course you couldn't have known about him."

"I knew all I needed," Julie replied quietly.

"But don't you know what they sent him to prison for?" she asked in an overly-shocked voice. "How could you marry a man like that?" She shuddered dramatically.

Julie looked right into the woman's face. "I know that lies sent him to prison. Nothing more."

The haughty gossip raised her eyebrows, glancing to the fullness of Julie's dress. "That is his baby you're carrying?" she snipped.

"It is and I'm proud of it. Are you always this rude?" she asked, turning away and firmly taking Keith's hand.

All the way back to the Stone's house, Julie was quiet. Too quiet. As Martha took Keith into the kitchen for a treat, she could no longer restrain the tears that burned in her eyes. She was still sobbing quietly when Martha returned.

She was ashamed to let her friend see the tears, but could not stop. Martha put a mothering arm around her shoulders. "There, there, child. I know how bad that was for you, but you mustn't. It's bad for the baby."

"I don't care about me, but it's all so unfair to Jess! He's been so good to me and he's worked so hard. Must they always talk as if he was some kind of animal?"

"People like Mildred are just nasty, vicious gossips. Unfortunately, there are a lot of people with too little to occupy their time, so they butt into other people's lives. But don't think all the folks in town are like that." She gave Julie a warm squeeze. "Here now. Dry your eyes. I just saw the men turn in the front gate."

"You won't tell Jess?" Julie asked urgently.

"No. Of course I won't," she said gently, patting Julie's shoulder.

Seconds later, they heard the sound of boots on the porch and Julie recognized the familiar, musical ring of Jess's spurs. Quickly, she straightened her dress and patted her hair, hoping her eyes weren't too red.

Doc and Jess were laughing as they entered the room, as if sharing a private joke. "....and you should have seen their faces!" Doc finished.

"What have you two been up to?" Martha asked.

"Well, you know that rodeo they're having today? I was down taking a look. Jess found me there and decided to get in on the bronc riding. Some of the men were bragging, standing around making things rough on him. After he put his entry money down, they told him he'd drawn John Duncan's roan. You know that horse hasn't been ridden by any of them.

"I got the distinct impression they figured they'd have a horse laugh on Jess after the horse threw him." Doc chuckled to himself and continued. "Well, Jess rode the roan, right to a standstill, then trotted him, gentle as a lamb, right over to the bunch that gave him the trouble, got off and handed the halter rope to Art, who started the whole thing."

Jess smiled. "I thought he was gonna bust wide open. Even swallowed his chew."

"The boys got their laugh, but it wasn't on Jess! Art and his boys took it pretty well, though. Art came over afterward with the prize money, gave it to Jess and shook hands with him, pretty agreeable, at that. Things may settle down after all with these knot-headed folks around town."

"Julie," Jess said, "let's go back to the mercantile. I promised myself that the pelt from Carcajou would buy you a cook stove. And now that I've got a little more cash, I want to pick up a few more things we've been lacking."

"A cook stove?" Julie gasped. "I can cook alright in the fireplace." She thought of cattle, brood mares, and the land.

"No. I want you to have a stove, to make things easier on you. You've got plenty to do, and with the new baby and all..." He squeezed her hand.

Spring and early summer were good to Jess and Julie. The icy winds and hardships of winter were all but forgotten in the warm summer breezes that stirred the grass in the meadow. Now, Jess found more and more to do close to the cabin, as Julie's time drew nearer. For more than two months, he had been building pasture fence, corrals, and a chute. True, they still only had the milk cow, her this-spring's calf, and the three horses, but Jess was not building for today. He was building for the future. He even built a tall fence around Julie's lush garden to keep out the elk, moose, and deer. And now that she was nearing her time, he found extra time to keep it weeded and well watered.

He looked up from the wood he was splitting for next winter. The place really was beginning to look like a ranch now. He felt a swell of intense satisfaction as he glanced up the trail for the hundredth time that day. Doc said he'd bring Martha up to stay with Julie, to be with her when her time came. Although their baby wasn't due for a week or so, Jess would rest easier when Martha was there to be with her.

Sinking the axe into the chopping block, he gathered an armful of kindling and stove wood to carry to the cabin. He looked to where Keith played, near the garden fence, with the little wooden horses and cattle Jess carved for him at Christmas, and he felt a glow of well-being. He was truly blessed.

The smell of fresh bread drifted out onto the porch, reminding Jess it was almost dinner time. He felt glad he bought Julie that kitchen range for it made her work easier now. But his hunger was forgotten when he saw his wife. She was leaning heavily on the table, pale and drawn, panting for breath.

"Julie!" he cried, frightened. He dropped the wood in the middle of the floor, unmindful of the mess, and rushed to her side.

"I'm alright." She smiled wanly to ease his worry, but there were lines of pain in her face. "The baby's just going to come a little sooner than I thought. The second one sometimes does that. We'll be alright, as long as you're with me."

After getting Julie into bed and making her as comfortable as he could, Jess went to bring Keith in. *Damn! I've helped birth horses and cattle, but never a woman...and this is Julie! What if something...Damn! If only Doc and Martha would get here!*

Any other time, Jess would have felt the danger or heard a slight sound, but his senses were wholly absorbed with the coming of their baby.

"Hazzard!" A hate-filled challenge rang out, shattering the peace into glass-like pieces.

Jess stopped, his heart turning to ice. Unbelieving, he turned toward the voice. Jerry Tripp stood before him, unshaven, brutal, with naked hatred glittering in his flat, hard eyes. Jess figured him long hanged and buried by now. It was like seeing a ghost, a ghost of the past.

"Go get your gun. I'm gonna kill you today." The man, no longer a boy, wasted no words. His intent was clear.

Jess glanced swiftly to the cabin and back to Tripp. God, not now!

"My wife's in there, havin' a baby." Jess's voice was cold and strangely hard, choking in his throat.

"Get it, or by damn, I'll kill you where you stand!" His voice was vicious, past his years. "I don't give a damn about another half-breed bastard being born. Get it." He paused a second. "They say she's a real looker. Maybe when you're dead, I'll hang around here awhile, so we can get acquainted. She can find out what it's like to be with a real man! When I get done with her, she won't be so hoity-toity!"

Jess's jaw hardened, his eyes a deadly blue mixture of fire and ice, knowing he must kill this man or be killed and leave his wife in deadly danger. Even if he was shot, he must make his shot true and kill this man. He turned toward the cabin to get his Colt.

"An' Hazzard," he hissed. "If you get any ideas of takin' a shot at me from the house..." He yanked Keith from behind him. "...I'll kill him."

Jess's heart leapt with fear for his son. Wordless, he nodded curtly, and walked to the cabin.

Before opening the door, he forced himself to relax, forced down the anger, the tenseness. Bending down, he kissed Julie softly.

"How're you doing?" he asked, almost in a whisper, knowing that this might be the last time in this life he saw her.

"Fine." Her smile held a touch of strain. "It just can't decide whether to come now or not."

Jess walked past her to the fireplace, where his gun belt hung. He hesitated only an instant before he picked it up, remembering Keith out there with that madman.

"Jess? What is it?" Fear was in her voice.

"Nothing much. Coyote out by the calf pen." He could not look at her as the knot came into his chest. Suddenly, he desperately wished he had kept in practice. It had been months since he even worn the gun! Now their lives depended on the swiftness of his hand.

As she watched him tie the holster down and flex his gun hand, she knew the Colt was not for a coyote. Terror gripped her throat. Not now! Oh God! It couldn't happen now! She choked down a scream, feeling it in her soul.

Jess longed to hold her to him once more but was afraid to make her even more anxious. He looked at her for a long moment, seeing her fear, not daring to stay longer, because of it.

"I'll be back, Julie," he said gently. Then he stepped outside to meet Jerry Tripp.

There was no trace of boy in Tripp any longer. Little things, the worn, dark smoothness of the holster, the way his hand instinctively dropped close to it, told Jess he had practiced long and hard with that pistol, practiced and lived for only one thing. To kill him. Had he worked hard enough? Jess also knew Tripp had an edge, for in his own heart was fear. Fear for Julie, Keith, and their unborn child tangled his heart. This was the first time he walked to meet a man with fear clutching his insides, and he knew fear, for whatever reason, was death. He forced it away from him with a vengeance. It was his only chance.

The afternoon was still as the two men faced each other. Even the birds ceased chirping, giving the air a deathly feel.

Tripp's eyes shined with savage eagerness as he let Keith go, feeling gratified for the hours that had put calluses on his gun hand, had stained the walnut grip of his .44 with sweat. A labor of hatred. Now, instead of a target, Hazzard stood before him, hand taut, inches from his gun. He was blind to everything, save that slender hand and a spot on the left side of Hazzard's shirt. Blind to the small child, who, afraid, ran toward his father.

Scarce seconds passed as Jess waited for Tripp to make his move, but he thought of Julie and all they had here in their small valley. One fraction of a second too slow and all would be lost to them forever. His eyes watched Tripp's eyes intently, for he knew they would signal his move.

His concentration was shattered, as he felt Keith grasp his legs. And he saw the look come into Tripp's eyes and his hand flash toward his gun. Fear for his son stabbed into him like a knife as Jess violently pushed the boy away from him. Away from danger.

A shot crashed, echoing across the lake and Jess spun from his crouch, squeezing off two roaring shots in reply. In pushing Keith from him, it cost Jess a second in drawing but it also caused Tripp to miss his shot. And it cost him his life.

For it was he, who now lay in the dusty yard, gun clutched in his twitching hand.

"Jess!" Julie screamed from the cabin, "Jess!"

But he couldn't answer. His heart felt as though it stopped. Keith lay sprawled, as he had fallen. Jess turned toward his son, stricken, and as he took a step, Tripp slowly, painfully, raised his gun with a shaking hand as he died, squeezed the trigger.

Jess staggered forward as the shot hit his back. He tried to take another step toward the child but he fell hard. He tried to raise himself, not truly comprehending what happened, as his body trembled from shock and sudden weakness. Keith was only a few feet from him now and Jess could see a spot of blood on his head, pooling onto the dry ground.

Oh God, no! No! He couldn't see the boy breathe! Reaching desperately for him, Jess was gripped with biting pain that took away all else. His arms could no longer hold his weight and he fell heavily. He tried to raise himself again, but was unable to. He could hardly breathe. All he could do was lie there and look at Keith's still, pale face. *The blood...only a small spot. God, why doesn't he move?*

He heard a horse in the misty distance of his pain. Trying to focus his eyes through the dimming fog, he saw Doc Stone running toward him, Martha, hurrying to Keith.

"Doc...Keith..." Jess's words were a harsh rattle, bringing bits of foamy blood to his mouth as he passed out.

Rapidly, Doc loosened Jess's shirt and pulled it off. Inches to the right of the center of his back, blood welled rapidly, sliding down his side, giving no sign of stopping.

Martha ran to her husband, carrying his bag. How could this have happened to them? "How bad is it, Simon?" she asked with fear in her voice, knowing what the foamy blood meant.

"I don't know yet. Doesn't look good. It looks like it went through his lung. You better go find Julie. See if she's alright."

For nearly an hour, Doc worked there in the dust, tying severed blood vessels that were sending blood pulsing from the ragged wound and packing the torn hole in Jess's scarred back.

Then, still wearily working to bind the wound, he heard Martha walk up behind him. There was nothing more that could be done in the cabin.

"Martha, could you drive over to Sean's before it gets dark? I'm afraid we're going to lose him this time. I know Sean would want to be here."

Chapter 29

Although it was past noon, the sun had not yet broken through the veil of mist around the lake. There was no breeze and even the pines were still. At the cabin, up the hill, Sean waited, out of sight through the fog.

Even where Jess stood, the mist swirled around the three graves at his feet. He had been there since early morning. Or was it yesterday? Or last week? He felt no pain from the gunshot wound. He was too numb to feel. He could just stand looking down. *Keith. God, he wasn't quite two and dead from a bullet.* His eyes moved to the next rock covered mound. Then he shut them and his jaw convulsed. *Julie. My life. If I had been at her side, maybe both she and the baby would have lived.*

For the thousandth time he cursed the speed of his gun hand, which drew those such as Jerry Tripp. *If only it was me here, under those rocks, instead of them!* The grief he felt was too much to bear.

His eyes burned and his throat felt tight as he looked out to the lake they loved. How often they sat right here, on this grassy knoll, watching the eagles soar above the still waters. The tears inside him would not come.

We only had a little more than a year. One summer. A summer of eagles. Julie and Keith My whole world. Jerked away at once. What is there left? He worked his hand. Damn it. It was so senseless!

Suddenly, he felt cold. He shivered and turned up his collar. With one look back to the three silent mounds of dirt and rock, Jess turned and walked slowly up the hill toward the cabin, feeling like an old man.

The cabin held so many memories for him. His throat constricted as he thought of the emptiness of it now. As he stood in the dark doorway, he heard Keith's laughter as he played with his wooden horses and cattle in the dust speckled sunlight of the window, and heard Julie's voice calling to him.

Our love. So many things, too-often unspoken, but strong. Too strong to be put down by anything. Except fate.

No. He couldn't stay here in this hollow cabin. Not where he could still smell the pine and wind fragrance, feel the touch of her cool hand, and the warmth of a little boy's soft hair. Jess moved to light a lamp, trying to clear away the shadows of the night, the ghosts in his mind. But even the light was not enough. He looked around the room, corner by corner. *The work of my own hands. The room where she died. Was that the work of my hands, too?* His throat tightened. He could still hear her scream his name, over and over again. But he could not come. He was lying in the yard with a bullet in his back, strangling on bloody foam, his fingertips inches from his still son.

Oh, God. Why? Did he speak the words or was it his mind, screaming? Breathing roughly, he poured the kerosene from the lamp on the floor, splashed it on the walls. Striking a match, he watched all he had left in this world burst into roaring flames.

Even with the intense heat he could not bring himself to leave. It was as though some force held him. Through the suffocating inferno, he could hear Sean calling him, but he could not go. He could not leave.

Then he heard Julie talking. He wanted desperately to hear what she said but could not make out the words. Sean answered and Jess again strained to hear. His mind seemed foggy, tired.

Then, in the heat of the roaring blaze that consumed him, he could feel her close to him once again, her cool hand close on his, leading him from hell. He closed his eyes and sighed. This then was death.

"Jess?" Julie spoke again.

He closed his eyes, remembering she was dead.

"No!" he whispered in agony.

"Jess? Oh Jess...come back to me." She was crying now, like in the dreams he had of her, long ago. And it was killing him. It felt like she was beside him. *No!* He knew she was not.

He turned his head into the flames, but the heat seemed less intense. Almost cool. He opened his eyes in surprise. It was light, but there were no flames. No smoke. In confusion, he tried to focus his sight. He seemed to stand still while the whole room spun crazily.

For the first time, he was wracked by pain. Pain that made him gasp, that sharpened his vision and cleared his mind.

Sean was sitting next to him, unshaven, looking drawn and tired. Uncertain of reality, Jess turned his head, trying to look around him.

On the other side of the bed sat Julie, half-asleep, holding his hand, stroking his fingers. Afraid to speak, to destroy what must be an illusion, a figure from the spirit world, he closed his hand on hers, feeling the softness of her again. *Am I dead? Is she?* Bewildered, he tightened his grip, not wanting to lose her again.

Then he saw her start as she felt his grip. Her eyes opened in hope. He saw tears well up in her eyes, felt them hot on his bare arm, saw her look into his eyes, and knew where he was, that what he felt was real.

Julie dropped to her knees beside him and kissed him. "Oh Jess! I love you!" Cool hands pushed a strand of dark, sweaty hair from his taut, thin face. "I love you so!"

"Julie," he whispered as he struggled to hold her close. This moment belonged to them alone. All he could feel were here lips on his, her hands on his shoulders, and their love.

Then a shadow of confusion and fear contorted his face as he tried to sort out reality from the phantoms of his dreams. "Keith?" His eyes searched for an answer.

She gently touched his face to reassure him. "Jess, he's alright. He just hit his head on a rock. Keith, the baby, and I are all just fine." She felt tears come to her eyes, thinking of the eight days he laid there, delirious with pain and fever, a muttered word and incoherent phrases telling the story of his hallucinations. She was helpless, unable to reach him, to tell him they were alive. And she was so afraid he would quit fighting for his life.

He seemed to understand as his grip on her hand relaxed, and his eyes closed with a sigh. Fear struck her and she looked to Sean, her heart pounding.

The big man's eyes held a gentle smile. "It's okay. He'll be able to rest now. And start to mend."

Jess slept until the next afternoon. Even then, he did not wake fully. Vaguely, he was aware of sounds from the other room. Chairs scraping, many voices, some familiar, some he did not recognize, all murmuring in conversation. He felt uneasy, but terribly weak and tired. Even breathing hurt almost more than he could bear.

Later in the day, he became aware of Julie again at his side, holding his hand. Her gentle stroking helped smooth away the pain. He opened his eyes. The lantern burned with a golden, homey glow. *It must be night. How long did I sleep?* Then he remembered the voices, and was worried.

Their eyes met and she smiled down at him.

"I heard voices." He struggled to speak and she sensed his uneasiness.

"No Jess, it's alright. It's exciting! Men are here. They've come to help. Some women too, bringing food. Sean, Ernie, Doc, John Miller, men from town, people from ranches. Even the sheriff and a young deputy from Carter City. They heard and they came to help. They're putting up our hay, cutting wood for this winter."

"What?" he rasped.

She nodded, dancing past him to the open window, her skirts blowing in the breeze. Even in the dusky light, she could see the tall, fat stacks of hay by the barn and out in the meadow. "It's going so fast, too! Word spread. First there were four or five; the men from around here. Then more came, and their wives. There's ten teams now, besides ours! And we set places for twenty men and boys today. Six wives were here, too, bringing loads of food."

She returned to his side. "Jess. It's going to be alright. Do you understand me? Everything is alright. I have something to show you." Then she smiled shyly at him and slipped quietly from the room.

The impact of what Julie told him finally struck Jess. *Is it finally over? The hatred, the bigotry, the next gunman? Was Jerry Tripp the last? Truly the last?*

When Julie returned, she held a small, blanketed bundle in her arms. Sitting down close, she lay the new baby next to him. With great effort, he eased the blanket back from the baby's tiny face with his gentle, wondering fingertip. As he looked from the delicate face to hands no bigger than his thumb, then back to his wife, the complete joy he felt was sharper, more intense, than any pain he ever knew.

"Well? How do you like your daughter?" Julie asked, gently kissing his hand that held hers.

"Daughter?" he whispered. As he looked into her loving eyes, the first tears he could remember came into his eyes. There was no need for words.

The next day, Jess felt stronger, in less pain. One by one, his friends, old and new, stopped in to visit, to encourage him, and to see for themselves he would recover. Sean was first and returned again in the afternoon.

"There's a man outside, who wants to see you, if you're feeling up to it," the big man said quietly. "He's been here for two days but wanted to wait until you were more able."

Jess nodded, wondering who it was who needed permission to see him. Sean left and minutes later, the door opened. There was the sound of hesitant steps and Matt Tripp stood beside his bed, hat in hands.

Jess's throat tightened and he drew a deep, painful breath. Jerry Tripp's father! The gray-haired man looked older than he did when Jess last saw him. More stooped, beaten.

"Mr. Tripp." Jess nodded a tentative greeting.

"Mr. Hazzard." The old man stood humble before Jess, not the avenging father. "I've come to apologize to you for my son...and my part in what happened to you." Mr. Tripp's voice quivered slightly. He was a man not used to apologizing. "I can't make excuses for him, for what he did to you, or for me trying to keep him from hanging. He was my youngest son. Come to me when I was older than most. Like your children." The old man swallowed hard. "I lost my first boy to an accident. He was a good boy. Gentle, strong, obedient. Maybe the way Jerry turned out was my fault. Maybe I spoiled him too much after James was killed and my wife died. I don't know." He looked at Jess, his eye pleading. "Why does anyone's son turn out bad. He was just plain no good. And I overlooked it...made excuses to people...defended him...even bailed him out of trouble, time after time. Kept hoping something would change him." Tripp's voice cracked and he bit his lip.

"I believed him...and the stories I heard about you. Killer. Ex-con. Outlaw half breed. So I justified him in my mind. Until I couldn't anymore. I finally knew he was no good when he killed a deputy, a friend of the family, to escape and come here to try to kill you. I've come to send his body back to be buried...and to say I'm sorry for my part in it. Maybe if I'd have..."

Jess held out his hand. "It's alright. No man wants to believe bad of his children."

"Will you forgive me, then?" The old man looked into Jess's eyes with new hope.

"There's nothing to forgive. We've all made our share of mistakes."

Gratefully, Matt Tripp gripped his hand, swallowing hard with emotion.

Then he released Jess's hand as he reached into his coat pocket. "I've met your family and your friends. Seen what you done here. I've got something for you. They tell me you want to buy the old Judson range, next to yours."

Jess nodded, wondering.

"I bought it two days ago." Then at seeing the disappointment fleet across Jess's face, quickly continued. "I bought it to be sure you'd have it. I know what land means to a man. What it means to lose it." He unfolded papers, holding them where Jess could see. "I know you won't accept it as a gift. But you can buy it from me for what I paid for it, whenever you can. A little at a time, with no interest." Mr. Tripp saw Jess was about to protest.

"Stop. Please let me do this for you. I bought it for very little. The out-of-state heirs were happy to be rid of it. It'd go a long way toward making me feel better, and to atone for all my son and I are responsible for. Please. These papers are all drawn up legal, in case something should happen to me. Please accept my offer."

Jess was briefly torn between not wanting to be beholden to any man, pity for the old man's feelings, and the flood of joy at the possibility of owning the wilderness land he treasured. He looked into the man's eyes and finally nodded.

"I'll go now. You read those papers when you feel stronger. I've already signed them in front of a witness. You do the same and send one copy in to the bank in Lawson. They're expecting them. Just pay on it when you can, whatever you can spare. I know it takes money to run a ranch."

Mr. Tripp saw the weariness in Jess's pale face, knowing how much pain his son had caused him, this time and before, and took his leave.

Alone, Jess turned his head to look out the window. Outside, far away, the sun flooded the mountains with golden light. Life was suddenly very good. The killing, the hatred, the bitter dreams were finally over.

It was a good day to begin again.

Bragg

A rider is lucky to get one great horse in their lifetime. I've been lucky to have two. Both were Morgan stallions.

My last stallion, Bragg, is pictured in the old photo, above. He was the inspiration for the Hawk Jess Hazzard rode in the story. He was a spirited, gentle horse with intelligence that was almost supernatural; a little horse that could do it all, and do it well.

We rode together for hundreds of miles throughout the mountains of Montana and Wyoming's Upper Green country, the rough setting for this book. When his time came, he was buried with love in the mountains of Montana on our own little ranch.

I miss him to this day.

~Jackie

Dear Reader,

Thank you for reading *Summer of the Eagles.*

If you enjoyed it, please stop by Amazon or Goodreads and leave a comment or review. It can be just a sentence or two or as long as you like. Reader opinions really do matter, and are very much appreciated!

Thanks again!

~ Jackie

Coming June, 2015: *Autumn of the Loons*

After a lifetime of pain and struggle, Jess Hazzard finally hung up his gun, buried his demons, and found happiness in the mountains of west Wyoming with his dear wife, Julie, their daughter, and her young son from a previous marriage.

Life was good until the day he returned home to find the love of his life brutally beaten and raped, and their son, Keith, kidnapped.

Now Jess must master his rage and strap on the Colt Frontier he long prayed he would never again have to wear, to pursue a ruthless madman and his vicious gunmen, save their son, and avenge Julie's violation.

To receive email notification about Jackie's books, including when *Autumn of the Loons* and other titles in the series become available, please email your request to jackieclaybooks@masonmarshall.com or follow us on Twitter. @masonmarshallpb. or on Facebook (Jess Hazzard Series at www.facebook.com/JessHazzardSeries) or (Mason Marshall Press at http://on.fb.me/1IB5JzP)

Your email address will be kept strictly confidential.

Made in the USA
Monee, IL
24 November 2021